BLOOD FOR BLOOD

MICHAEL EARHART

For Misty

PROLOGUE

Roger McLean had no idea that his death was just up the street, less than fifteen minutes away.

Deciding to get some work done before he took Sam out for lunch, he put his feet to the floor and stretched until his back crackled, cast a quick glance to his wife's side of the bed. It was empty, but that was fine. *She's probably out back in the garden,* he thought, and then put on his sweat pants and a T-shirt and went downstairs.

This weekend was the first in a long while that the two of them had the house to themselves. Little Abigail, who'd just turned two, was staying the weekend with Sam's mother. Roger missed the little booger, even though she'd only been gone now for a little over twelve hours, but he was enjoying the peace and quiet that swept in with her absence, and he would be sorry to say goodbye to it come Sunday evening when they went down to pick her up.

Outside, with his killer turning onto his street and trying to find an out-of-the-way place to park, the sun was bright and warm, and the breeze drifting in through the open windows in the living room as Roger made his way toward his office was heavily-scented with lilac. Roger loved that smell. It reminded him of his grandmother who, every spring, always had a vase full of freshly-cut lilac branches sitting on the kitchen table out at the old farm.

In the kitchen, he poured himself some coffee and went to one of the windows next to the cherry-stained French doors that led out onto his back patio, smiling as he watched Samantha on her hands and knees pulling weeds around the edge of her flowerbed. She couldn't see him standing there, oblivious as she was to everything except her precious flowers. The sun struck her honeyed-gold hair in a brilliant sheen as it trailed down her back in a long, single braid. She was wearing shorts and a blouse with one of his work shirts over it, loose and unbuttoned, humming to herself as she worked.

His smile turned sad. *How am I gonna tell her? Will she understand I had to do it?* He thought she might, but it would be a hard sell. Still, he loved her more than anything in this world, and he wasn't about to lie to her anymore, especially when it came to money. *I'll make her favorite breakfast and we'll talk it through. She'll forgive me. She has to.*

He turned to make his way back toward his office and the mountain of paperwork waiting for him. He was crossing into the living room when he heard his wife talking to someone. *Probably Winnie, or her crazy old grandmother,* Roger thought. Both women lived together in the house next door, on the other side of the privacy fence he had installed last year. Not thinking any more about it, he walked into his office and flipped on the light.

Samantha screamed.

It was enough that it froze him in place. The birds that had, just a moment ago, been chirping through the open windows were deathly quiet now. A cold sweat broke out all over his body. Before he could open his mouth to call out or turn and go see what the problem was, Samantha screamed again, louder this time, only to have her cries cut off suddenly, violently, by a very loud *BOOM* that seemed to shake the house.

4

Roger started to tremble then. A young man raised in a Christian home, where the only violence he ever knew were from the movies and cartoons he'd watched as a kid, had no idea what to do.

I need my phone, he thought suddenly, because now he believed he knew what that awful sound had been, and he was scared.

He turned toward the coffee table where he'd placed his phone when he came off the stairs and saw a man come through the French doors leading out into the backyard and step into the kitchen wearing a black leather jacket, black gloves, black pants, black boots; a military shotgun, also black, rested in his hands. His face was covered with a black ski mask.

"No!" Roger sobbed, and then the gun went off again, blowing his kneecap apart like a rotten apple struck with a baseball bat.

He screamed. Searing pain ripped through him. He found himself floundering on the floor, clawing at the carpet as the stranger with the shotgun stood over him silently, his eyes glittering chips of stone through the holes in his ski mask.

"Please!" Roger begged, trying not to look at his mutilated leg as it trailed behind him like a bloody dead thing on the floor. *"Please, don't do this!"*

The man didn't say a word. He simply reached into his coat and drew a Glock 9mm fixed with a heavy duty sound-suppressor.

"I just need more time!" Roger pleaded. His mind, steeped as it was in a fog of sluggish pain, suddenly realized what this was all about, only too late. "Oh God, *please!*"

The silenced Glock made a dull, hollow *pop*, sending a bullet punching through the flesh and muscle of Roger's upper back. The wound, now spreading blood over every inch of his torn T-shirt, burned like someone was putting cigars out on his skin.

He rolled onto his back, screaming, though he couldn't hear his own voice. He could taste his own blood, though; he choked on it, spat a gob of it out onto the carpet, but more kept coming up.

"Nothin personal, Roger," the man in the ski mask said. He leveled the Glock, and then another bullet struck Roger in the side of the face and turned off the lights.

CHAPTER ONE

1.

Bolan looked at himself in the clouded sliver of mirror. The face looking back was hard to recognize. The blue eyes were the same, but the smooth, angular face of the boy who first walked in here was now a chunk of chipped concrete set atop a thick bull neck, with a jaw the shape of a shovel blade; the black hair was shaved down to the scalp to a fine fuzz. There were scars, too—both seen and unseen —that weren't there twenty years ago when those heavy doors first slammed shut behind him.

Twenty years. Where did the time go?

He had started his bit on an aggravated assault charge; five years for putting a man in a wheelchair with a baseball bat. The other fifteen were tacked on after he beat another inmate to death in the showers. Three of them had come at him, all at once. Two of them ended up spending a week in the prison infirmary; the one who started the whole thing died with a crushed skull.

During the hearing, the prosecutor told the judge the charges of manslaughter were justified, considering the brutality involved. "Mr. O'Brien had the chance to walk away and refused," the prosecutor had argued, standing there dressed in his thousand dollar suit and three hundred dollar haircut. "We feel self-defense does not apply under the circumstances. Because of that, and given Mr. O'Brien's violent history both inside and outside of the prison system, the State would recommend the court accepting the plea agreement as written."

The judge asked him if there was anything he would like to say before she handed down the sentence. His lawyer, with a sourly amused expression on his face, advised he keep his mouth shut. Bolan did as he suggested, telling the judge he had nothing else to say. The judge, looking bored by all of this, handed him another fifteen years like she was calling out Bingo numbers.

2.

"O'Brien."

He turned to the officer standing on the other side of his cell door. The man's massive head seemed to fill the long, narrow, rectangular window. He was black as an African chief, good-looking, physically fit, holding a clipboard in his huge dark hands.

"I'm ready," Bolan said. He clenched his hands at his side to keep them from shaking.

That big, dark face never looked up. It might've been a pagan idol carved from mahogany. "Pack your shit, then. You got five minutes."

"I won't need five," Bolan said. "Ready when you are."

3.

Down at processing they dressed him out in a plain white T-shirt, a pair of state blue jeans, and a pair of blocky brown work boots; he was cut a check for $350.75 (all that remained on his commissary account), and handed a bus ticket back to his hometown. The shirt they gave him was a little big, but it could not conceal the broad shoulders, massive chest, and heavy arms knotted with corded muscle. Standing at six feet and five inches, he towered over the sweaty fat guy sitting behind the desk.

"You got twenty-four hours to get in touch with your P.O.," the officer said. He slid a manila envelope with Bolan's release paperwork and contact information for his local parole office across the desk. "You understand?"

Bolan said that he did.

"You have a bus ticket?"

"Right here." He held it up in his large, scarred hand.

"How nice for you." The officer shot him a sour frown. He slid a pen and Bolan's release papers across the desk. "Sign here, here, and here." With each *here*, he jabbed the paper with the blunt tip of his sausage-like finger.

Bolan signed. "There you go." He slid the pen and papers back across the desk and smiled as big and beautifully as a child on Christmas morning.

The intake officer pointed toward a steel door sheathed in shatterproof glass. "Go through there and wait for the buzz. After that, good luck to you." A smile slithered across the man's doughy face. "See you in a month."

Bolan's return smile was unsettling and without humor. "You'd better hope not," he told the man, and then he turned, went to the indicated door, waited for the buzz, and stepped out into the free world.

4.

The prison van dropped him and a few others off at the Greyhound station at around six in the morning. He cashed the check at a 7-Eleven across the street. The cashier gave him a funny look when he showed her his Department of Corrections I.D., but she counted out the $345.75 (minus the $5.00 check cashing fee) and told him to have a great day with a smile that was genuine but still a little nervous. Bolan understood and didn't hold it against her. He took his money, bought a paperback from one of the racks next to the register, and walked across the street to wait for the bus.

It was a three hour wait, and another two-and-a-half hour ride south. He was tired but couldn't nap because of his nerves. He tried to read the book but his mind kept wandering and the words started to look like alphabet diarrhea, so he gave up on it and just sat back and enjoyed the ride, watching as the world flew by his window at seventy miles per hour.

He remembered he had a picture in his pocket. It was the only thing he made sure to carry with him out of that hell hole. Taking it out, he carefully unfolded it and just stared at it with a smile slowly stretching across his face. The girl in the photo was his daughter, Samantha. She was pretty; tall and lean, built like a tennis player. Blonde hair to her shoulders. She had his eyes—the same Irish blues his old man had given him.

He studied the girl in the picture, feeling the stinging pain of twenty wasted years taking a bite out of his heart. He'd never met her in person. Sara, his girlfriend at the time of his incarceration, had been pregnant and never told him. She wrote him a letter his second week in lockup telling him it was over, that she wanted nothing more to do with him. She'd never mentioned she was pregnant, though.

Maybe she didn't know at the time, was a thought that recurred in his mind often over the years. *Or maybe she just never wanted me to know about it.* That thought also crept up quite often, and over time it seemed the more likely explanation of the two.

Either way, Samantha had taken it upon herself to contact him during his last thirteen months in the joint. She sent him a letter explaining who she was and her desire to get to know her father. She said she had a two-year-old daughter of her own named Abigail. Abby was in the picture with her mother, a child with a child of her own. Abby had red-gold hair and the exact same blue eyes. She was beautiful. So was her mother. They both looked happy and it made him happy to see them like that.

Samantha's letter had come as a shock to him, but he had

promptly answered her back and a regular correspondence had begun. He got a letter from her almost every week, and every time he got one from her, he sent one back. It was mostly him answering questions she had about him and his family—where she came from, medical history, things like that. He told her why he was locked up and for how long, but she didn't seem scared off by it. She told him her mother would freak out if she knew they were talking (*Shit a gold brick* were the exact words, he remembered with a grin), but she didn't care about all that. She wanted Bolan to come and see her and Abby and her husband. Roger was his name. Seemed like a good guy from what Samantha had told him. He worked in the roofing business, owned his own truck and tools and ran a nice crew. They sounded happy together, in love. Bolan found that the more Samantha told him, the more he wanted to know.

Being in prison all those years had made him give up hope of ever having a normal life; and he'd learned in the early years it was easier to cut ties with those friends and what little family still spoke to him and just focus on trying to make it on the inside. He never thought he would have a family again because he never really believed he would make it out of prison alive. But this last year, since learning he actually had someone out there, he'd decided to calm it down, so to speak. He took to reading his Bible (Samantha liked to send him scriptures to read in her letters, and he'd done so) and going to church; and he found his mind, oddly, turning towards some semblance of a future. After almost a year of them talking back and forth through letters, he felt he actually *had* a future.

He put the photo back in his pocket. Before he knew it, the bus driver announced over the intercom that they would be arriving at their destination in about thirty minutes.

Last stop.

CHAPTER TWO

1.

The bus station was downtown, right across the street from the courthouse where he'd been convicted of aggravated assault and sentenced to five years in prison when he was only nineteen. The man he had beaten was in a wheelchair now, or so he had been told. Bolan thought about him as the bus came to a jerky stop and wondered if he was still around. He wanted to say he felt bad for what he'd done to the guy, but he couldn't. The asshole had been putting his hands all over Sara at a party after having too much booze and blow, and when Bolan told him to piss off, the prick yanked a knife and Bolan went berserk. Somehow he'd managed to take the knife away, breaking the man's fingers and arm in the process, and then he went to work on the guy's face, smashing his teeth and jaw. After the guy went to the ground, holding what was left of his face together with his hands, a very drunk and out of control Bolan took a baseball bat from the trunk of his car and came back and went to work on his legs, breaking one of his knees and pelvis in about five different places. He'd been standing over the guy when the cops finally showed up and surrounded him in a ring of gun barrels, yelling for him to get on the ground. That had been the last time he saw Sara, crying on the porch while they handcuffed him and forced him into the backseat of a police cruiser.

He stepped off the bus and looked around. Samantha told him in her last letter that she would be at the bus station waiting for him and, if she wasn't, to go ahead and walk to another address she'd given him, located right downtown. Against his protests, she and Roger had rented him an apartment—an entire year's lease paid for upfront. He was not a particularly prideful man, but he wasn't one for accepting charity, either. Samantha, however, had insisted, and his cell mate (a guy named Derrick, who was serving thirty-five to life for killing a woman during a robbery) had told him all about life in a nasty halfway house, so he relented and accepted the offer.

The sidewalk was empty. No sign of Samantha or her husband. That was fine with him. It was a warm May morning and the fresh air had never smelled or tasted so good. He thought maybe a long walk was just what he needed.

The bus driver followed him off and went to the side of the bus, opened a hatch, and started chucking luggage out onto the curb, humming to himself as he did so. Two other people then made their way off the bus: a young girl of about fifteen and a fifty year old man with a short, gray beard and wearing a Desert Storm Veteran's hat.

"Any luggage, buddy?" the driver asked. He was a short, stocky black guy with big hands and a friendly face.

Bolan shook his head. "No, man. Thanks."

"You have a great rest of your day," the driver said, and them clomped back up into the bus and shut the door. He gave the big diesel engine a few good revs, and then disengaged the parking brakes with a screech, and the Greyhound began its long slog to wherever, belching black exhaust from its pipes. Bolan watched it go, briefly wondering where it was headed next, and then turned his attention back across the street.

2.

He walked up and down the street of the downtown area, surprised at how little things had changed in the last twenty years. The Blockbuster Video where he used to rent Nintendo games as a kid was gone, replaced with an O'Reilly's Auto Parts store now; the cars passing him on the street were shinier, sleeker, but pretty much everything else was the same.

He dug in his back pocket for an envelope in which he kept all of his important information and opened it, searching for a piece of paper he'd kept safely guarded while inside the joint. Finding it, he unfolded it carefully, reading the address Samantha had given him to himself over and over. He was trying to remember exactly where Market Street was and couldn't. And then he remembered a friend of his in middle school he used to skateboard with had lived on Market, and it all came flooding back. He started walking towards downtown, repeating the address to himself as he went.

It brought him to a line of storefronts. There was a beauty shop called Melanie's Makeover, a candy store named All That's Sweet, a restaurant called the Tuscan Kitchen that allowed you to eat at umbrella-tables outside on the sidewalk, and a bakery with the name

Sugar Mama's written in a bright pink arc on the big display window out front. Bolan chuckled at that one.

Confused, he walked up and down the street several times, looking at the address on each of the buildings, but he wasn't seeing anything indicating an apartment.

Has to be above one of these businesses, he thought.

"You new in town?"

He turned towards the voice and saw an older man with thick wavy hair leaning against a wall smoking a cigarette. He was painfully thin with stooped shoulders, and wore a flannel shirt tucked into a nice pair of jeans and bright white tennis shoes. A thick pair of glasses rested on the bridge of a nose that looked like it had been broken more than a few times.

"Excuse me?" Bolan asked.

The old man nodded towards the piece of paper Bolan was holding. "You look lost," he said. "I asked if you were new here."

"No, I'm not. Just been away a while. I'm looking for an address and I can't seem to find it."

"What's the address?" He took a long drag off his smoke and then casually tapped his ash onto the sidewalk.

"It says 33 ½, but I'm not seeing it anywhere." Bolan walked over and showed the man the piece of paper with Samantha's loopy handwriting on it.

The stranger gave the paper a disinterested glance and then pointed with the first and second fingers of his right hand, the stub of his cigarette jutting out between them. He was pointing at the entire row of storefronts in a short sweeping gesture that made the cigarette tremble slightly between his knuckles.

"That side of the street is even numbers," he said. "See?"

Bolan saw.

"33 ½ is behind me." He indicated the building against which he was leaning by stabbing a thumb over his shoulder. Bolan saw that the man was standing next to the doorway of a barber shop called Rick's. "I'm Rick," the man said with a big, yellow-toothed grin. "That address is the apartment above my place."

"Are you the landlord?"

Rick laughed, shook his head. "Hell no. That's Merle. Old bastard owns the whole building. I pay him rent, same as everyone else on this block. Nice enough fellow." He paused, grinned sourly. "Until you're late. Then the *old bastard* part kicks in." He grinned hugely, took another puff. "You lookin to rent the place, it's already gone."

"I'm the one who rented it."

Rick gave him a queer look. "You don't know where your own apartment is?"

"Someone else rented it for me," he admitted, a little rankled by the guy's tone.

Rick nodded to say he understood. "Pretty little blonde woman? I saw her talkin to Merle the other day. Nice young lady. Cute little kid with her, too."

"That's my daughter and granddaughter."

Rick looked at him with renewed interest. "Seriously? You started young, my friend."

"I was eighteen," Bolan said.

"Well," Rick said with a sigh, expelling smoke. He flipped his cigarette out into the street where it was caught by a warm gust and rolled into the gutter. "She's a fine young lady, if you don't mind my sayin so. Nicest girl you could ever meet. She and her husband come by all the businesses around Christmas time and give us cookies and cards and things. Good folks."

Bolan smiled. He'd never met Samantha, but he was suddenly very proud of her. It was a strange feeling. "Yeah, she's something."

"Well, I need to get back to it," Rick told him. He held his hand out for a shake. "Name's Rick Bernhardt. It was good talkin to you."

Bolan shook his hand. It was like grabbing hold of a tangle of old roots. "Bolan O'Brien."

Rick paused, his eyes narrowing behind his glasses. "You wouldn't happen to be related to Mary O'Brien, would you?"

The smile faded from Bolan's face. "That was my mother."

Rick shook his head gravely. "Shame what happened to her. Lung cancer, wasn't it?"

"Yeah."

Rick shook his head again. "Damn shame. She was friends with my wife, Laura. She would come over for coffee sometimes, play cards. Nice lady. Had a temper, though."

Bolan remembered. He nodded. "Yeah, she did."

"Small world, huh?" Rick smiled again, his lips peeling back from his huge, nicotine-stained teeth. "I've jawed out here long enough. My next appointment's due any minute now. Say, you ever need a haircut, come see me. First one is on the house. The rest you pay for, like everyone else."

Bolan absently ran his hand over his shaved scalp. "Won't need one for a while, but I'll remember that."

"You take care," Rick said, and then went inside.

Next to his barber shop door was another door Bolan hadn't noticed until Rick had left. It said 33 ½ in faded black letters on a worn wooden plaque fixed to the center of the door. He gave the knob a little turn and it opened to a long narrow staircase that went straight up into darkness. Putting the piece of paper back in his pocket, he took the stairs two-by-two.

CHAPTER THREE

1.

The apartment Samantha had rented for him was much bigger than Bolan had expected when looking at the building from the outside. It had fifteen foot ceilings and hardwood floors and it smelled like fresh paint and drywall. Compared to the cell he'd been living in the last twenty years, he felt like he was standing in a stadium.

There was an old green couch pocked with cigarette burns in the living room with a small table and lamp for furnishings; a refrigerator in the kitchen and one of those two-in-one washer and dryer hooked up in a small utility room next to the water heater in the back. One small bathroom with a tile floor and clean shower, sterile-white walls. A vanity mirror hung over the sink with three large bubble bulbs that gave off a soft yellow light. The bedroom, farther back, was small, with a single window that looked out into the alley at the red brick building next door.

In the kitchen there was a Post-it Note on the Formica counter top. It was from Samantha.

Hope this place will be fine. It's small but it should help get you started. There's some leftovers in the fridge. I'll come by and restock it with some groceries on Friday. Also, in the drawer next to the sink is an envelope with a debit card and my phone number and address

in Cambridge. The debit card has $500 on it for some walking-
around money until Roger can get you started at your new job.

He stood there staring at the note for a long time, feeling the
sting of tears.

2.

He went downstairs and asked Rick if he could use his phone.

"No problem, neighbor," Rick said as he was finishing up
around a client's ears. The man in the chair was an old guy, mid-60s
to early-70s, and the two of them had been talking about going
fishing when Bolan walked in.

"I still say Minnesota has the best damn fishin I ever saw," the
old timer in the chair was saying as Bolan picked up the cordless
phone and dialed Samantha's number. "Caught a trout one time that
weighed almost fifty pounds."

"You're a damn liar, Bob," Rick said, without missing a beat.

"No I ain't!" Bob insisted. "It's true! That sombitch weighed a
good fifty to fifty-five pounds, as sure as I'm sittin in this shitty chair
of yers."

Rick turned him around so he could examine himself in the
large plate glass mirror behind them. "That *shitty chair,* as you so
eloquently call it, Bob, makes me money, so watch your mouth.
Now, that'll be twenty-two dollars."

Bob pushed himself up out of the barber chair with a groan,

went for his wallet. "Twenty-two dollars," he said morosely. He fished out a twenty and a ten and handed them over. "Damn highway robber you are, Rick. And to think I saved your ass back in 'Nam."

Rick rolled his eyes. "No you didn't, Bob. It was *me* who saved *your* ass from stepping on a Punji stick. If it weren't for me, you'd have some Vietcong's shit-poison in your blood and would've died." He snatched the bills out of Bob's hand and turned to the counter.

Bob looked over at Bolan and gave his huge wrinkled head a wag, smiling. "Believe this guy?"

Bolan smiled back, but he was hardly paying any attention. He kept getting Samantha's voicemail. She wasn't answering. He thought about leaving a message, but then decided against it and hung up.

"Thanks, Rick," Bob said, slipping his meaty arms into the sleeves of a light jacket. "Even though your memory about 'Nam is gettin a little soft, yer a helluva barber."

"Well, thank you, Bob," Rick said, opening his cash register and dropping Bob's thirty dollars in with the rest. He fished out eight ones. Closed it with a bang and turned to Bob as the old man was getting his hat from the peg by the door, holding the bills out in front of him. "See you in two weeks, you old shit."

"Stick it up yer ass, you thievin prick." Bob smiled wondrously. He took a look at the eight singles in Rick's hand and nodded. "Keep the change for your tip, though I'll be damned if you deserve one the way you treat your loyal customers." He gave Bolan a wink, told him to have a good one, and then left.

Rick watched him leave, shaking his head with a faint smile, and then reopened the register and dropped the ones back inside. "He does that every time," he said, shutting the drawer. "Bob likes to tell stories and complain, but he's here every two weeks like clockwork. Hell of a machine-gunner, back in the day." He smiled to himself, as if savoring some long-distant memory, then looked at Bolan. "Don't you have cell phone?"

"No."

"Thought everybody had one of those things these days. Well, you ought to get one. Save you a trip down those steep-ass stairs." He reached for a black plastic broom leaning against the wall and began cleaning up clumps of Bob's gray hair off the rubber mat around the chair.

Bolan thought the idea of getting his own phone was a good one. "Where do I get it?"

Rick stopped sweeping and gave him a peculiar look. "You been living in a cave or something?"

Bolan was caught off guard by this. He frowned. "No. Why do you say that?"

Rick shrugged, went back to sweeping. "I don't know. Seems like everybody knows you can buy a cell phone at Walmart these days." He glanced up, looking at Bolan over the tops of his glasses.

There was a shrewdness in his eyes—a *knowing*—that made Bolan uncomfortable. "Maybe not someone who's been . . . *out of town* for a while, I guess."

He and Bolan exchanged looks. Bolan didn't respond, just stood there in the doorway, still as a hugely-muscled statue.

"I'm not judging you, son," Rick said finally, "but you got the penitentiary smell all over you. That why your girl rented the place upstairs in her name?"

Bolan's expression might've been carved out of stone. Then he nodded shortly. "Yeah."

Rick bent and swept the rest of the hair into a dust pan, grunting as his knees popped. "Thought so. How long were you inside?"

"Twenty years."

Rick gave a little whistle of surprise. "Damn. What did you do?"

"Aggravated assault."

Rick emptied the dust pan into a waste basket and looked up. "Twenty years for *assault?*"

"I wasn't a model inmate," Bolan said stiffly.

The old guy didn't seem too bothered by this. He simply nodded. "Well, your business is your own, I guess. I don't mean to pry, son, it just comes with the job. You'd be surprised how much people tell their barber."

Bolan didn't understand why anyone would tell their barber something like that, but he nodded anyway. "Yeah, well, I don't."

"I understand that." Rick put the broom back in its place against the wall and took off his apron, hung it over the back of the chair. "I'll give you a lift."

"You don't have to do that."

"I know I don't. But it's my lunch break and I need to pick up some things so I don't have to do it after I close. Come on." He snatched his keys from a hook near the door and Bolan followed him outside.

3.

Rick took him across town to the local Walmart in a sky-blue Cadillac that had probably been new around the time Jimmy Carter was president. It was in pristine condition and Rick was extremely proud of it.

"Got this baby as a graduation gift when I got out of barber college," he said, giving the steering wheel a loving pat with his hand.

"It's nice," Bolan agreed, though he thought it stank like an ashtray and old aftershave on the inside.

Rick grinned from the driver's seat, the wind coming through his window blowing his hair crazily around his head. "Thanks. It's good to know there's still people with good taste in this world." He reached down and turned the radio up as Johnny Cash came on singing about falling into a burning ring of fire. They drove the rest of the way in silence.

Inside the store, Rick pointed him towards the electronics section while he took a cart and did some shopping for himself. After about twenty minutes of trying to decide which phone to get, a Walmart employee helped him pick out a relatively cheap smart phone and a prepaid plan that gave him unlimited talk, text, and web. Bolan thanked him, paid for it, and then went to the parking lot to wait for Rick.

Rick came out with a cart full of odds and ends about ten minutes later. Bolan helped him load the bags into his trunk and they left.

4.

"Hey, if you're needing some work, let me know," Rick said as he killed the Cadillac's engine. "I could use a little help around the shop. Pay is shit, but it's something, at least."

"What would I be doing?"

"Sweeping, mopping, emptying the trash—shit I hate doin."

Bolan grinned. He liked Rick a lot. "I'll think about it," he said. "Thanks for the ride."

"What're neighbors for?" Rick flashed his big nicotine grin. He shook a cigarette out of his pack and offered Bolan one. Bolan told him he didn't smoke and Rick shrugged, lit it, and then said it would probably kill him one day and popped his trunk.

Upstairs, it took Bolan a minute to figure out how to use the phone he'd bought. He put Samantha's number into his contacts and then decided to give her another try. The phone rang and rang, until her voicemail popped up again. It was strange, hearing her voice telling him to leave his name and number and she'd get back to him. She sounded so grown up. He opened his mouth to leave a message at the beep, but then hung up and thought to try his luck again a little later. If he couldn't get ahold of her in another hour or so, he decided, he would find a way up to Cambridge and knock on her door.

He didn't have to wait long. He went to the bathroom to take a leak. When he was coming back down the hallway, he heard his phone ringing. He picked it up and looked at the screen. It said SAMANTHA across the top. Oddly, he felt a flutter of sudden fear in his chest and almost didn't answer it.

"Hello?"

"Who is this?" The voice was female and hostile right off the bat. Not what he was expecting at all.

Confused, he said, "I was looking for Samantha."

"Yeah, I figured that since this is her phone," the angry woman on the other end shot back. "Who the hell is this?"

Bolan felt flustered for a moment, not really knowing what to say. "Bolan. And you are?"

A long pause. He could hear the woman breathing on the other end. "Wait, wait . . . *who?*"

Bolan sighed. He didn't have the patience for this. "Look, I told you who I am. I'm looking for Samantha. Can you just let her know I called?"

"Bolan," the voice mused, as if tasting the name. "Bolan *O'Brien?*"

"That's right. Who is this?"

"I can't believe this."

Bolan felt the heat rise in his face. He wasn't in the mood to play games. "Who is this?" he demanded again.

"This is Sara," the woman said, "Sam's mother."

He froze.

Sara.

He hadn't recognized the voice at first, but now that he had a name to put to it, it was definitely her. He felt his heart crawl up into the back of his throat. "Sara?"

"Yeah," she said with a heavy sigh.

"It's been a long time." His throat was dry. Made it hard to swallow.

"I'd say about twenty years or so. When did you get out?"

"Today, actually."

She laughed, but it was an unpleasant sound. He thought he detected a sob somewhere underneath it. "Of course you did. What do you want?"

"I told you, I wanted to talk to Samantha," he said. "She was supposed to meet me this morning and never showed."

That laugh again, like a bitter little bell. "Yeah, I'm not surprised."

He frowned at that. "What's that supposed to mean?"

"Nothing. Look, I don't know how you got her number or how she even found you, but she's not here."

"Okay," he said. "I'll call back later."

"No," she told him, almost yelled it. "She won't answer you then, either."

Now he was starting to get angry. Was she really going to sit here and play these stupid games, after all these years? "Look, I get it. You don't want her to speak to me. Fine. But it's not really up to you. She's an adult, and I'm still her father."

Sara burst into a fit of laughter that hurt his ear. He pulled the phone away quickly, his frown deepening. She sounded crazy.

"It's not up to you, either," she said finally.

"I'm hanging up."

"Wait!"

He paused, his fingertip hovering less than an inch above the little red dot that would end the call. "Sara, I don't have time for this shit."

"Where are you?"

"My apartment."

"Where is that?"

"Downtown."

"Can you come over some time this afternoon?"

He could feel his heart thumping in his temples. "I guess. I don't have a car, but I can walk."

"I live on Cherry Street," she said. "You still remember where that is?" The question was sarcastic, a jab to get under his skin. He ignored it.

"Just give me the house number." He went into the kitchen and found a pen and the Post-it notepad Samantha had used. "Go on," he urged, holding the phone against his ear with his shoulder. She gave him the number and told him she would be there the rest of the day, and then hung up.

CHAPTER FOUR

1.

The address brought him to a small, two-story house. It was gray with white trim, a nice little place. A dusty red, four-door Buick sat in the small gravel driveway like a tired dog.

Sara saw him coming up the walk, came out onto the porch to meet him. She was standing in front of the door, arms crossed under her breasts. Her blonde hair was longer than he remembered, pulled back into a ponytail that fell between her shoulder blades. And she looked *good*. She was thirty-seven, a year younger than Bolan, but she looked much younger. She looked stronger than he remembered, too—athletic, like she could hold her own against any tennis pro of her choice. Her jeans were snug but not too tight, and the sweatshirt she wore hung loosely about her shoulders and looked a bit too warm for early May. And her face—once babyish with a spatter of freckles across her cheeks and nose—was lean and sharp, almost hawkish. She wasn't wearing any makeup, either, and looked all the better for it. Her gray eyes followed him keenly, like a female bird of prey sizing up her next kill, as he made his way towards her.

"I'll be damned," she said as his boots clunked up the sidewalk. Now that he was closer he could see her eyes were red and puffy, as if she'd been crying. "They actually let you out."

He stopped and just stood there, his large, muscular arms hanging at his sides like lengths of knotted rope. He had no idea what to say all of a sudden. "What do you want, Sara?"

She shifted her weight from one foot to the other. "I want to know how you got Sam's number."

"She gave it to me," he replied coolly.

"I wasn't aware you two were speaking."

"About a year now."

"It true you killed a man in prison?"

He considered her question. He saw no reason to lie about it. He nodded.

"I guess beating a man only *half* to death wasn't enough for you, huh?"

"Fuck off."

"Fuck *you*, Bolan!" Her voice was loud and shrill, and it made the old man painting his fence across the street stop and turn in their direction. "You left me here all alone after what you did! How fucking *dare* you come here!"

"You *told* me to come over here, remember?" *What the hell's the matter with her?*

"Oh, go fuck yourself!" She began to cry now. Brought her hands up to her face. Bolan could only stand there. Finally, she

33

seemed to get herself together. The look she gave him was cold and full of hurt.

"When's the last time you spoke to her?" Something in her voice trembled. She seemed to be on the verge of some sort of breakdown. Bolan could almost hear the thin ice cracking beneath his feet.

"Two weeks ago," he said. "I just got her number this morning. She was supposed to meet me at the bus station, but never showed." He suddenly had a bad feeling.

"And she gave you her number *this morning?*" The question was an odd one. At once it sounded hopeful and scathingly skeptical.

She's losing her freaking mind.

"Sara," he said carefully, "what's going on?"

"She's not here." Her chin started to quiver. She was about to come apart in a very bad way and he didn't like the feeling he got washing over him from head to foot—the feeling that some unseen force was about to take a giant piss down his back.

He took a step toward the porch. "Sara, what's the matter? Where's Samantha? Did something happen?" He looked down at the toys scattered across her porch, and suddenly that bad feeling deepened. "Is Abby okay?"

Sara's shoulders sank as she put her fist to her mouth and squeezed her eyes shut. Tears popped out through the slits in her eyelids and rolled down her cheeks.

"Sam and her husband were murdered three days ago," she managed to say. And then she *did* come apart. A wracking sob rippled through her. She sank to her knees on the porch, holding her face in her hands, shoulders shaking up and down as she wept. Her voice became a long, low, muffled wail that sent a knife of despair into the meat of his heart.

"What the fuck are you talking about?" He suddenly felt very cold and numb all over.

Sara went on crying. "Someone broke into their house and shot them," she managed. "It was the first date they'd been on since Abby was born, and I offered to babysit." She lowered her face into her hands and uttered a moan that suddenly made him feel sick to his stomach. He couldn't speak, just stood there dumbly looking at her.

Sara went on. "I got the call the next morning, and when I went over there . . ." She choked on the words, swallowed, said, "The police were loading their bodies into a truck. They asked me to come down to the morgue and make a positive identification, so I went. And the whole time I was driving over there, Abby was in her car seat singing some little song and I kept thinking this was all a big mistake, just a big fucking mistake, and that when I got there the bodies would have someone else's faces on them. But then they pulled back the sheets and I saw my little girl . . ." She buried her face again, her shoulders shaking. "Bolan, it looked like someone blew her in half! They shot her and she looked like something that had been hit on the highway and just left there! It was . . ." Her voice lowered to barely a whisper. *"It was awful."*

35

She continued talking, but it turned into a mishmash of blubbering nonsense as Bolan's mind reeled at what he'd just heard.

This wasn't possible. He never even got to meet her. *Murdered?* Fuck no. This was a dream, had to be; a bad, twisted sort of nightmare where, when he finally awoke, he would be sweating and wide-eyed and wanting to puke for the first few seconds because it would *feel* real, but it *wouldn't* be real, because no matter how bad things get, this sort of shit just didn't happen in real life.

Only it did. And it was happening to him right now.

He turned back to Sara, suddenly remembering the day they had met in high school. Bolan and some friends had sneaked out of third period to smoke a joint in the parking lot in his friend Corey Ramsey's car. Well, it was Corey's dad's old Cutlass, but Corey was sure his old man was going to let him have the papers once he graduated. They'd all climbed into the car—Bolan and Corey and Tommy Newsome—and were about to spark it up when someone knocked on the back driver's side window. All three of them jumped and nearly screamed like girls, until they saw Sara Lewis and her friend, Holly Nolan, looking at them through the window and laughing. Bolan had known who Sara was, but this was the first time they had ever actually hung out. Corey let the girls into the car (he'd had a thing for Holly since like the second grade) and the five of them got stoned out of their minds. On the way back into school, Bolan asked Sara if she wanted to go to a movie some time and she told him yeah, that would be cool. Then they both giggled and somehow Bolan ended up being her boyfriend for the next three years.

2.

"Sara." His voice came out in a dry croak. *"Sara."*

She stopped and looked up at him, her face as raw as an open wound. "What?"

"I'm sorry."

They stared at each other, looking across a twenty-year chasm yawning between them. She nodded, and all the meanness just sort of drained out of her like a water balloon with a hole in it. "I know," she said shakily. "I'm an asshole for not telling you about her."

He shook his head. "No, you did the right thing. I was no good for you. Your mom and dad knew it, too. Hell, I think *I* even knew it."

Sara stood up and hugged herself as if she had suddenly caught a chill. She took a cigarette from a rumpled pack in her back pocket and offered him one. He shook his head. She lit it, took a few puffs.

"I was really scared back then," she said. "I didn't know what to do. I didn't even know if I was going to keep the baby. And that night, the night you got arrested, I showed up at Tommy's party to tell you I was pregnant. When I saw you were already half-drunk, I chickened out and couldn't tell you. Then the fight happened, and they arrested you, and I guess . . ." She stopped and looked down at her feet, blinded by tears. "I guess I took it as a sign or something."

Bolan remembered that night clearly, despite the fact he was well-lit by the time Sara had shown up. She had wanted to tell him something, something important, and he had told her to wait until he got another beer. She had stormed off and went out onto the porch where Marcus Baxter was doing some blow with a couple of guys from another town whom Tommy had invited. Bolan didn't know exactly what went on out on that porch, but when he went out to see what was wrong with Sara, he saw Marcus grabbing her boobs and laughing and Sara was cussing at him and trying to push him off. That's when Bolan, a young hothead full of liquor, decided to intervene, and things went south pretty quickly.

3.

A red Ford F-150 pickup truck pulled up into the driveway and parked behind Sara's Buick. Bolan looked over and saw a thin man in his early-to-mid-forties step out and approach the porch. He was walking cautiously, eyeing the big, tall stranger warily.

"Sara," he said. He saw she had been crying, but he didn't seem at all shocked by it. "Honey?"

Sara looked over and gave him a weak smile. The cigarette had burned to a crooked ash between her fingers. "Jim. Hey."

Jim was a good seven inches shorter than Bolan, wearing a blue work shirt with his name written on a white tag above the left breast pocket and a battered brown baseball cap dark with sweat stains. He was very tan, like he spent his every waking moment in the sun, with a shaggy mop of graying brown hair and a goatee.

"Everything alright?" he asked as he neared the edge of the porch and stopped. He looked with concern at Sara, and when his eyes got to Bolan his expression of concern changed to suspicion almost instantly.

"Everything's fine, Jim." Sara seemed to notice her cigarette had burned down to almost nothing and flipped it out into the yard. "This is Bolan O'Brien. Sam's father. Bolan, this is Jim Bowman."

Jim's reaction was that of a man who had just been bitten by something nasty. He stiffened in a cartoon-like way and his eyes widened slightly.

Must've heard the stories, Bolan mused to himself. "Hello," he said.

Jim nodded, keeping his distance. "Hey."

Bolan looked from Jim to Sara. "I'm going to head out," he said, taking a step back. He could see the love Jim had for Sara, and the look on Jim's face when their eyes met told him that he wasn't welcome here as far as Jim was concerned. "Sara?"

"Yeah?"

"Would you mind if I came to the funeral?" He knew he had to get out of there right now or he was going to start crying like a child. Something inside of him had torn, and that tear was quickly growing larger by the second.

Sara gave him the most pitying look he had ever seen on another human being's face, and that made it so much worse. The anger she'd exhibited towards him earlier—it was like it came from a completely different person. She nodded slowly. "Of course. It's Saturday. We can give you a ride."

Jim didn't seem too enthused by this idea, but he nodded. "Yeah, man."

"I'd better go." He looked at Jim and lied through his teeth. "It was nice meeting you." He turned back towards the street.

"Bolan?"

He stopped, looked back. It took everything he had not to take off running down the sidewalk. "Yeah?"

"Would you like to meet your granddaughter?"

For the first time, the idea that he was a grandfather struck him like a hammer to the chest. *I'm only thirty-eight years old,* kept ringing in his head. When he tried to speak, his words caught in his throat and he suddenly didn't know what to say or do. He simply nodded.

Sara smiled, pointed towards Jim's truck. Bolan looked and felt his heart flutter. He could see the top of a child's car seat through the open window. "Come on," she urged him, motioning him over. "She's sleeping right now."

Bolan walked across the yard towards the truck like a rusted Tin Man badly in need of oil. He approached the window and saw little

Abby lying in her seat, head tilted upward, her eyes closed, mouth open in a pink O, snoring softly in the gentle bar of sunlight falling in through the back window of Jim's Ford. She was wearing a blue shirt with Spongebob on the front and little pink shorts. Her chubby little legs were propped up against the back of the driver's seat, her tiny toes poking out of the tops of a pair of sandals. She was holding a stuffed Winnie the Pooh in the crook of her arm.

Bolan just stood and stared at her, as if she'd just fallen out of the sky. Her long, reddish-blonde hair fell against her round face in thick ringlets.

"She's beautiful."

"We're going to be taking care of her from now on," Sara said softly, trying to avoid waking her. "Roger's parents live in Arizona and they don't come around very often. The state has already granted us temporary custody until the court hearing."

Bolan took one last look at Abby, filling himself up with the sight of her, and then told them he had to go. He was turning towards the sidewalk when he felt Sara grab his arm and he stopped. She gave him a hug. It startled him. He didn't know how to react at first, but then he slowly returned it, wrapping his massive arms around her and holding her for a second, taking in the smell of her hair. It was a mixture of cigarettes and lavender shampoo.

"For what it's worth, I'm sorry," she said quietly, the side of her face pressed against the muscles in his chest. "I'm so sorry."

He released her and nodded. Without another word, he left them both standing there and didn't look back.

CHAPTER FIVE

1.

The funeral home was empty when they arrived.

Sara walked him over to Samantha's casket. The mortician made it so that nothing from the chest down could be seen, due to the amount of damage the shotgun blast had done to her at pointblank range. Her blonde hair was done in ringlets, and just the right amount of makeup had been applied to make her look like some life-sized doll. The dress they picked was white with little yellow flowers all over it, like something out of the spring collection at a high-end clothing boutique.

In a matching casket next to her, Roger lay dressed in a fine, navy blue suit with a red tie. He normally wore glasses. Here he didn't have them on, however, and the left side of his face was caked heavily in clumpy makeup, making him look slightly disfigured in the soft overhead lighting. Bolan had a grisly suspicion that Samantha's husband had been shot in the side of the face before he died. Standing over the two of them, he suddenly felt like a complete ghoul.

He shifted his eyes back to his daughter, lying so still and stiff. "She's pretty," he said more to himself than anyone else, but Sara took this as if he was talking to her.

"She was always such a girly-girl," she said softly, lightly running her fingertips along the hem of her daughter's dress. "She was my world." She began to choke up and put her fist against her lips, squeezing her eyes shut against it. Bolan stood there feeling like his hands were made of thumbs and he didn't know what the hell to do. A quick glance over his shoulder, he saw Jim near the foyer in a black suit and tie, watching the two of them like a hawk.

"I wish I could've gotten to know her better," he said quietly. He felt the tears beginning to sting his own eyes. "I wish I could've been there." Then he felt Sara's hand slowly slide into his, coiling around his fingers and knuckles like a little soft, warm animal and give him a gentle squeeze; exactly the way she used to when they would go to the park and spend an hour or so just walking and talking before they sneaked off someplace to make love.

He looked down at her, puzzled a little. She was looking back at him, but out of the corner of her eye. Her head never moved.

"I'm glad you're here now," she said.

"I wish I wasn't, to be honest."

"I know."

2.

He rode with Sara and Jim to the cemetery. It was awkward, to say the least. Bolan sat in the back of the extended cab with his big hands lying in his lap, watching the world passing by his window as they drove out of town and onto the highway. Jim and Sara made some small talk back and forth, but that eventually dried up and the ride was quiet until Jim decided to turn on the radio. Bolan caught him glancing back at him every so often in the rearview mirror, and he suddenly wondered if this guy was going to be a real problem.

After five miles of cornfields and farms where herds of cows grazed lumpishly under the mid-morning sun, they turned into a large cemetery encircled by a tall, wrought-iron fence.

Bolan remembered the place well. His cousin had been buried here just a year before he went to prison. Joey had died in a drinking and driving accident. He and some friends had been hitting it pretty hard all night. They decided to go on a beer run at eleven-thirty, and did so at around a hundred and ten miles per hour. Joey had been in the back seat and two of his friends had been in the front when they took an almost ninety-degree curve in the road without so much as tapping the brakes. The car wrapped itself around a two hundred-year-old oak tree that gave no fucks and was crushed like an empty Pepsi can. Joey had been ejected from the car through the rear windshield, dead with a broken neck before his body hit the road. The last time Bolan had seen him was here, just before they lowered his casket into the cold, dark earth. He still harbored a bitterness towards his cousin, he realized as Jim slowed and followed the procession of mourners through the cemetery's entrance, because his death was one that could've been avoided if he'd just not been so damn stupid.

Isn't that most of us, in the end? He wondered on that, and hoped not.

3.

The preacher spoke at the graveside about Roger and Samantha, about their involvement in the church and how loving they were as parents, promising everyone listening that they had secured their place in Heaven and were, even now, walking on streets of gold. When it was over, everyone stepped forward and paid their respects, tossing flowers or saying a little prayer, and then they turned and gave Sara and Jim a hug or a handshake, passing over Bolan with curious looks as they made their way back to their cars.

Once they began lowering the caskets into the ground, he turned away and found Jim's truck and decided to wait here for Sara until it was all over. He didn't feel he had a right to stand there beside her after all these years, and he hated himself for it.

After almost an hour, Sara finally appeared, walking like a mournful spirit through the tombstones, her black dress flowing around her in rippling shadow. When she reached the truck, she lit a cigarette and leaned back against the passenger door next to Bolan.

"Do you have any plans tonight?" she said after a long silence. The cemetery was quickly emptying out now.

"No," he said.

"We're having a get-together later. Some food and beers, nothing big. You're welcome to come."

"Jim doesn't like me."

Sara blew out a cloud of smoke. "Jim's overprotective. He loved Sam like his own daughter, and absolutely *adores* Abby." She glanced up at him. "And he's heard the stories about you."

Bolan looked at her. "From you?"

She shook her head. "Not all of them. There's people in town who still remember you. Some of them keep up on things, and you killing a man in prison is almost legend."

Bolan crossed his arms. His long legs were also crossed in front of him, capped with the big blocky work boots the state had issued him upon his release. Right now it was the best he had, but he still felt like he didn't belong here.

"I didn't kill the guy for fun," he said moodily. "The prick came at me in the shower with two of his buddies and a shiv. I did what I had to do, and I'd do it again."

"*That's* why guys like Jim are nervous around you, Bolan."

"I didn't tell *him* that."

"You don't need to. Your eyes, the way you carry yourself— they say it loud and clear: *Don't fuck with me.* You need to loosen up a bit."

"I don't know how to do that."

She flipped her cigarette into the grass. "I know, Bolan, but you're not in prison anymore. Sam rented that apartment for you because she truly believed in you. She never told me she found you, but if she was writing you for a whole year, then she had hope for you. The best thing you can do right now is to start living your life. Do it for her, if not for yourself."

He thought about that, and it frightened him when he realized he had no idea how to do it. It was a strange feeling, not knowing how to live. He'd spent so long just trying to survive that *actually living* had become something of an enigma; something for other people, not him.

"I'll try," he said.

She smiled up at him. "That's all I ask. So how about it? You coming over later?"

He considered it, and then shook his head. "I can't. I need some time to think about what I'm going to do. Maybe some other time. Okay?"

She put her hand on his broad, muscular forearm and ran her fingertips lightly through his arm hair, the way she used to do when they were dating. It sent a shiver all the way up the side of his face.

"You do what you have to," she said. "We may not be together anymore, but we're *in* this together, just the same."

He reached down and grabbed her hand in his; and for a moment they looked at each other, again like two people gazing out across a vast ocean of time and space.

He said, "Sara—"

"Everything alright?"

Bolan's mouth snapped shut. Jim had appeared as swiftly and silently as Satan. He was standing near the front of the truck, his eyes watching their touching hands with cool disapproval. Sara jumped a little and pulled back, smiling awkwardly as she stepped forward and gave him a peck on the cheek.

"Everything's fine, honey," she said. "Bolan said he won't be able to make it tonight."

Jim looked at Bolan as Sara opened the door and climbed up into the truck. "What a shame," he said sourly, and then made his way around to the driver's side door.

CHAPTER SIX

1.

A few blocks away from his apartment, just across the street from the library, was the city police station.

Bolan hesitated outside the building, remembering the night he'd been arrested all those years ago. The arresting officer had brought him down here to take a statement. Bolan had still been drunk and his shirt stippled with Marcus Baxter's blood. It was in one of the interrogation rooms inside this very building that they told him he was facing a felony charge and possible prison time, and *that's* when the reality of the situation had set in for him. It wasn't the handcuffs cutting off his circulation and making his fingers feel like they were being stung by a hundred angry wasps, or the ride across town in the back of the cruiser that smelled like a mixture of disinfectant and old vomit. No, it was in that room—sitting across the table from the officer taking the report while his head started to pound and his bladder became engorged with all the booze he'd drank since early evening—that he knew his life would never be the same again.

He remembered that moment now, and shivered; thought about turning around and just going home, but he couldn't. Someone inside might have the answers he needed, and he wasn't going to run away from them. He opened the door and stepped inside.

2.

The lobby was painted drywall and darkly-stained wood. A large plaque with the pictures of every police officer on the roster hung on one wall. Each officer's name and rank was displayed just below their picture, with the current Chief of Police sitting above them all like the portrait of a king. Bolan didn't know any of them as he scanned each and every face (he was looking for the guy who'd arrested him that night and couldn't find him), though a few might've been people with which he'd gone to school.

A table stacked with some old magazines sat against the far wall next to an ugly plush chair. A few feet to the right was a heavy wooden door leading into the back, next to which stood a windowed counter with a little silver bell sitting off to the side. He looked through the glass and saw empty desks and dark computer monitors and wondered if anyone was actually on duty. He tapped the top of the bell and recoiled a little when it rang. In the small, empty hallway it was startlingly loud.

He waited a moment to see if anyone would come and investigate the ringing bell, and when no one did, he turned and went for the door.

"Can I help you?"

A woman roughly his age was now standing behind the glass in a dark blue police uniform. She had her hair done in a boy-cut and she was looking at him with a bored expression.

"I just had a few questions," he said.

"Do you need to report a crime?"

"No."

"Okay, then, what's your question?"

Now that he was here, he didn't know exactly how to ask what he wanted to know. "My daughter and her husband were killed a few days ago in Cambridge."

"I'm sorry to hear that." And she was, he could tell.

"Thanks. Anyway, I know this isn't the right jurisdiction, but I was wondering if you people maybe had some information on it."

She looked at him, her curiosity deepening. "Information? Like what?"

"I just wanted to know if the Cambridge police had any suspects they were looking at."

"Unfortunately, you would have to ask them about that, sir. You could call them or go into the station and ask to speak with the detective assigned to the case. Other than that, I don't know what else to tell you."

He nodded. It was pretty much how he thought this would go, but he had to try. "Thanks."

"Are you okay?"

He looked back at her and thought for a second she looked familiar, but he couldn't place her face. Then it occurred to him that she had been one of the jailers who'd booked him in the night he was arrested, all those years ago. He was positive it was the same woman because he could remember thinking at the time she was too young to be working in a jail. She obviously didn't share his recollection, though. She was looking at him as if she'd never seen him before in her life.

And why would she remember me, anyway? How many people had she seen come and go over the years? Probably a lot.

"Yeah," he said. "I'm fine."

"You said your daughter and her husband were killed. Was it a violent crime or an accident?"

"Violent. They were shot in a home invasion."

The officer looked appalled. "I'm sorry."

"It's fine, really. Thanks for your help." He went for the door again, and she stopped him again. He turned back and she slid a small white business card under the glass.

"This is the name and number of Detective Shelby Carlson," she said. "He's my cousin. Give him my name and he can patch you through to whoever you need to speak with."

Bolan took the card, turned it over in his hands, inspected the writing on the one side, and then put it in his pocket. "Thank you.

And what name do I give him?"

"Molly," she said. "Officer Molly Daniels."

"Thank you, Officer Daniels."

"You're welcome. And again, I'm sorry for your loss."

"Me too."

3.

Bolan waited until he was inside his apartment before making the call. He took out the card Officer Molly Daniels had given him and dialed the number.

"Cambridge Police Department, how may I direct your call?"

"I need to speak with a Detective Shelby Carlson."

"One moment."

A brief silence.

"This is Carlson."

"Yeah, an Officer Molly Daniels gave me your name."

"Okay. Something I can do for you?"

"Well, I was wanting some information about a home invasion that happened about a week ago."

"Buddy, you're going to have to do better than that. We're up to our eyeballs in homicides, robberies, and in-broad-daylight home invasions around here."

"It was a young couple. Roger and Samantha McLean."

"Hold on."

More silence, but it was shorter this time.

"I'm sorry, sir, I'm not the detective on that case. You'll want to speak with a Detective Palmer."

"Palmer?"

"Yes. I can patch you through to his office. I think he's still here doing some paperwork or something."

"That would be great. Thank you."

"By the way, how do you know my cousin?"

"I don't. I met her this morning and asked her how I could find some information on this and she directed me to you. Nice lady."

"She's like a little sister to me. I'll patch you through. You have a good day."

"You too."

After a minute or two, an older, gruffer voice said, "Palmer here."

"Detective Palmer, I was calling about the home invasion that happened the other day. Roger and Samantha McLean were the victims."

"Do you have some information pertaining to the case?" The rough voice suddenly sounded interested, almost hopeful. It gave Bolan a sinking feeling he didn't like at all. *If he's hoping I have something to share, then he doesn't have anything.* He prayed he was wrong, but he didn't think so.

"No, sir, I was actually hoping you could give *me* some information."

"And you are?"

"Bolan O'Brien. Samantha McLean was my daughter."

"Hold on a sec." Bolan could hear him clacking away on his keyboard. "Says here a James Bowman is the father, Sara Lewis the mother."

Bolan didn't recognize the name, but then he remembered that a lot of people named James went by Jim. "He's the stepfather. I'm the biological father. It's a long story."

"It always is."

Bolan had to bite his tongue on that one. "I was wondering if you could maybe tell me a bit of what happened."

"I don't see why not. But to be honest with you, Mr. O'Brien, there's not much for us to go on at the moment. Mrs. McLean was in the back of the house, apparently working in her garden, when an individual dressed in black and wearing a black ski mask entered the backyard through the gate in the privacy fence and shot her at pointblank range with what we believe to be a 12-gauge shotgun."

He remembered what Sara had said, about Samantha looking like she'd been blown apart, and the way the mortician had made it so none of her was visible from the chest down. He shuddered.

"Mr. O'Brien?"

Bolan took a deep breath. He was standing at one of the living room windows with his eyes closed. "Go on, Detective."

Detective Palmer cleared his throat. "Yes, well, at the same time Mrs. McLean was shot in the backyard, another individual forced his way through the front door, where he then shot Mr. McLean three times—twice in the chest and once in the forehead, just above his right eye."

He remembered the heavy, clumpy makeup on Roger's face and suddenly felt ill. "Was it a robbery?"

"That's the thing, Mr. O'Brien, nothing in the house seemed to be touched. Mr. McLean's wallet was sitting on top of the dresser in the bedroom with over three hundred dollars still in it. None of his credit cards were taken, either."

"How do you know they were wearing ski masks?"

"The neighbor who called 911 saw the man who entered the backyard through the fence."

"And there's no way to tell who it was? With cameras everywhere, and satellites, you people are still stumped by a fucking *ski mask?"*

Palmer bristled at that. "Mr. O'Brien, I told you we're doing everything we can. You need to have a little patience, as hard as that may be right now."

"Did Samantha and Roger know who attacked them?" Bolan went on without missing a beat.

"I don't think so, no."

"Do you have any suspects at all? I'm no cop, but this seems to me like they may have been targeted."

"We have a few leads, but I'm not at liberty to discuss the details in an ongoing investigation. I hope you can understand that."

"Is there anything else you *can* tell me?"

"I'm afraid not, Mr. O'Brien. Like I said, I can't discuss the details of an ongoing investigation."

"So you have no idea who actually shot my daughter and her husband?" Bolan could feel the heat in his face rising—that sick, helpless feeling in the pit of his gut.

"Mr. O'Brien?" Palmer said, avoiding the question.

"Yes?"

"I'm sorry as hell this happened to your daughter. I would love to tell you the same bullshit we always say, about how we'll catch these guys and we'll make them pay for what they did, but the scum-sucking truth of it is that we're severely understaffed and underfunded, with the city council tying our hands at every turn. If someone doesn't come forward with a definite I.D., or video, or *something,* then the chances of us finding these assholes are pretty slim. Nothing was left at the scene; and believe me, we've poured over every inch of every room. Not a single hair or fingerprint that didn't belong to the McLeans has been found. The killers even took the empty shell casings before they left."

Bolan was stunned by the man's candor, the amount of raw, infuriating honesty. "I understand, Detective." *But I don't like it one fucking bit.*

The detective sighed, his breath rattling. "The way I see this playing out is like this: one of these lowlife shitbags is going to get caught for something down the road. They're going to want to make a deal to save their own ass. When that happens, they'll tell some story about a guy they heard who shot your daughter, and they'll offer to give up his name just so they won't have to sit in prison where they belong for the next ten-to-twenty years."

"That's not very comforting."

"No, it's not, but that's how this shit usually goes in cases like this. Or sometimes the universe corrects itself and the man who shot your daughter and son-in-law ends up dead with his throat cut in some piss-stained alley, or with a needle sticking out of his arm. Either way, it's going to work itself out."

Bolan didn't know what to say to that.

"Look," Detective Palmer went on, "give me your number. The moment I hear anything, you and Miss Lewis will be the first people I call. Okay?"

"Okay." He gave the detective his number, thanked him, and then hung up.

That night, as he lay on the couch in his living room and watched a small spider crawl its way across the cracked ceiling fifteen feet above him, he realized just how different the outside world and prison really were. If a man wronged you in prison, you knew right where to find him, and there was a very easy—and bloody—solution to right that wrong. But out here, in the real world, he was powerless to do anything.

And it pissed him off.

CHAPTER SEVEN

1.

He decided to take Rick up on his offer of a free haircut and maybe ask him about the job he'd mentioned.

"Come on in," Rick said when the door opened. It was nine in the morning and the shop was empty. It smelled like coffee and aftershave.

"Hope I'm not bothering you."

Rick shook his head, folded the paper he'd been reading and put it on the counter next to his clippers and combs. "Not at all. Mondays are usually pretty slow until around three or four. What can I do for you?"

Bolan looked at himself in the mirror. His hair had grown out quite a bit since he was released from prison and he had started to grow a beard. It was thick and black with just a few tiny tell-tale grays here and there.

"That free haircut still on the table?"

"Yes, sir," Rick said, smiling broadly. He gestured for Bolan to sit in the chair, then grabbed one of those body bibs and snapped it around his thick bull neck. "And the beard? Goin or stayin?"

Bolan moved his head up and down, side to side, examining it in the mirror. "I think I'll keep it. I like the way it looks."

Rick nodded. "Me, too. Not on my face, mind you, but it does bring out the color in your muscles." He chuckled at his own joke and grabbed a spray bottle. "How we doin the hair?"

"Part it on the side and trim it up around the ears and back."

"You're the boss."

They chatted while Rick worked, talking about everything from the weather to taxes to the rising price of gas, none of which concerned Bolan in the least.

Finally, Rick was finished and began to clean the back of his neck and around his ears with a soft brush. He held up a small hand mirror to let Bolan see both sides of his head, asking if that's what he wanted. Bolan looked at it, liked what he saw, and told him as much.

"Free of charge," Rick said as he stood up from the chair, "but next time it'll be twenty-two dollars."

"Okay," Bolan said. "And how about that job you offered? You still need someone to sweep and take out the trash?"

Rick washed his hands and dried them on a towel. "Sure. As long as you understand I can't pay you more than fifteen an hour."

"That's fine," Bolan said, relieved. He had a meeting with his parole officer on Friday and this was one less thing he had to worry about. "When do you want me to start?"

Rick turned and grabbed the black plastic broom and tossed it to him. "How about now?"

Bolan caught the broom. "Thanks, Rick."

"See how thankful you feel when you see your first paycheck, son."

They both laughed.

2.

Bolan was busy sweeping hair into a pile at 4:30 in the afternoon a few weeks later when Rick returned from running some errands and told him to come out back with him. He put the broom aside and followed the barber through a small hallway cluttered with boxes to a metal door with a bright green EXIT sign over it.

"Where we going?" he asked as Rick put his hands on the door and pushed it open.

"Just hold onto your balls, son," Rick said as he stepped out into a small gravel lot behind the building. This area was for private parking. The only way in or out was through a small alley running beside Rick's shop.

Bolan followed him outside. Rick's sky-blue Cadillac was sitting directly in front of the door. The barber pointed to another car next to it. This one was an old gray Chevy Nova that had a little bit of rust around the tires. The gray wasn't even paint, Bolan saw, but primer.

"What do you think?" Rick asked.

Bolan shrugged. "About what?"

Rick frowned. "The car, stupid. What do you think about the *car?*"

Bolan walked around it, looking it over the way a man might look over a questionable buffet spread. "It's pretty cool, I guess."

"It's a piece of shit, but the papers are clean. Here." He took a set of keys from his pocket and tossed them over the hood. Bolan caught them with both hands. "Man needs some wheels of his own, don't you think?"

Bolan looked at the keys, looked at the car, and then at Rick. "Are you serious?"

Rick gave him a wicked grin and nodded. "Damn straight. It's yours. No strings attached. Well, there is *one* string."

Bolan frowned. "What is it?"

"You ever want to get rid of her, you give her back to me. Understood?"

"Rick, I can't take this." He offered the keys back.

Rick waved it away. "Nonsense!" he said. "It's my car and I can give it to whoever I want to. I *want* you to have it. Part of your job now will be to run errands for me so I don't have to. That alright with you?"

Bolan didn't know what to say. He crossed the space between them, his boots crunching dully in the gravel, and gave the old man a hug that made his back crackle.

"Careful, you freakin ape," Rick sputtered, pushing him out to arm's length. "I'm not as spry as I used to be."

"Thank you so much, Rick," Bolan said, deeply moved by the gift. No one had ever given him anything so great in his entire life.

Rick waved this away, too. "Don't worry about it. She's all yours now. I had a friend of mine rebuild the engine and transmission. She looks old and broken down on the outside, but everything under the hood is top notch. I want you to have her, son. You've gone through enough bullshit in this life, I felt it was time you had something positive to focus on."

Bolan looked at him, felt his eyes welling up. Rick saw it and nodded gravely.

"I heard about your daughter, and I'm sorry as hell about it," he said. "This car don't mean jack shit stacked up next to something like that, but I wanted to do something other than just give you my condolences." He nodded at the car. It sat in the small gravel lot like some dangerous, crouching animal waiting to be unleashed. "I first got her when I returned from 'Nam in '75. This one's a 1969."

"Thank you, Rick. This really means a lot to me."

Rick shoved his hands into his front pockets. "To the both of us. Now get your ass back inside and sweep up the mess I made. She'll still be waiting for you when you clock out at six." Then he turned, grinning like the Cheshire Cat, and left Bolan standing there, alone, with his new ride.

3.

He found himself driving out to the cemetery where Samantha and Roger were buried. He didn't plan it, didn't even realize that he was heading there until he was pulling in through the big wrought-iron gates and slowly cruising along the narrow asphalt lane towards the back corner where they shared a large marble headstone in which both of their names were engraved.

He cut the engine and got out, approached the huge headstone that gleamed in the sun like polished glass.

ROGER AND SAMANTHA MCLEAN, the top of it read. *LOVING PARENTS AND SERVANTS OF JESUS CHRIST.*

He stood there quietly, hands in his jeans pockets, listening to the wind sigh through the trees around him. Somewhere far off a dog was barking happily.

"I just wanted to come out here and tell you both how thankful I am for what you did for me," he said out loud. It was awkward for him, talking to a stone. He was never much of a believer in ghosts or spirits (at least not the way they were portrayed in movies and horror novels), but he did believe in God—to some extent—and thus reasoned that if there really was such a thing as God, then there must also be a place for someone's soul to move onto when they died. And he felt that if there was even the *slightest* chance Samantha and Roger could hear him, then he needed to say it.

"I wish there was something I could do. I'm so sorry for what happened to you." His vision began to blur and he felt the tears pouring from his eyes like warm blood from fresh wounds. Wiping them away, he lifted his head to the sky and closed his eyes, trying to get ahold of himself.

If only I had been here, he thought, and not for the first time. *If only I would've listened to Sara that night.*

But he knew that the kid he'd been back then would've never listened to anyone, no matter how much sense they might've made. His mother, whom he could never remember a single day without a beer in her hand, had always told him that he was the biggest mistake she'd ever made, and that he was going to end up in prison one day. *"You're either going to kill somebody, or somebody's going to kill you because of your temper,"* she would lecture him, her eyes large and dark and mean, sunken into her bony face from years of heavy drinking, holding her beer in one hand and the cigarette that would eventually kill her in the other. *"You're just like your dad, Bolan—a fucking hotheaded loser. And that's all you'll ever be."*

He opened his eyes and looked down at the headstone. Someone had placed some flowers at the foot of it. They hadn't been there long, either. *Probably Sara,* he thought. And then, irritably, *Or Jim.*

Reaching his hand out, he ran his palm across the curved top of the stone, feeling the rough granules on his skin like thousands of sharp, microscopic teeth.

"I'm going find out who did this," he suddenly said out loud. The tears were dry now, glazed around the edges of his eyes. His voice took on a coldness that was strange to his own ears. "I'm going to find them and make them pay for what they did."

He stepped in closer, leaned down and gave the large carved *S* of Samantha's name a light kiss. It was like kissing an old, bloodless scar.

"That's one thing I can still do for you."

He lingered for a few moments more, listening to the birds singing in the boughs of a nearby elm tree, and then went back and slid in behind the wheel of his car. Giving the headstone one final, long look, he sealed his intentions within his heart and brought the engine to life with a roar, put the car in gear, and slowly rumbled his way back out onto the highway.

CHAPTER EIGHT

1.

Over the next several months, Bolan worked for Rick in the barber shop sweeping, mopping, emptying the trash, and running whatever errands the old man needed done. One afternoon he'd gone to lunch and grabbed the two of them some burgers from Wendy's. When he came back, the shop was empty and quiet. He called out to Rick as he shut the door behind him, but there was no answer. Worried, he sat the bag of food down on the counter top. Went into the office in the back and found Rick with his face in the toilet in his private bathroom, vomiting violently.

"Rick, you alright?"

Bolan assumed he'd caught a flu bug, or maybe ate something that didn't agree with him, but when Rick finally pulled himself shakily to his feet, looking pale, Bolan saw blood spattered around the inside of the bowl—thick, nasty streamers of it. There was also blood on Rick's lips, in his mustache, and he wasn't fast enough with that raggedy handkerchief he always carried to wipe it away before Bolan saw it.

"What's wrong with you?"

Rick blew the question off as nonsense. "You sound like a

Nancy."

"I don't care." Bolan followed him out of the bathroom and back into the office. He didn't like the way Rick just sort of collapsed into his chair behind his desk. "Tell me what's going on, Rick."

Rick waited for Bolan to sit down. "I got cancer," he finally said. "Stomach." He tapped his belly, just above his naval.

"Damn," Bolan said after a long moment of silence. He was looking down at his big hands. "I'm sorry to hear that."

Rick chuckled. "Yeah, me too. Doc says I need to be taking chemo. I told him to fuck right off."

Bolan didn't argue with him. When he was seventeen, a year before his arrest, his Aunt Jan had died of breast cancer. The doctors convinced her to take the chemo therapy treatments, telling her it increased her chances of going into remission by almost eighty-five percent. She believed them, took the treatments, and died eleven months later. But not before she'd gone through the worst pain Bolan imagined a human being could ever experience. She lost her hair, both of her breasts, and weighed less than ninety pounds when she finally took her last breath. What he saw lying in that hospital bed— hooked up to every machine the hospital had, it seemed—looked nothing like the vibrant, loving woman he'd known his entire childhood.

"How long do you have?" he asked quietly.

Rick shrugged. He was already starting to bounce back from his nausea. "A few months. Maybe a year, if I'm lucky. I don't really care."

Bolan looked up sharply. "You don't care?"

"Not one bit."

"Why not?"

"Because I'm done with this life," Rick explained matter-of-factly. "And I don't mean in a suicidal way, either. I mean, I've lived a good long while, got to marry the greatest woman God ever created, and I've run a successful business now for the last thirty-five years. My bills are paid, my affairs are in order, and I see no reason to prolong the inevitable. As far as chemo goes, I want to enjoy the time I have left and not be poked with needles and filled with poison while some moron doctor pats me on the head and tells me everything is gonna be fine. No sir, not me."

Bolan thought he could understand that. "I'm behind you, whatever you want to do," he said.

Rick looked at him and smiled. "Thank you, son. Means a lot."

They were quiet for a moment, both of them wrestling with where to go from here, when Rick's eyes rolled up to Bolan's face. His expression was serious.

"What about you?" he asked.

"What do you mean?"

"Learn anything about what happened to your daughter and son-in-law?"

Bolan shook his head. "I've been calling that detective every week for months now. He's starting to get annoyed, I think."

"Fuck him," Rick said nastily. "They still don't have a clue who did it?"

"No." Bolan looked up, shrugged his heavy shoulders. He remembered the promise he'd made at the cemetery and choked down a lump of dull, helpless rage. "There's nothing I can do."

Rick considered him a moment. "What do you *wanna* do?"

"Make them pay." His voice had the tone of a judge passing down a death sentence.

"Okay," Rick said. He sat forward, his chair squeaking beneath him. "All you need to do is find out who they are."

"How do I do that?"

"Well, you said Samantha and her husband were big into church and doing the Lord's work, right?"

Bolan nodded.

"Start there."

"At the church?" Bolan almost laughed. Rick's stone-cold expression smothered the urge.

"Think about it, son: nobody just up and kills someone like your daughter without a reason. You said it yourself—they left Roger's wallet and credit cards just fucking sitting there."

"What does that have to do with it?"

"They were *targeted,* Bolan. That means someone knows something. Someone *always* knows. Place to start is to talk to someone close to them."

"The preacher," Bolan said.

Rick grinned. "Now you're getting it."

2.

Against his better judgment, he decided to call Sara.

"Hello?"

"It's me."

"Bolan? What's going on?"

"I was just wondering how you were holding up," he lied, suddenly feeling very awkward.

She sighed. "Feels like I haven't slept in days."

"I hope it's not too late, me calling," he said.

"No, not at all. I was just sitting here going over some bills and shit. How have you been?"

"Working for Rick. Trying to get on my feet, you know?"

"Rick?"

"He owns the barber shop below my apartment."

"Oh. That's cool."

"Yeah, I just sweep up, run some errands—that sort of thing."

"I thought I saw you driving a few weeks ago," she said. "A gray Nova or something. When did you get your license?"

"Rick gave me the car, but he wouldn't put it in my name until I took the test. A few months ago."

"Well, I'm happy for you, Bolan. I truly am."

"Thank you," he said.

"So, what's up? Something you need, or were you just worried about me?" She sounded like she was being sarcastic, but it was hard to tell.

"Any way I could come by?"

She was quiet. He could hear music playing softly in the background. Finally, she said, "Come on over. But don't make me wait too long."

"Alright. Be about twenty minutes."

"Okay." She hung up.

3.

There was a lamp on in the living room when he knocked. He waited a moment, heard her feet shuffling behind the door.

"Hold on," she said, and then the rattle of a chain lock being loosed and the door opened. Her hair was piled on top of her head like golden foam, and she was wearing a long, salmon-colored nightgown with no bra underneath. Her nipples were standing out of the silky fabric like push-pins. "I was about to go to bed." She stepped aside, welcoming him in.

"I got here as fast as I could." He stepped into the living room. It smelled of potpourri and cigarettes. A large aquarium sat on a table along the far wall, lit up bright blue and swirling with colorful fish. The television was off and a radio was quietly playing Phil Collins in the background. *She always did have good taste in music.*

"Have a seat," she said, motioning towards a large leather sectional couch as she went to the kitchen. "Want a beer?"

"Sure." He sat down, placed his hands in his lap. He suddenly didn't know what to do with himself.

She took a beer from the refrigerator and handed it to him as she sat down beside him. He could smell her perfume. Vanilla. Same thing she used to wear all those years ago. She had a cigarette between her fingers and snuffed it out in an old glass ashtray that looked heavier than a brick. It was piled with old butts, not all of them hers by the looks of the various filters. He suddenly wondered if Jim was here and thought this might've been a bad idea after all.

"Welcome to my home," she said, her words slightly slurred as she waved her hand around the room. He could smell the vodka on her breath even before she picked up her glass and took a sip. Now he *really* thought he might've made a mistake.

"Look, if you're busy, I can come back later."

She lowered the glass and looked at him, puzzled. She was buzzed, alright, though still a ways from being full-on drunk. "Why would you do that? I look busy to you?"

"No."

"You're fine, Bolan. Relax." She emptied her glass and sat it on the end table next to her. When she turned towards him, she was smiling. "You said you wanted to talk," she said.

"Yeah, I guess I did."

Her smile widened a little. She adjusted her nightgown so that it tightened against her breasts. "I thought maybe you just wanted to fuck."

Stunned, he just looked at her. He felt a rush of heat in his face and neck and started to get up. "Maybe I should go."

She put a hand on his arm and gently pulled him back down. "I'm just messing with you. I have a man. Jim. I told you about him. He's a good guy."

"I don't want to start any trouble for you."

"You're not. Now sit the fuck down and relax." She reached down and grabbed the beer from between his legs and took a drink from it before handing it back to him. "You want to talk, let's talk." Then she looked at him, her smile faltering a little. "What did you want to talk about?"

He was looking down at his hands, feeling like a nervous boy in the principle's office again. "I guess I just wanted to know about the last twenty years. I want to know who my daughter was." He could feel the sting of tears, and when he looked up at her, she was crying, too. Tears were rolling down her cheeks, but the rest of her face was calm and motionless; she was like a statue crying in some dark and lonely garden.

"Well," she said after a moment or two, calmly wiping the tears away with the palm of her right hand, "Samantha was a free spirit. Always looking for the next adventure. But she loved people, always trying to help someone if she could. That's what I really loved about her. She was sweet."

"I never met her face-to-face," he said quietly. "She started writing me out of the blue. It took me by surprise, really. About a year before I was supposed to get out, I was walking back from my job in the kitchen when a guard stopped me. He had a letter in his hand and told me someone must love me, after all." Bolan smiled at the memory. He and Officer Delbert always went back and forth like that. "I hadn't gotten a letter from anyone in years up to that point. I remember looking at the name on the front of the envelope and my fucking hands started shaking. It said *Samantha McLean*; and I can remember thinking that I didn't know any Samantha McLean, and yet somehow, deep down, I knew this letter was going to change things."

"How so?" Sara had turned and folded her legs underneath her and leaned forward, resting her elbows on the insides of her thighs. Her legs were long and smooth and muscular, and Bolan forced himself to look away. Not much farther up and he could see she wasn't wearing any panties, either.

"I don't know," he said, focusing on the aquarium across the room. Some big fish was lazing on the side of the tank, warming itself beneath the overhead light. "Something just told me I needed to read that letter, so I made my way back to my cell and took it out of the envelope and devoured every word. I had to read it like five times just to convince myself it was real. Anyway, I wrote her back and she started sending me a letter every week after that. She wanted to come and see me, but I wouldn't let her."

"Why not?"

He shrugged. "I just didn't want her seeing me like that."

"You should've."

Bolan nodded slowly. His voice was thick with regret. "I know that now."

They were quiet for a long moment. Bolan could hear the

bubbling of the aquarium's water filter and Bruce Springsteen now on the radio singing about glory days.

"Wanna see some pictures?" she asked suddenly, jarring his eyes away from the huge fish that was now slowly circling a Spongebob Squarepants figurine at the bottom of the tank.

"Like baby pictures?"

She smiled and stood. The hem of her gown slowly rode up and he turned his face away. Memories of the two of them making love flooded back to him suddenly, and he shifted uncomfortably in his seat.

"Me and Sam made a scrapbook together last year," she was saying as she bent over and rummaged through a drawer in her computer desk. "This was just before they released me from the hospital."

She opened it and showed him a picture of herself holding Samantha in her arms. The baby was sleeping, wrapped in a fuzzy Mickey Mouse blanket and wearing a pink beanie cap. Sara looked tired, but her eyes had that motherly glow that was absolutely beautiful. He grinned, in spite of the fact he felt a stab of regret that his head wasn't floating and smiling over her shoulder in the picture.

"She was so little," he said, rubbing his thumb gently over the surface of the photo.

"Little?" She laughed. "She was twenty-two inches long and weighed almost eight pounds." She turned and looked him. "She

ended up taller than me by almost six inches. Got it from you."

They spent the next hour or so flipping through the book, looking at frozen memories of which he was never a part. Here was a picture of Samantha on her first day of kindergarten, wearing a pink Hello Kitty backpack; and over here she was in the first grade, dressed as an elf for the school Christmas play; and another picture a few years later at her first high school dance. She was wearing a cornflower blue dress and her blond hair was braided around her head and she looked absolutely stunning. Bolan felt as if a hand made of ice was squeezing his heart. If he stayed much longer it might burst.

"I think I need to go." He shifted the scrapbook from his lap into her hands and sat forward, resting his forearms on the tops of his knees.

She looked at him, confused at first, and then understanding dawned on her face and she closed the book and sat it on the end table next to her empty glass.

"I'm sorry," he said.

"I get it," she said. "We can go through this stuff another time."

He stood up, feeling like an asshole. "Thank you."

"No problem." She reached up, took his hand in hers.

They lingered that way for a moment, and then he gently slipped his hand free and went for the door. He opened it, and then turned and looked at her. Just before stepping out onto the porch, he said, as casually as he could manage, "What was Samantha's pastor's name?"

"Why do you want to know that?"

He shrugged. "I thought I might go to the church she went to and talk to him. Maybe learn more about her, I guess."

"That sounds like a good thing. I don't have his name off the top of my head. Hold on."

She went to the desk and rummaged through the top drawer until she found what she wanted. "This is his card," she said, handing it to him. "He gave it to me when Samantha was baptized."

Bolan took it, turned it over in his fingers. *Grace Fellowship Christian Church, Reverend Jacob Murphy,* it said, and had a list of numbers he could call.

"That's a mouthful," he said.

"They're good people," Sara said. "Church isn't exactly my thing, but if it was, I'd probably go there."

"And this is the guy who preached at her funeral?"

"Yeah."

He slid the card into the back pocket of his jeans. Then he looked at her, feeling a wave of regret and sadness washing over him. "Give Abby a kiss for me, will you?"

She nodded. "I promise."

He went to step outside. He put one foot out the door and then turned back around.

"What is it?" She could tell he wanted to say something.

Taking a deep breath, he said, "I wish to God I could go back to that night again."

She was puzzled at first, then shook her head. "Bolan, don't. What's over is over."

But he had to say it. Been waiting to say it now for twenty years. "It eats me up, Sara. Everything I missed, everything I gave up because of that one fucking night of stupidity. I'm sorry. I left you with a little girl to raise all by yourself, and now that little girl is dead and we're sitting here as if I have any right to feel loss or pain or sadness over it. I never meant for any of this to happen. I wish I could take it all back."

She placed her small, warm hand on his shoulder. "You have every right to hurt just as much as I do," she assured him. "Maybe even more than me. I at least have my memories. And they were good ones."

He nodded. "I have to go."

He turned and stepped off the porch and onto the sidewalk. Made his way down to the street where his car was waiting. Sara didn't say anything else, just watched him go. By the time he got behind the wheel and put the key into the ignition, he'd resigned himself to the road he had to follow now, whether it was right or wrong. If it was the last thing he ever did, the ones who killed his little girl were going to die.

CHAPTER NINE

1.

Jacob Murphy, Pastor of Grace Fellowship Christian Church, watched as the dull gray Chevy Nova came rumbling off the highway, it's tailpipes crackling and popping, and he suddenly had a bad feeling.

The aged muscle car turned into the parking lot and came to a stop. The driver killed the engine and sat there for a second—a large, faceless shadow behind the steering wheel. The pastor was bundled up in his big, fur-trimmed parka, his breath smoking in the freezing air as he laid salt along the sidewalk for this Sunday's service. A week before Christmas, it was bone-breaking cold, with roughly two inches of ice and snow covering everything in a thick crust, with more snow expected in the coming days.

He watched expectantly as the driver's side door opened. A foot encased in a large black harness boot emerged from the Nova's dark interior. It was attached to a long leg clad in fitted blue jeans. A moment later the driver got out and stood in the frigid cold, removing his sunglasses and tucking them into the collar of his black T-shirt as he looked around in a leisurely, curious fashion.

"Can I help you?" Jacob asked, setting the big, rumpled bag of salt crystals down on the sidewalk.

The driver turned his head and looked at him. There was something oddly familiar about him—those volcanic blue eyes and high cheekbones—but he knew he'd never seen this man before in his life. The guy was a giant, standing almost six and a half feet tall, and even the heavy jacket he wore (brown leather, wide collar trimmed in tan fleece) could not hide the fact he was muscled like a bull.

"I'm looking for the pastor here," the man said in a deep but friendly tone. His black hair was cropped short and neatly combed to the side, his beard thick and heavy.

"That's me." Jacob smiled as he approached, holding out his hand. "They call me Pastor Jake."

The driver of the Nova returned his smile and shook his hand with a grip like iron. "I was hoping we could have a talk," he said.

"Sure thing," Jacob said cheerfully, though that bad feeling was still there, worming its way through his gut. "Come inside where it's warm."

"Thank you."

That's how Bolan met Pastor Jake.

2.

"Would you like some coffee?" Pastor Jake asked as he hung his parka on a rack in the back corner of his office. The room was small and tidy, with dark wood paneling and a frosted window that looked out across a snowy field, beyond which a woods seemed to stretch away endlessly to the horizon. Bolan could see a small herd of three or four deer snuffling in the snow for food about a hundred yards from the window.

"No, thanks," he said, taking a seat in a chair in front of the pastor's desk. "I drank like a half a pot this morning already. I think I can feel my hair growing."

The pastor chuckled. "Wish I could say the same." He bent his head forward, giving Bolan a good view of his pinkish scalp shining through his thinning, sandy-blond hair. "Started losing it when I hit twenty-five. That was almost twenty years ago now."

Bolan looked the man over. He was short and heavy, but not morbidly obese, wearing a thick, light brown sweater and dark brown slacks. *He looks like one of my old English teachers in high school,* he thought.

"I'm sorry for just dropping in on you like this," he said as Pastor Jake made himself comfortable behind his desk.

Pastor Jake waved this away. "Oh, that's perfectly alright. That's what I'm here for. Not just for the church, but the community as a whole. I didn't catch your name."

"Bolan O'Brien."

The pastor seemed to mull this over, and then shook his head slightly. "Sorry," he said with an embarrassed chuckle, "but you look familiar to me and I cannot for the life of me think of where we might've met. Your name doesn't ring any bells, either."

"My daughter's name was Samantha. Samantha McLean."

The smile faltered. "I'm so sorry for your loss, Mr. O'Brien."

"Just Bolan. And thank you."

"Yes, Bolan. Sam told me a lot about you in the last year before she . . ." He trailed off, not exactly sure how—or *if*—he should finish the statement.

"Was murdered." Bolan did it for him.

"Yes. I'm really sorry for your loss—for *all* of our loss. Sam and Roger were fine young people, a good family, and they were instrumental in growing our outreach program here at Grace Fellowship."

"I don't care about any of that," Bolan said, a little colder than he'd intended.

Pastor Jake's mouth snapped shut. A look of sudden concern crossed his face. "Do you mind telling me what you *are* here for, Bolan?"

"I have some questions."

The pastor spread his hands open on the desk in front of him. "I'll help in any way I can."

"I want to know who would kill a couple of kids like Samantha and Roger, to start."

Pastor Jake blinked. "Well, I'd say only some pretty disturbed people would do such a thing."

Bolan nodded. *On that, we agree.* "The police said it was a home invasion."

"That's what we were told, too."

"Except that nothing was taken from their home."

Pastor Jake's brow wrinkled at that. "That's strange."

"That's what I thought. I'm no cop, but it tells me that someone wanted them dead for a reason."

The pastor looked genuinely unnerved by that. "You mean, you think someone *targeted* them?"

Bolan nodded. "I do. I can't prove it, but I know it."

Pastor Jake grew quiet. His hands were now folded in front of him as if in prayer. At last he looked up. "Someone they *knew.*" It wasn't a question.

Bolan felt his heart leap up at that. He sat forward in his chair. "Did my daughter or Roger get involved in something they shouldn't have?"

Pastor Jake eyed him warily. "I think they might've," he said to Bolan's complete surprise. "Roger, at least."

"Tell me," Bolan said. "I need to know."

"That would violate the promise I made to Roger."

"I don't care about that, either. I need to know what you know."

"I've been wrestling with this for almost a year now," the pastor said with a heavy sigh. "But I don't want to wrestle with it anymore."

"Then tell me," Bolan urged. He was one step away from lunging over the desk and yanking the man up by his throat.

The reverend took a long, deep breath, and said, "Roger came to me last January. For a few weeks before that—right after Christmas, I believe—he seemed very agitated. I never asked any questions, thinking he might tell me in his own time. So I watched him and waited. Then one day after service he waited until almost everyone in the church was gone and asked me if we could come to my office and talk. I said sure, let's go, and he went on to tell me that he'd gotten into some trouble with some very bad people."

Bolan nodded. "Go on."

"He told me his business was going under and that he needed some money. He went to the bank but was turned down for a small business loan due to some things he'd defaulted on in the past when he first got out of college. He told me he'd found someone who offered to loan him the money at an outrageous interest rate. I told him not to do it, to trust in God and let *Him* provide for his family, but Roger said he needed the money *now*."

Bolan felt a chill settle in his heart. "What did he do then?"

"He took the money," Pastor Jake said with grim finality. "Everything seemed fine after that, only he never told Samantha about it."

"She didn't know anything?"

The pastor shook his head gravely. "Not that I am aware of. A month or so went by. Roger came to me—he was pretty shaken up—and said he had gotten in over his head."

"How much did he owe?"

Pastor Jake shrugged. "I don't know how much he actually borrowed. He wouldn't tell me that. Just said they were threatening him and his family."

"What did Roger do about it? Did he go to the cops?"

"No," the pastor said. "He was too scared. Said they'd threatened his family and that they would kill Sam and his daughter if they even smelled a cop."

"And what did you tell him?"

"I told him to contact the police," he said. "I threatened to do it myself if he didn't, but Roger freaked out and made me promise as his pastor that I would keep my mouth shut."

Bolan didn't say anything. Just sat there as still as stone.

His silence made the pastor nervous. "I should've went to the police with what I knew," he admitted, "but Roger would've just denied it all and taken his family and left. You never met him, Bolan. You have no idea how scared and irrational he was. I was afraid he would do something *really* stupid and get them all killed anyway." He put the palm of his hand against his forehead in a gesture of distress. "I'm so sorry."

After giving the pastor some time to get himself together, Bolan asked, "Do you know who these people are?"

Pastor Jake grabbed some Kleenexes from a box on the corner of his desk, blew his nose and wiped his eyes. "I only got one name out of him."

Good enough. "What was the name?"

The pastor looked up sharply. He heard something in Bolan's tone he didn't like. "Why?"

"Why do you think?"

Pastor Jake shook his head. "No. No, I won't be a part of *that*."

Bolan was on his feet, reaching across the desk before the man could even blink. He used his left arm to sweep the books and computer onto the floor with a loud crash, and then grabbed the pastor by the throat with his right hand. He squeezed until something in the pastor's larynx gave a hollow little *pop*, and lifted him out of the chair as easily as if he weighed no more than a small child. The muscles in Bolan's arm stood out in thick cords, visible even through the heavy brown leather of his jacket sleeve.

"The name," he hissed through gritted teeth. "Now."

Pastor Jake's face went from pink to fire engine-red as he feebly beat at Bolan's thick wrists with the palms of his hands. *"Please!"* he croaked, *"Lemme go!"*

"The name," Bolan repeated, lifting him a few inches higher. He had him against the wall with his feet dangling over the carpeted floor.

"B-Benny!" the pastor croaked. *"He said his name was Benny!"*

"Last name?"

He shook his head rapidly back and forth. *"That's all he said, I swear!"*

"Where did they meet?" The reverend made a little gagging sound. "Come on, Pastor. Where did they meet?"

"A bar in Cambridge! Twenty-fifth Street!"

Bolan loosened his grip and let the pastor down as gently as he could. The man was bent over, hands on his thighs, coughing and hacking, sucking in big gobs of air. When Bolan got to the door of his office, he stopped and turned around. Pastor Jake was now standing upright, eyes floating in pockets of red, puffy flesh, his hand rubbing at the front of his throat.

"You keep your mouth shut about this," he warned. "Otherwise, they'll never find your fucking head."

Pastor Jake flashed him a mean, animal look of contempt. *"Just get out of here!"*

Without looking back, Bolan turned and went to his car.

3.

Rick listened quietly, taking an occasional sip of his beer as Bolan told him everything he'd learned from the preacher. When he was finished, the old man shook his head. "I'll be damned."

"You know this bar he mentioned?" Bolan asked. His beer sat untouched on the table in front of him.

Rick nodded. "The Shamrock." He went silent again, thinking. Then he stood up, the legs of his chair screeching on the kitchen floor. "Come with me a minute."

He led Bolan to his bedroom at the back of the house. They were standing in front of a gun safe that looked to Bolan as if it weighed as much as an elephant. Rick silently punched in the combination on the electronic keypad and popped it open.

Bolan gave a little whistle. "These are all *yours?*"

"Of course they're mine. Who else would they belong to?"

The safe had several guns standing in racks in a nice, neat row. Bolan counted six rifles, four different handguns, and three shotguns of various barrel-lengths, all of them polished and cleaned and looking as if they had just come off a showroom floor.

"Quite a collection," he said.

"It's alright, I guess." Rick reached into the safe, took one of the rifles. "Ever see one of these?"

"In almost every war movie in the eighties," Bolan said with a laugh.

Rick chuckled, flipping the gun over in his hands. "Yeah, well, there's a reason for that. This is an M16A1," he explained. "I carried this baby in the jungles of Vietnam back in the late sixties and early seventies. You wouldn't believe what I had to go through to smuggle it back stateside. Here." He tossed the rifle with both hands. Bolan caught it, amazed at how lightweight it was. "Merry Christmas."

Bolan liked the look and feel of it. "You serious?"

"Aren't I always?"

"Thanks."

"Thank me after you blow this Benny fucker's head off." He paused, then stabbed a finger at Bolan. "And don't get caught with the fucking thing."

Bolan looked up. "Won't they be able to trace this back to you?"

Rick laughed dryly. "Not likely. It's not in any database, but that won't matter if they pull *you* over with it." In the bottom of the safe was a large stack of ammo boxes of various calibers. "Grab some of those and follow me. Not those, the 5.56 hollow points. That's it. Now, come on."

"Where are we going?" Bolan asked, cradling four of the boxes against his chest.

But Rick wasn't waiting around. The barber's oversized snow boots were clomping their way into the hall and already crossing the kitchen to the back door. Bolan went after him.

4.

Rick led him out to the barn. The cold, December wind came howling across the fields and cut through the both of them like a blade of ice. Bolan shivered.

"What're you doing?" he asked as Rick selected a key from his ring and unlocked the heavy doors. The smell of old hay and stale manure rolled over him, a sweet and pungent odor that wasn't at all unpleasant. Rick had told him he used to own a few horses before Laura died, but that he'd had to sell them off to pay for her sudden and unexpected funeral after she'd collapsed of a heart attack.

"We're gonna go find this Benny prick," Rick said. There were two rows of horse stalls running on either side of the barn. Sitting in the middle was a black GMC van, partially covered in a blue tarp. Rick yanked it away, coughing as a cloud of dust settled over him.

Bolan just looked at him.

Rick saw the look, and bristled. "Don't you give me any shit, damn you. I'm coming along to make sure this goes smoothly."

"*What* goes smoothly?" Bolan stepped into the barn, still

lugging the M16.

Rick didn't answer. He climbed in behind the wheel. Reached across the passenger seat and opened the door for Bolan.

"What're we doing here, Rick?"

"I told you," Rick said, and started the engine. "We're gonna find Benny."

"You mean *right now?*"

"You got something else to do?"

Bolan didn't.

5.

As it turned out, finding Benny wasn't as easy as simply going to The Shamrock and waiting for him to show up. For one thing, Bolan had no idea what the man even looked like. Second, there was no way to know if the guy frequented the place on a regular basis. Bolan said as much to Rick as they took their seats at the bar.

"I suppose we should ask around," Rick said.

"Won't that make the guy suspicious?"

"The man's a criminal, son. He's suspicious by nature."

"Yeah, but you look like you could be a cop."

Rick turned on him with genuine hostility. "Go fuck yourself."

Bolan grinned. "I'm serious. How do we ask around without scaring the guy off?"

Rick just shrugged. Behind them, the clack of pool balls seemed to mingle with the beats coming from the juke box.

After about an hour, Bolan was ready to call it a day. His head hurt from the beer and the constant noise of the place, and his back was starting to cramp. "Let's get out of here," he said.

"We need to at least ask someone if they know the guy," Rick insisted. He rapped his knuckles on the bar top. *"Bartender!"* The man looked up from the crossword puzzle he'd been brooding over now for the last hour or so, and made his way down to their end of the bar.

"Whaddya need?"

"I was wondering if Benny was around," Rick said bluntly.

The bartender was tall and skinny, with long hair and an obscenely-long beard that hung almost to his belt buckle. Brightly-colored tattoos covered both his sinewy arms from wrist to shoulder. From the vibrancy of the colors and the attention to detail, Bolan was convinced it wasn't prison ink.

The bartender bent forward at Rick's question, cocking an ear towards him. "Who did you say?"

"Benny," Rick said, a little louder this time, but not so loud that anyone outside of their little huddle could hear him. "I was told I could find him here."

The man frowned at the mention of the name, his eyes instantly bright and suspicious. *Shit,* Bolan thought. *We've already lost him.*

"Don't know no Benny, man," the bartender said. "Sorry."

"You sure?" Rick moved his hand and suddenly there was a hundred dollar bill, folded longways, between his first and second fingers.

The man's eyes lit on the money. He looked from the bill to Rick's face. "I might know him," he said shrewdly, "if there's another one where *that* came from." He nodded toward Rick's hand.

Rick reached into his flannel jacket and produced another hundred, coupled it with the first, and then flattened them out on the bar in front of him. "How about now, asshole?"

The bar tender scooped them up and made them disappear into the front pocket of his jeans. "Guy named Benny comes in here once in a while," he said, keeping his voice low. His eyes bounced around the room behind Bolan and Rick cautiously as he spoke. He pointed to a stool at the end of the bar where it dog-legged. "Sits over there and takes bets on the games." He nodded up at the large flatscreens on the wall above the bar. Each one had a different sport playing while they were sitting there.

Bolan frowned. "He's a bookie."

The bartender shrugged. "I don't know, and I don't want to. He pays for his drinks, never starts any trouble, and I don't ask questions. But I saw some of the dudes who come in here to meet with him. Not the kind of guys you fuck with. Get my drift?"

Bolan and Rick exchanged looks. Rick then turned and said, "I have another fifty for you if you don't tell him we were asking about him." He pulled out another bill and slid it across the table to the man's waiting hand.

"No problem," the bartender said. He snatched up the money as if he half-expected Rick to change his mind and yank it away. "I never talk to the dude about anything other than what he wants to drink and the weather. I prefer it like that."

"And what would it take for you to call him and get him here?" Bolan said.

The man's expression soured. "Never fuckin happen."

"Maybe I owe him some money, want to pay him," Bolan said.

"Then you should already have his number."

Bolan studied the man's face, fighting the urge to smash it to a red ruin. "Call him now."

The guy seemed to think it over, said with a hard grin, "You fellas have a good night," and then turned back to his crossword puzzle.

It was a complete and open dismissal, and Bolan wasn't having it. His right arm shot out like a piston and grabbed the man by the hair on the top of his head, and then, with both hands, he brought the bartender's face crashing down hard on the bar top, which suddenly startled Rick, who recoiled with a hiss of *"Shit!"* between his teeth. Over the blaring music, no one heard the man's nose break like a dry twig against the counter, and if anyone bothered to look over at all, they would've only saw Bolan and Rick talking to the man as he seemed to be bent over and reaching for something under the bar.

Bolan kept his sledge-like fist knotted in the man's long, greasy hair while leaning up and over him, applying pressure to the back of his neck with his heavy forearm. He leaned in close, so that his mouth was almost against the guy's right ear. Blood was running out of his busted nose.

"If I have to tell you to call him one more time, I will break one of these bottles and shove it down into your fucking skull," Bolan said with deadly softness. "You understand?"

"Fuck!"

He tightened his grip. He could feel the roots of the man's hair popping as they slowly pulled away from his scalp. "I asked you a question, asshole."

"Yeah, yeah, I get it! Fuck, man! Lemme go!"

"Dial the number."

The bartender reached into his back pocket and took out his phone. As Bolan had suspected, the guy was on better terms with the bookie than he'd first let on. He had the number dialed in just a few seconds.

"Put it on speaker," Rick told him. He'd regained his composure now and seemed to be enjoying the man's distress immensely.

Through the speaker, Bolan heard a man answer, say, "Hello?"

"Benny?"

"Of course it is, dickhead. You dialed my number. Whaddya want?"

Bolan leaned forward, applying pressure to the bartender's already strained neck. Any more weight on it and it would snap like a pencil.

"I gotta guy down here wants to make a bet," the bartender said, doing an excellent job of keeping the pain out of his voice.

"You called me for *that?*"

The bartender's right eye rolled up to Bolan. "He says he wants to drop five on tomorrow's Vegas match. I'm lookin at him right now. He's carrying a fat stack. Thought you'd be interested."

A long pause. Bolan and Rick exchanged looks. The bartender was shitting himself.

At last, the man on the other end said, "Alright, sure. Tell him to meet me there at the bar tonight, nine o'clock."

Bolan could feel the relief sweep through the bartender. A long, low shudder ran from his head to his feet. "Alright, dude, thanks," he said to the bookie. "Have a round on me when you get here, for the interruption."

The bookie on the other line chuckled. "I always did like you, Tom. See you at nine." Then he hung up.

Rick winked up at Bolan, tapping the bar with his knuckles as he turned his stool towards the door. "Good man," he said to the bartender and got to his feet.

Bolan released him, grimacing as a few strands of the guy's hair stuck to his fingers. He wiped them off with a napkin. "I'm coming back at nine. You do anything to screw with us, and I'll cut your fucking head off."

The bartender had a rag to his face now, soaking up the blood still pouring out of his mangled nose. His eyes were wet and runny, but he nodded and said he understood. Bolan gave him one last look of warning, and then followed Rick out to the van.

CHAPTER TEN

1.

"So what do you think?" Bolan asked as they drove out of town. It had started to snow. Ice crusted the edges of the van's windshield in jagged swathes.

"We need to get shit ready," Rick said. His breath smoked in the air in front of him.

"Ready for what?"

Rick turned and gave him a hard look. "His interrogation." He didn't say any more, and Bolan didn't ask.

They didn't speak another word the whole way back to Rick's farm.

2.

By 8:30, roughly five hours since their conversation with Tom the Bartender, they were back at the bar, sitting in the frozen gravel lot out back. They'd spent the entire afternoon clearing out one of Rick's old horse stalls (he'd been using them for storage over the years and had accumulated quite a lot of crap), getting it ready for their unwitting guest.

"Let's get this show on the road," Rick said suddenly after

consulting his watch.

Bolan left the rifle Rick had given him at the farm, choosing to carry a knife instead. He'd found it in the barn in a steamer trunk full of stuff from Rick's time in 'Nam, and when he showed it to him, Rick said he used to carry it in the jungle with him while on patrol.

"Can I have it?" Bolan had asked. It was big and heavy, serrated to a saw-toothed edge on the backside of the blade.

Rick gave the knife a disinterested look and shrugged. "Sure, I don't give a shit."

Bolan figured if this went south and the police got involved, he would get a hell of a lot less time being in possession of a knife than a gun. "What's the plan?" he said.

"We go in, make sure we have our guy, then get his ass out here into the van."

"How do we do that?"

Rick thought it over, lightly drumming his fingertips against the steering wheel. "Wait until he goes to the bathroom and force him out that door there." He pointed to the back entrance behind the building on the other side of the small, square-shaped parking lot. "Soon as I see you, I'll open the doors."

Bolan looked at him. "You think it'll work?"

"Big as you are, you shouldn't have any problems manhandling the prick," Rick assured him. "Besides, he puts up a struggle, I'll point this at his head and let him know it would be smarter to relax and do as he's told." He placed his .45 gently on the dashboard in front of him.

Without another word, Bolan got out and crossed the lot, his boots crunching heavily in the snow.

3.

There was a man sitting at the end of the bar when he walked in, exactly where Tom the Bartender told him he would be.

As Bolan neared the bar, Tom (now wearing a bandage across his battered nose and sporting two black eyes) signaled him with a slight sideways nod of his head, indicating a lean man of average height sitting at the end where the bar bent into its signature L shape.

"That's him!" Tom muttered under his breath as Bolan took a spot three stools down from where the bookie was sitting. He thought he caught the tail end of an insult thrown in there for good measure, but he let it slide. Tom had earned the right to be pissed off.

Bolan ordered a beer. He could feel the adrenaline starting to pump now. After clearing out the stall all afternoon, he'd been tired. Now he was wide awake.

Risking a quick glance, he saw the man named Benny was wearing a dark brown leather long coat over a white paisley button-down shirt and black jeans. He couldn't see the man's shoes, but if he had to bet on it, he guessed they were something made of leather and probably expensive. He was clean-shaven. His hair was slightly longer, greasy, combed straight back from his broad forehead. When he smiled, his teeth were crooked and slightly yellowed.

Now, how the hell do I get him outside?

Bolan sat and thought it over for a few minutes, taking a mean little pleasure in watching Tom the Bartender squirm under the tension. He was pretending to wash the same mug for the last twenty minutes, his eyes bouncing from Bolan to the man at the end of the bar, and back again. Benny, on the other hand, was more interested in watching the game on one of the flatscreens, sucking down beer and chomping on peanuts while making marks in a little notebook he took from his left breast pocket. He didn't seem to notice the bartender's trepidation in the least.

I've got to get him outside somehow. There has to be a way.

As if he'd read Bolan's mind and decided to play along, the bookie suddenly got off the stool and put his phone in his pocket. "Catch me up if I miss anything, will ya?" he asked Tom, nodding towards the TV. "I'm gonna take a piss."

The bartender briefly glanced at Bolan and then gave the bookie a nervous smile and nodded. "Sure thing, pal."

"By the way," Benny said, stopping on his way to the bathroom. "What the fuck happened to your face?"

Tom swallowed, looked from Benny to Bolan, and then back to Benny. Bolan felt his gut tighten and thought maybe the bookie might notice that little sleight of the eyes, but Benny just stood there waiting for an answer, a little smirk on his lean, hawkish face.

"Damn bottle of Jack fell off the shelf earlier," Tom said smoothly. "Cracked me right between the eyes."

Benny considered this, laughed. "Ain't that some shit?" Then he shook his head, chuckled, and walked past Bolan towards the restrooms in the back.

It's now or never.

Tom seemed to see the sentiment in Bolan's eyes and gave a quick little nod behind the bookie's back. *Do whatever you're gonna do and get the fuck outta here,* that nod seemed to say.

Bolan put his beer down and got up. He shadowed his prey until the man reached his hand out to push open the men's room door, and then grabbed him by the throat, shoving him hard up against the wall. The bookie, caught off guard, made this little garbled *urk* sound in his throat as he tried to beat Bolan's hands away and free himself, but he might as well have been fighting off a grizzly bear. Bolan was too strong and too aggressive, and when he slammed his forearm into the side of the bookie's head, all the fight drained out of him and he sank to his knees.

"You fuckin hit me!" the bookie managed to get out just before Bolan hauled him back up to his full height and planted a knee with the force of a battering ram into his guts, ripping the air from his lungs in a sickening, wet whooshing sound. He sank right back down

to his knees, letting out a long, thin, whistling gasp in place of a scream.

"Who the fuck are you?" he wheezed when he was finally able to draw in a breath. His eyes were watering and his cheeks and head were as a red as a brightly-polished apple.

"Shut up," Bolan said calmly and coldly. He took a quick look back towards the pool tables to see if anyone was watching. Thankfully, no one seemed to give a rat's ass about what was happening near the restrooms. "We're going for a little ride. Keep your mouth shut or I'll break your jaw. Understand?"

Benny shook his head. "No, I *don't* understand! Who the fuck are you?"

Bolan yanked him to his feet a second time. He reached into the man's jacket and pulled his piece from where it sat snug inside a plastic, carbine fiber holster clipped to his belt. It was a Glock 9mm. He quickly shoved it down the front of his pants and covered it with his jacket.

"That's *my* fuckin piece!" Benny spat, and he wriggled to try and break free.

Bolan slapped him with an open hand across the jaw, hard. The force of it snapped Benny's head back so that he had no choice but to look up into Bolan's moody blue eyes.

"One more word, and I'll open you from throat to crotch." His fist was curled around the haft of the combat knife when he brought it up close to Benny's face and laid the tip against his cheek, just below his right eye. "You understand *now?*"

Benny's eyes bulged. He nodded vigorously. "Yeah, yeah! I got it!"

Bolan shoved him towards the door at the end of the hall. "Let's get some fresh air, then."

Benny crashed through the back door and tumbled into the parking lot with all the grace of a pig in a tutu. It wasn't until he saw the van with its back doors open that he realized just how much trouble he was in.

4.

It was cold in the barn, especially for Benny. He was sitting in the center of one of Rick's horse stalls, strapped to a chair with zip ties cinched around his wrists and ankles. A piece of duct tape covered his mouth, and there was nothing keeping his balls warm except for his boxer shorts. The rest of his clothes were in a pile in the back corner of the stall.

"This is how it's going to go," Bolan told him as he leaned against the side of the stall, one foot planted on the nail-studded wood behind him, his big arms crossed over his chest. The M16 was leaning against the wall next to him. Benny's eyes brightened with fear when Bolan brought it in with him.

"I'm going to ask you some questions. You're going to answer them. Simple. You refuse to answer, I hurt you. You *still* refuse to answer, I start cutting pieces off you, one-by-one." He reached behind him and drew the large knife from its scabbard on his belt. "Am I making myself clear?"

Benny eyed the long, scarred blade fearfully. He nodded and mumbled something.

"I'm going to remove the tape," Bolan said, sheathing the knife. "You scream, and I cut your fucking nose off. Clear?" Benny nodded. He was sweating, and he stank like fried chicken grease. "Good." Bolan tore the tape off in one hard yank. If Benny had been wearing a mustache, it would've come off with it.

"Ouch!"

"No louder than that, and we'll get along fine," Bolan said, wadding up the tape and tossing it into a corner. The stall smelled like old hay and dust, with a ghostly hint of horseflesh. "Are you ready?"

Benny looked at him, on the verge of tears. "W-who are you, man? I ain't never seen you before in my life."

"Want to jump right in, huh?" Bolan nodded. "Fine. I'm the father of a woman you murdered at the end of last April."

Benny frowned. "I don't know nothin about no murder, man. I don't kill people."

"Liar." Bolan raised the knife.

Benny flinched back against the chair. "Listen, man! I didn't kill

110

anybody! I'm a business man, that's all!"

"It's your *business* I'd like to talk about." Outside the stall, Rick was rifling through some old clutter he'd kept out here in storage. Benny was listening and suddenly looked scared again.

"What's that old man up to back there?" he wondered with big, wet eyes.

"Don't worry about him," Bolan said. "You worry about me."

Benny shivered. "I'm freezing my ass off, man! Can I at least have a blanket or something?"

Bolan bent down, planting his hands on his knees so that he was eye-to-eye with Benny. "You're not getting *shit* until we're done."

"Okay, okay. It's cool. Look, I'll tell you anything you want to know. Just get me a blanket or something, alright?"

Bolan straightened. "Rick?"

"Got one right here," Rick grunted, and then something came flapping over the stall's wall and landed with a heavy thud on the ground next to Benny's chair. Both Bolan and Benny looked down at it at the same time.

"*Hell* no, man!" Benny cried when Bolan picked up the horse blanket and showed it to him. "That fuckin thing's probably crawlin with mice or fleas or some shit!"

Bolan threw it over his shoulders. He wasn't wrong, either. The

blanket stank like dirt and mouse turds. "Best you're going to get."
He adjusted the blanket on his shoulders so that it covered most of
his upper arms. There were holes where mice had chewed through
the fabric, and faint stains that might've been anything. "Better?"

Benny looked anything but better. "I guess."

"Good. Now let's begin."

"Whaddya wanna know?"

"Who killed my daughter and her husband?"

Benny shook his head. "I don't know who you're talkin about,
man. Give me a name or somethin."

Bolan's face hardened. "Their names were Samantha and Roger
McLean."

Benny thought this over for a second, his eyes moving back and
forth as if he was reading a file in his memory Bolan couldn't see. "I
never heard of 'em, man. Honest."

The knife came out with a viciousness that made the keen blade
hum. The tip hovered just half an inch from Benny's nose. "You'd
better tell me what I want to know, or I'm cutting it off." He gave his
nose a little prick with the knife. Benny jerked back as if something
jumped out and bit him.

"I swear, man! I never heard those names before!"

Bolan, switching gears, said, "You approached Roger in the

Shamrock. The two of you started talking. Sometime during the conversation you mentioned that you give out loans."

Benny's eyes flickered at that. He nodded. "Yeah, that's right. I met him at the bar."

"So you remember him?"

"Sure. He was looking to borrow twenty grand, or something like that. He offered one of his trucks as collateral. I told him I'd have to call my boss."

"Did you?"

Benny nodded. "Of course. I can't loan out that kind of money without consulting upper management, you dig?"

"Your boss gave the okay?"

Benny nodded. "It's a lotta money."

"What's your boss's name?"

Benny stopped. His mouth snapped shut. He shook his head. "Man, they'll kill me if I tell you that."

"*I'll* kill you if you don't."

Benny was quiet for a long time, his head bent down so that Bolan couldn't see his face. Finally, he said, "Vincent."

"What's his last name?"

"Vincent Manga. He's the head of the Manga Family. They run

a smuggling operation outta Express Continental. You probably seen their trucks on the highway. They're a big deal throughout the Midwest. He runs the whole fuckin show."

Bolan left the stall, came back with a dusty stool Rick had dragged out when going through his things. He planted it on the floor in front of Benny and sat down. "Tell me about it."

Benny took a deep breath, let it out. "Vincent's family is originally from Detroit. His daddy is some big shot mob guy up there, or so I've heard. He's also like eighty-something. Nobody down here has ever seen the old man." He shrugged. "Vincent runs his entire operation down here and ships the money back up north."

"What do they smuggle?"

Benny looked at him like he was stupid. "Guns. Drugs. Dirty cash that needs cleaned, that sorta shit. Vincent uses the legitimate side of his business to hide it."

Bolan mulled this over. "Tell me about you and Roger."

"Guy came to me wanting to borrow twenty large, like I said. I didn't want to help him at first, but I told him I would see what I could do."

"Why didn't you want to help him?" Bolan asked with a frown.

Benny shrugged. "I dunno, he seemed too young, desperate. I thought to myself, no way this dude's gonna pay it back. It felt wrong."

"Go on."

"He asked me about the money. I told him I'd have to give my boss a ring. I did, and Vincent gave the okay, only he wanted something else."

"What did he want?"

"He wanted Roger's trucks," Benny said. "To smuggle shit across the border. He figured the kid bein an American and a small business owner, the Border Patrol would overlook him."

"Guy like Roger wouldn't draw that much attention," Bolan agreed.

Benny nodded grimly. "Exactly."

Bolan was quiet. He was going over everything in his mind, not wanting to miss anything. Finally, he asked, "How did Roger know to come to you? From everything I've seen, he wasn't the type to know guys like you."

Benny seemed mildly offended, but he let it pass. "Kid started askin people around the bar, real subtle and shit." He uttered a sarcastic little grunt. "Tom heard 'im, gave me a call."

"And Vincent told you to give this dumb kid twenty grand, just like that?"

Benny was nervous now. "N-no. He wanted a face-to-face."

Bolan's eyebrow arched. "Roger met with him?"

Benny nodded. "Yeah. Vincent wined and dined 'im, started askin him about his business—how many trucks he had, how big were they, that sorta shit. Then he gives the kid the money in this fat envelope, tells him he's got thirty days to pay it off. With interest. Only this dumb fucking kid comes back a month later, tells Vincent he can't pay it all back in time. But that was the plan, see; because *that's* when Vincent made him the offer, about using his trucks. He fuckin *knew* the kid wouldn't be able to pay that shit off in a month. So he promised to wipe the debt clean if Roger did a run for him. Only Roger told him to go fuck himself, and here we are."

Bolan looked at him, surprised. "He actually said that?"

Benny shrugged. "Not in those words, but it's all the same to Vincent."

Bolan was looking for any indication the man might be lying. All those years in prison, he'd seen every sort of liar and conman there was; he knew when someone was trying to run a game on him. As far as he could tell, though, Benny was either telling the truth, or he deserved an Academy Award.

"Are you saying it was Vincent who ordered my daughter to be killed?" he asked finally.

Benny nodded. "That's what I've been sayin. Vincent is the one who put the word out when Roger told him to screw off. And once Vincent gives the green light, he don't just kill *you*. He kills your whole family."

Bolan was quiet, thinking. Benny watched him for a moment, then fidgeted in his chair. He said, "If you're lookin for some payback, you can forget it. Vincent is heavily protected—both inside *and* outside the law. You dig?"

"Nobody is untouchable," Bolan said. *Prison taught me that.*

"Whatever, man. Yer funeral."

Bolan stood up from the stool, approached Benny with the knife in his hand. Benny saw it and instinctively recoiled back against the chair. "How do I get to him?" Bolan asked.

"I just told you. You don't." His eyes were following the knife like a hypnotist's finger.

"There has to be a way," Bolan said. "How do *you* meet with him?"

"I rarely ever see the man in person," Benny admitted. "But if I was to put in a good word for you like I did Roger, he might wanna meet with you. I must emphasize the word *might*. To be honest, Vincent can be unpredictable. No tellin what he might do at any given point."

"Can you make it happen or not?"

"You have to be one scary motherfucker to impress *these* cats," Benny warned. "They don't just take in anyone off the street. You need to have the type of skill set they're lookin for."

"How about a man who spent twenty years in prison for beating another man to death? Would that impress them?"

Benny chuckled at that. "That's right up their fuckin alley. But you don't get it, man. This ain't yer daddy's mafia and shit. These people are *modernized*. They own people at the bank. They pay off cops, judges, lawyers, politicians. They have *hackers* these days, for fuck's sake. They're a mega-corporation you never hear about. They do their homework, too. You can bet they'll be running your name through the NCIC the moment I give it to 'em."

Bolan smiled. It was unpleasant. "I won't need some bullshit cover they can see through."

Benny frowned. "What the fuck does that mean?"

Bolan squatted down in front of him, lifting the knife. Benny recoiled a little as he reached down and cut the zip ties off his ankles. "You got Roger in, you can get me in," he said slowly.

"I don't know, man," Benny said, rubbing his wrists ruefully. "This is a dangerous fuckin game, my friend."

Bolan stood to his full height, holding the knife down at his side. "Give them my name, let them do their background check. They won't be disappointed." He paused, then said, "What about the other two?"

Benny frowned, cocking his head to one side. "What other two?"

"The police think there were two men who broke into

Samantha's house," Bolan explained. "One went into the backyard through a privacy fence, the other kicked in the front door. I want them, too."

Benny thought this over a second, then said, "There's a few guys Vincent likes to use for things like that. I'll have to check around."

"I want their names and their faces, Benny. Both of them."

"They're probably private contractors," Benny said. "That'll be a little more difficult."

"You find out who they are. I don't care how."

"They'll kill me, too, if they find out I'm snoopin around."

Bolan gave him a hard look. "You just worry about getting me their names."

"And if I don't?"

Bolan placed the edge of the knife against the soft flesh of Benny's neck. "Then I'll have to kill you right now and figure something else out."

Benny swallowed hard enough that his throat clicked. "Easy, man. I was just askin." He licked his lips to moisten them. "I just have one request."

Bolan's brow furrowed. "What is it?"

"You go after Vincent, you'd better make sure he's dead. I'm serious, man. You don't go after a man like that and leave anything to chance."

Bolan agreed.

CHAPTER ELEVEN

1.

Christmas came and went, and no word from Benny. Bolan started to think maybe he'd been played. Then the phone rang.

"Yeah?"

"O'Brien?"

"What do you have for me?"

"I talked to Vincent," Benny said.

"And?"

"He wants to meet you face-to-face."

"You sound worried."

"The guy's a fuckin animal. Of *course* I'm worried. I just hope this doesn't end badly."

"Why do you just assume it will?"

"I don't know, man, maybe I'm just bein paranoid or somethin."

"When does he want to meet?"

"Tomorrow night. There's a truck stop up north going towards

Michigan off I-69 called the Hoosier Auto Truck Plaza. Know it?"

"I know it."

"Nine o'clock."

"Am I going alone?"

"No. Vincent wants me there, too." He didn't sound enthused by this at all. "Pick me up around seven."

"Fine. Give me your address."

"Oh, no. I'm not givin you my fuckin address. I'll be at the Shamrock."

"Alright. I'll be there."

"Yeah, me too." And Benny hung up.

2.

They'd been on the road for about twenty minutes when Bolan turned to him and said, "So what's the deal with you?"

Benny was huddled against the passenger door of the Nova, rubbing his hands in front of one of the heating vents in the dashboard. For a car as old as this, Bolan was impressed with how well everything worked.

"Whaddya mean?"

"It didn't take much for you to flip on your boss."

Benny didn't say anything.

"I have to admit, I was afraid you might be setting me up or something," Bolan said.

Benny's crooked teeth poked through a bitter grin. "You never know. I might be." Bolan fixed him with a withering glare. Benny suddenly burst out laughing, gave him a light, backhanded slap on the shoulder. "Relax, man."

Bolan glanced at him from the corner of his eye. He didn't like the sudden change in the man's mood. "So why are you doing this? What did Vincent do to you?"

It was dark inside the Nova. The sun had sank a few hours ago. Benny's face was lit up like a goblin mask by the dash lights. "Who said he did anything to me?"

Bolan shrugged. "I just figured, seeing as how you're helping me."

Benny turned and fixed him with a sour expression. "I had a knife to my throat, remember?"

"You don't now. Why go through with it?"

He didn't think Benny would answer. Then he said, "Let's just say you're not the only one to lose someone he cared about, and leave it at that."

"Fair enough."

Bolan turned the wipers on, swept the clinging snow off the windshield. The highway in front of him was mostly empty, except for a few semis and the occasional cop lurking with his lights off under the overpass.

3.

A short time later, he saw the truck stop sitting off to the right. The lot out back was full of semis—some of them idling with their running lights on, others dark and cold. There were eight gas pumps out front, with two pickup trucks and a small red car fueling up. Bolan avoided these, choosing to park along the side of the building where there were about a half dozen other vehicles spread out from each other. He picked a spot near the back so he could get a good view of the place and killed the Nova's engine.

For ten minutes they sat there with the snow swirling and blowing against the windows before a white Cadillac Escalade pulled off the highway into the truck stop. Its bright, halogen headlights swept across Bolan's windshield as it moved past the fuel pumps and then came to a stop in the parking lot, about three or four rows in front of him, just to his right. The driver was parked facing them, but the windows were tinted and the snow and the dark made it impossible to see anyone inside.

"That's gotta be them," Benny said softly beside him.

"You ever have to meet him like this before?"

Benny shook his head. "Nah. This is new."

Bolan watched the Escalade for a minute or two, until the other driver suddenly flashed his brights on twice in quick succession. They knew he was here, then.

Someone was getting out of the back of the Escalade. It was a big guy, wearing a winter overcoat with a heavy fur collar. He appeared to Bolan to be one of those men who, at first glance, looked fat and soft but were, in actuality, built like a brick shithouse. Kind of guy who could literally tear your head off and shit down your neck, if he was so inclined.

Bolan watched him approach with his head bent slightly into the falling snow. He rolled the window down when the man stopped just a foot or two from the driver's side door. The stranger lifted his head —a huge Cro-Magnon bulge with no hair and a face that looked as if it had been drawn on a caveman's wall.

"Good to see you, Benny."

"Hey, Vincent," Benny said nervously.

Vincent gave him a nod. "You takin any bets on the Super Bowl?" He never moved his head, but his eyes crawled over every inch of the Nova's interior, taking note of everything visible.

This guy doesn't miss anything, Bolan thought.

"Quite a few, yeah," Benny replied.

Vincent's face split in a smile that would frighten children at a single glance. "That's good. Glad to hear it." His eyes settled on

Bolan for the first time. "You O'Brien?"

"That's me."

Vincent nodded as if to say he'd figured as much. "Good to meet you. Benny here's been singin your praises, says you're the sort of guy I need workin for me."

Bolan looked at Benny. Benny shrugged. He looked back at Vincent. "I could use the work, to be honest."

Vincent gave the rusted Nova a cursory glance. "I can see that. Drivin around in this dinosaur, I'm surprised you can afford the gas these days." He shook his head the way a man might when discussing how far society has fallen. He then took a deep breath, expelled it loudly, and said, "I've done some reading up on you in the past few days. Impressive stuff. Took out three guys in prison all by yourself." It wasn't a question.

"I did what I had to," Bolan said.

"We all just do what we have to," Vincent remarked agreeably. He was just looking at Bolan in that unsettling way, studying him. "I want you two to follow me."

"Where?" Bolan asked.

"Someplace more private, where we can talk." He stopped and gave Bolan a huge grin, flashing his big, round, white teeth. "Don't worry," he added, "I'm not gonna kill ya. This ain't the fuckin movies." He gave the window sill a heavy rap with one huge hand

and then made his way back across the lot to the waiting Escalade. For a guy his size, he moved with a feline grace that was a little unsettling.

Benny waited until Vincent's huge frame disappeared inside the Cadillac and said, "You see what I mean? That dude's a fuckin monster."

"Yeah," Bolan agreed, and started the engine. *And he's going to die for it.*

4.

He followed the Escalade out onto the highway. They drove for about fifteen minutes and then turned off onto a back road lined with cornfields choked with snow on both sides. Another few minutes and they were turning into a large plot where an old barn stood all alone with a rusted windmill and a white-washed propane tank half-submerged in overgrown weeds. The house that used to be here must've been torn down a long time ago, because there was no sign of a foundation or anything at all to mark where it once stood.

A man got out of the Cadillac's front passenger seat. Approached the barn and pulled the doors open. He then stepped aside as the Escalade slid through the opening like a sleek, great white shark. Bolan was a few feet behind them. He waited until the guy standing outside waved in him, too. He pulled up right behind the Escalade and turned off the engine. Behind him, the barn doors closed with a loud bang.

For a second, Bolan felt the sting of panic rise up into the back of his throat. He looked in the rear view mirror and saw that the doorman was just standing there, watching the Nova from behind. He gave Benny a *here goes nothing* look, opened the driver's side door, stepped out.

"Welcome to one of my safe houses," Vincent said, his voice loud and deep inside the barn. "I have quite a few of these spread around so that the Feds can't bug my meetings. Hope you understand."

"I get it," Bolan said.

There was only Vincent and one other guy besides the one who'd opened the barn doors. The man standing to Vincent's right was tall and thin, much older than everyone else here. He wore a gray driver's cap, like one of those Irish gangsters in the movies, and a nice, long, black leather jacket that fell to the middle of this thighs. He was also watching Bolan with a mean, suspicious look, with one hand in his jacket pocket while the other hung loosely at his side.

"This here's my Uncle Lou," Vincent announced, indicating the older gentleman. Then he looked at the old man and pointed at Bolan. "This is the guy I was telling you about. Ain't he the biggest fuckin Irishman you ever saw?"

Uncle Lou looked Bolan up and down, unimpressed. "Saw bigger, back in the day."

Vincent chuckled at that, his small, mean eyes twinkling

merrily. "Uncle-fuckin-Lou—everything was better *back in the day.*"

Uncle Lou placed both his hands in his jacket pockets. He never took his eyes off Bolan.

Vincent tossed a nod over Bolan's shoulder. "The man behind you—Phil, get your ass over here—is my cousin, Philip. Uncle Lou's oldest son."

Bolan turned and the man named Phil walked past him and took his place near Lou. He seemed disinterested in all of this, even bored. He took a cigarette out of his coat and lit it. He was skinny like his father, with a head full of wild red hair he combed back from his broad forehead in waves.

"So that's everybody," Vincent said, bringing his huge hands together in an ear-splitting clap that echoed across the empty barn. Benny jumped at the sound, and Vincent seemed to take a moment of mean pleasure in it. "Now we get down to business. Benny, here, says you can handle yourself and that you can be trusted." He grinned. "I don't trust people as easily as Benny does, sorry to say. But I do need someone for a job. Think you can handle it?"

"Depends on the job," Bolan said. He didn't like the look the old man was giving him and instead focused his attention on Vincent.

"Job's simple: my cousin, Phil, is going to deliver something for me. He needs someone to drive him."

Bolan looked from Vincent to Phil (who didn't even seem to be in the same room, the way he was smoking and studying his nails), and then back to Vincent. "A driver? That's it?"

Vincent grinned, spreading his hands out in front of him. "That's it. You interested?"

"How much does it pay?" Bolan wasn't at all interested in the money, but he knew he couldn't look too eager to put his life in danger for free. They would smell a rat in an instant, and he would never leave this barn alive.

"It pays jack shit," Vincent told him, "but it gets your foot in the door. What do you say?"

Bolan glanced sideways at Benny. His skin was slicked with a thin sheen of sweat, despite the sub-zero temperature inside the barn. He looked back at Vincent. "Alright. I can drive."

Vincent beamed. "Excellent!" He turned to Uncle Lou. "Load his trunk and let's get the fuck outta here. Benny, you're coming with me. I have some things to talk over with you about the Big Game."

Benny flinched at the mention of his name, and then quickly regained his composure. "Sure, Vincent. Whatever you say."

"Phil, you know what to do. Show O'Brien here how we do things."

Phil took one last drag on his cigarette and snuffed it out on the heel of his shoe. "Of course, Vince. I got this."

"Wait a minute," Bolan said suddenly. Everyone froze in place.

Vincent's huge, ugly head slowly turned on his massive neck.

"What is it? Wasn't I clear enough?"

"So, do I have the job?"

Vincent looked at Uncle Lou, who simply shrugged and opened the back hatch of the Escalade. He took out what looked like a large Adidas gym bag (it was blue with white stripes) and walked it around to the back of Bolan's Chevy Nova.

"Pop the trunk," he said, pointing at Benny. Benny ran around to the driver's side, bent, and pulled the latch. The trunk popped open, Lou deposited the bag, and then slammed the lid down with a bang.

Vincent, meanwhile, was giving Bolan that unsettling smile again. "No," he said matter-of-factly, in answer to Bolan's question. "This is just the interview. If everything goes according to plan, we'll talk. If not, I know where you sleep." He laughed at that, and then climbed into the back of the Escalade, waiting for Uncle Lou and Benny to join him.

"Come on," Phil said suddenly, taking Benny's place in the passenger's seat. "We got a long drive ahead of us."

I guess I'm really doing this, Bolan thought, and then slid in behind the wheel.

CHAPTER TWELVE

1.

About three and a half hours later they were sitting outside a pawnshop on the south side of Detroit when Phil handed Bolan a gun.

"That's a .357 Magnum," he said proudly, tapping the big revolver. "You got a problem, you shoot it with this thing, and you ain't got a problem anymore. Dig what I'm sayin?"

Bolan looked at the gun as if it was a small, venomous animal. "You really think I'll need this? Vincent said I was just supposed to drive."

"It's just for show, man," Phil assured him. The man had spoken less than ten words to Bolan the entire drive north, and now he seemed to come alive—friendly, even. "Like they say, better to have it and not need it, than need it and not have it." He opened his door and paused with one leg outside and looked back at Bolan. "Just be cool, man. Vince chose me because I've done this a thousand times. Everything will be alright."

Bolan looked up from the gun in his lap and nodded. He felt like someone had just dumped a bucket of ice water into his belly. "Yeah, alright. Let's just get this shit done already."

Phil smiled, flashing his big grin like the world's most innocent car salesman. "My *man!* You got this." He got out and went around to the back, opened the trunk. Pulled out the Adidas gym bag, slung it over his right shoulder. He walked around to Bolan's window with a Beretta 9mm in his hand, checked the clip, and then shoved it down into his belt at the small of his back and covered it with his jacket.

"I need you ready to get us out of here when I come back out," he explained, his breath fogging the air in front of his long, thin face. "I'm gonna take the bag inside. Anybody follows me back out, or tries to get froggy and leap, you step out of the car and point that monstrosity at 'em. They'll take one look and run back inside. Got it?"

Bolan just looked at him, wondering how in the hell Vincent could place any amount of trust in this guy. He was a cartoon. The kind of guy who would do anything in school to get the approval of the "cool kids".

Phil saw the uncertainty in Bolan's eyes and mistook it for fear. "What's the problem?"

"Shouldn't I go in there with you? Hard to watch your back sitting out here."

"This place has a reinforced door in the back. Nobody they don't recognize gets back there to do business, you dig? I need you out here with the car running."

Bolan looked across the snow-blown lot at the pawn shop, and then back at Phil. "You expecting trouble?"

"I *always* expect trouble, man. Nature of the beast. But these guys are jumpier than your average scumbag, and I don't wanna take any chances something goes wrong. Just sit out here and wait for me to come back. Okay?" He gave the door a hard little rap with the back of his knuckles. "Relax, bro. You won't need to shoot anyone. These guys ain't gonna fuck around. They all know who Vince is. Just be cool. Keep the car running and be ready to get out of here when I get back. Okay?"

Bolan looked down at the gun, could feel the deadly weight of it. "Alright, man. Just don't take too damn long. It's freezing out here."

Phil shot him a smile and then began his walk towards the shop's front door, his shadow pooling beneath him in the glare thrown down by the parking lot lights.

2.

Ten minutes had passed with no sign of Phil. Bolan was watching the pawnshop when a sudden sick feeling came over him. He looked around nervously, checking his mirrors. It was just after one in the morning. This time of night, his was the only car in the lot, except for a blue Nissan parked only twenty yards away, crouching in the dark next to the building like a big, sleeping dog.

What the hell am I even doing here? This is fucking nuts. It crossed his mind to simply put the Nova in drive and take off, leaving Phil and Vincent and the whole business behind, but he knew he couldn't. Samantha and Roger deserved better.

He put his hand on the gear shift and began tapping it nervously with his fingers when Phil suddenly exited the pawnshop, minus the gym bag. He was walking hurriedly, occasionally looking back towards the shop over his shoulder, like he was expecting someone to follow him out.

Bolan's heart hit like a hammer. His eyes kept jumping from Phil to the door of the shop, and back to Phil. When Phil was about halfway between the pawn shop entrance and Bolan's car, the door to the pawn shop opened and someone stepped outside into the lot. This person raised his left hand to the side of his mouth and shouted out to Phil, who stopped and turned. The two of them had an exchange (Bolan couldn't make out anything they were saying above the blowing heater and the rumble of the Nova's engine), and then the man's right hand came up and that's when (too late) Bolan saw the gun. He couldn't see Phil's face, but it wasn't hard to imagine the smile melting away to a look of surprise as the gun made a dull *pop* and struck Phil somewhere in the abdomen. Bolan could see Phil's head turn downward as he looked at himself when the gun went off again, the second shot missing Phil only by a few inches.

That's when the reality of the situation settled over Phil and he turned with a round, white face of shock and began to run towards the waiting car. As he neared the front of the Nova, Bolan reached across the seat and opened the door for him. The gun went off three more times—*pop, pop, pop*—and Phil, his lips peeled back from his teeth in a terrified grin, dropped into the passenger's seat.

"Fuckin go!"

Bolan put the car in gear as the guy began to walk towards them with the semi-automatic pistol leveled at the windshield. He was of average height with a lean build, and wore baggy, stonewashed jeans with a large black hoodie. He trained the pistol on the passenger side of the Nova and yelled something Bolan couldn't make out.

"What the fuck, Phil?" Bolan had just enough time to get out before the man opened fire again.

The first shot completely spider-webbed the entire passenger side of the windshield. Phil was screaming frantically for him to hit the gas as the gunman fired again, this time striking the passenger door with the sound of a baseball hitting a metal garbage can.

That was all it took. Forget getting out of the car and pointing a gun at a man clearly ready and willing to shoot back. Bolan stomped the gas pedal to the floor. The Nova's tires screamed on the asphalt, slinging the car around in a perfect one-hundred-eighty-degree turn that Bolan would not have been able to pull off again if he had tried to do it on purpose. They were racing out of the lot and into the street as another round of gunshots caused the rear windshield to shatter like a bomb, spraying the back of Bolan's head and neck with hot shards of glass like tiny, biting teeth.

3.

"I'm hit, man!" Phil was screaming as Bolan blew through three red lights in a row. This time of night, the frozen streets were empty and dark. *"Oh God, I've been shot! I've been shot! Ohhhhh shiiiiit!"*

Bolan, wide-eyed and all sorts of confused, looked over and put a hand on Phil's shoulder, trying to calm him. The man's flesh was already cool and damp through his shirt.

"Just hold on!"

"I can't, man, it really hurts! Ahhhh!"

"What the fuck happened back there?" He looked over and saw Phil's right hand was slick with blood. The white button-down shirt he wore underneath his expensive leather jacket was nothing more than a sopping red rag. It was coming out of him fast enough to dribble onto the seat.

"I don't know! I walked in and gave them the bag, just like Vince told me to, and they started getting all sketchy on me and shit. I got a bad vibe, so I told them I had other business and had to split. Next thing I know, the dude with the hoodie tries to stop me from leaving the shop. I heard him say something to another dude under his breath, and then they started to follow me out of that back room."

The color was draining from his face at a frightening rate. The V-shaped veins in his forehead were bulging to the point of bursting, as if someone was making the Peace Sign with their fingers underneath his skin. His lips were peeled back from his teeth in a

137

cartoon caricature of pain that would have been funny under vastly different circumstances.

"I've got to get you to a hospital!" Bolan heard himself screaming. He didn't realize it until later that the passenger side window had been blown out and the wind was roaring inside the car as he pushed the Nova to almost 70 miles per hour down the street.

Phil shook his head violently. *"Not happenin', man! No fuckin hospital!"*

"Phil, I *have* to! You got blood in your mouth! You need a doctor!"

"You know where the Traveler's Resort Motel is, over on Bailey?"

Bolan blinked. He'd never been to Detroit in his life. "I don't know *shit!"*

Phil made a hurtful sound in his throat that sounded like a sob. His teeth were slimed with blood and his breath rattled wetly in his chest.

"Just take a right at this light up here," he said, pointing through the battered windshield with a blood-soaked finger. His voice was weakening rapidly; his skin was turning pallid.

I'm looking at a talking corpse, Bolan thought crazily.

"I got a room I use when I'm in town," Phil finished, digging in his jeans. He took the keycard and threw it up onto the dashboard.

"Room 109. Take me there."

Bolan was checking the rear view mirror and slowing his speed. The last thing he needed was to get pulled over. "Phil, you don't know me, but I don't think that's such a good idea!"

Phil pointed his own pistol at Bolan now, a gun he never had the chance to use in his defense. *"Just do what the fuck you're told!"*

Bolan glanced over, saw the barrel of the Beretta pointed right at the side of his face, and he nodded, suddenly feeling very calm. "Have it your way, asshole."

"That's right!" Phil shouted above the wind rushing in through the shattered windows, *"My* fuckin way! Now lemme make a call!" He reached into his front pocket and pulled out his cell phone. His finger was trembling and smearing blood all over the screen. "I know a guy who can help me, if anyone can. He'll know what to do."

"He a doctor?"

Phil nodded and began to dial the number, stuck the phone to his ear when the other line began to ring. A few rings and someone on the other end answered. Phil told the guy on the phone the address of his hotel room, and that he needed his services right fucking *now.* Phil then told him *of course* he would be paid, and then thanked him and hung up. With a bloody hand, he pointed up the street and told Bolan to turn left and follow the road until it came to a T, and then turn right.

A few minutes later they were pulling into the lot of the Traveler's Resort. Bolan got out of the car and ran to the passenger side door, opened it. *"Shit!"* he barked as Phil practically spilled out onto the asphalt like a Crash Test Dummy. He helped him to his feet, followed his directions to room 109, and then used the key Phil had given him to unlock the door.

The room looked like the set piece for a porno movie shot in 1975. It stank of mothballs and furniture polish. The TV on the dresser wasn't even a flat screen, just some old nineteen-inch hulk from the late '90s.

He took Phil to the bed and dumped him as gently as he could.

Phil screamed. *"Fuck!"* There was so much blood. To Bolan, it looked like it was pouring out of him from everywhere at once.

He stripped Phil's coat and shirt off and stepped back with a hiss of breath through his clenched teeth. There was a small black hole in Phil's right side, just above his gut. Blood, thick and dark, was bubbling out of it and onto the sheets beneath him.

He went into the bathroom and began to run some towels under the hot water, hoping he could do something to slow the amount of blood currently pumping out of Phil onto the mattress. It occurred to him in that moment that this was Vincent's cousin, and there was no telling how the man might react when he learned that Phil had been shot. And if he died? Bolan didn't want to think about any of that right now. *One damn thing at a time.*

Someone was knocking on the door as Bolan came out of the bathroom. He froze, his eyes bugging out of their sockets, his Adam's apple working up and down, though no sound came out of his mouth. Slowly, he went to the door and peered through the peephole and saw someone standing on the stoop.

It was a man, very short and portly, and he was sketchily looking around behind him before he knocked again, louder and more forceful this time. Bundled up in his furry parka, he looked like a small, upright bear who'd wandered in out of the woods and was lost. His breath smoked in the air around his head like a halo in the pale blue light falling from the motel's neon sign. Bolan closed his eyes, took a deep breath, and opened the door.

The man at the door gave no greeting, asked no questions. He immediately pushed his way inside, told Bolan to make sure the door was locked behind him, and then plunked down what looked like some kind of medical bag on the nightstand near Phil's sweat-soaked head. He took one look at the wound, gently lifting the bloody ball of waste that was now Phil's shirt, and then motioned for Bolan to follow him to a corner at the other end of the room.

"He's not going to make it," the stranger said bluntly. He had about four days' worth of stubble on his flabby cheeks and neck. His eyes were gigantic behind his small, round glasses, and he stank of bourbon. Bolan just stared at him.

"Did you hear me, son?" the man asked.

Bolan nodded. "There's absolutely nothing you can do? Nothing in that bag, there, that could help him hold out until an ambulance gets here?"

The man seemed to understand his distress. He sighed like a patient teacher dealing with a dim-witted pupil. "He's been shot in the liver. There's nothing I can do for him short of a miracle, and miracles are *not* my forte. Frankly, I'm surprised he made it this long."

Both men turned and stared wide-eyed towards the bed as Phil moaned weakly. From here, by the window, Bolan thought he looked like a corpse already. His skin was ashen and oiled with sweat, and his entire lower body was dark with blood. Outside, the scream of passing semis off the highway rattled the window panes in their cheap frames.

"Look, man, you have to do *something*." He was thinking about Vincent, how he might react when he learned his cousin was killed on Bolan's watch. It could very well throw his plan to kill Vincent into the shitter for sure. "If this guy dies, it's *my* ass."

The man seemed sympathetic, though Bolan perceived it to be something well-practiced and completely devoid of sincerity, like a doctor telling you you're going die but at the same time everything was going to be okay.

"As I said, I cannot. He is a dead man, even if you dial 911 right now." The stranger stopped and looked around the room, and then his eyes slid back up to Bolan. "Which I would not do, if I were you."

"What do you suggest?" It was supposed to be sarcastic, but he genuinely wanted to know.

"My advice?" the man asked, as if this was the first time anyone had ever wanted such a thing from him. "I don't know what happened here, and I don't wanna know. Turn the TV up, slap a Do Not Disturb sign on the doorknob, and then ditch and torch your car." Then he paused and looked Bolan straight in the eye and all the feigned sympathy was gone. "And don't ever mention that I was here. Not ever. Understand?"

Bolan looked at him. "Who are you, anyway?"

The man was sweating and nervous, gathering up his medical bag and using the sleeve of his parka to wipe down any surface he might've touched on his way to the door. "I came over here when he called me. That's the arrangement I have with Vincent and his crew. I upheld my end of that arrangement, and now I'll be on my way." He stopped at the door, holding it open as the sounds of the night— semi horns and sirens—swept in with the cold. "Tell Vincent he can keep his money. This shit ain't worth it."

Bolan turned to Phil when the door slammed shut behind the strange little man. He stood over his bedside and called his name three times before he realized that Vincent's cousin was dead as a door nail.

4.

Like a man deathly allergic to sunlight, Bolan began running around the room, closing the dingy blinds and ripping the cheap curtains over the windows. The room was plunged into darkness. He suddenly felt cold. Looking at the waxing corpse of Phil just lying there on a sweat-soaked, blood-stained bed made him feel like he was in a morgue in one of those crime shows on cable television.

What am I going to do?

Somewhere a phone rang.

Bolan's breath left his body in a hiss. He felt his heart crawl up into the back of his throat. He was looking at the push-button phone on the nightstand beside the bed, under the lamp.

The phone rang again.

He took a step towards it, his hand reaching out to grab the receiver when he froze and wondered who the hell would be calling this room at this moment. And then it occurred to him that it wasn't the phone on the nightstand that was ringing. It was Phil's cell, still in his hand.

He walked slowly around the bloody, stinking mess, wrinkling his nose. Phil's bowels must have let go when his heart stopped because he stank like shit. The ringing phone was in his right hand, now a cold, waxy claw.

Don't answer it, he told himself, but for some reason he was reaching down and prying Phil's rigid fingers back like a hunter opening a bear trap. The name on the caller ID said VINCE—just like that, in all caps. He let it ring once more, then closed his eyes, swallowed, and answered it.

"Yeah?"

It was Vincent, all right. "I assume since you're answering my cousin's phone that he's dead."

Bolan looked down at Phil. His eyes were glassy now, staring up at the ceiling with his mouth open. A fly was crawling along his cheek. *Why would he just jump to an assumption like that?*

"I'm sorry," Bolan lied. He could not have cared less for Vincent's loss. "He's been shot."

Vincent was quiet for a moment. Bolan could faintly hear the thump of music in the background, but not much else. "I want details," Vincent said at last. Strangely, he didn't seem the slightest bit angry.

Bolan told him how it went down, exactly the way it happened. He spoke in a low, flat tone, trying to sound sympathetic but not doing a very good job of it. When he was done, Vincent said, "Looks like there's a job opening for you after all. You interested?"

Bolan swallowed. "I just told you—"

"That my cousin is dead. Yeah, I know. *That* was the job. Now, you interested or not?"

Bolan was confused. He suddenly wondered if this was really happening or just some weird dream. "You're going to have to explain this to me, man."

Vincent's tone hardened. "I don't have to explain shit to you, O'Brien. But I can see you have some questions, and rightly so." He cleared his throat away from the phone. "My cousin Phil was a rat, plain and simple. I have it on good authority that he was working with the Feds. They offered him immunity just three days ago if he was willing to roll on me and some other guys, his own father included. That bag he was carrying?"

"Yeah?"

"The money in that bag is what I paid to have it done."

"You're telling me that you had your cousin deliver the payment for his own assassination?"

"Pretty fucked up, huh?" Vincent cackled like a little boy being tickled.

Bolan didn't know what to say to that. He just stood there, watching the fly crawl over the bridge of Phil's nose and disappear on the dark side of his face. *Who the hell is this guy?*

"O'Brien? You still there?" He could almost hear the man grinning like some bloodthirsty clown.

"I'm here."

"So, you want the job or what?"

He was still trying to wrap his mind around what he'd just learned. "Your Uncle Lou—"

"My uncle is the one who gave the green light," Vincent snapped impatiently. "What the fuck do you care, anyway? This was your big moment—your test—and you passed with flying colors. I told you back at the barn: if everything went according to plan, we'd talk. Well, everything went *exactly* as I'd planned, and now we're talking."

Something else dawned on Bolan at that moment, but he was too freaked out to be angry about it. He said, "I could've been killed. Your guy shot the shit out of my car."

Vincent chuckled. "Relax. Jimmy is a pro. If he wanted you dead, you'd be dead. That's why we use him for things like this. He had to make it look good."

Jimmy. Good to know. "So what happens now?"

"First things first," Vincent said, his tone indicating he was ready to get down to business. "Where's Phil's body?" Bolan gave him the name and address of the motel. "Okay," Vincent went on, "I'll send someone to collect him. They'll bring you a car and take your old piece of shit to the scrapyard. No one will ever find it when my guys are done with it, I can promise you that."

Bolan felt a little sad to hear that. He'd really grown attached to that car. And he would have to tell Rick what happened. "Alright."

"You stay put until my guys get there," Vincent told him.

"When they *do* get there, you drive down here to me. We got some business to discuss. Any questions?"

Bolan couldn't think of any. The fly was sitting in the jelly of Phil's left eyeball. It made his skin crawl to look at it. "No, I got it."

"Good." He paused. "And O'Brien?"

"Yeah?"

"Don't go running off on me, now."

"I won't," Bolan said.

He gave Bolan his address, and then hung up.

CHAPTER THIRTEEN

1.

Bolan waited in that motel room with Phil's slowly ripening corpse for what felt like days. When the sun finally cracked in an eastern sky as cold and fragile as frozen glass, a hard knock on the door shook him out of his lethargy. He was sitting in a chair as far away from where Phil was lying as he could get (there was a sour smell coming off him now, like old cheese sitting out in the sun), and when he heard the knock, he got up and went to look through the peephole.

Two men stood at the door, bundled against the freezing temperatures in heavy coats and scarves. One was wearing a baseball cap so Bolan couldn't see his face, and the other—the one who'd knocked, presumably—was balding with a neatly-groomed beard.

"Who is it?" He had the .357 behind his back, hammer cocked.

"Vincent sent us," the balding man with the beard said softly into the door.

Bolan lowered the hammer on the revolver and opened the door. "Come in," he said, stepping aside to allow the two men entry. Both accepted without a word and came inside. "He's over there."

They each looked Phil over without a word between them. The

one in the baseball cap was carrying some kind of black leather case. The bearded one handed Bolan a set of keys with a nod towards the door.

"Car's outside," he said. "Black Jeep Cherokee. Tank's full. Vincent wants to see you." And by *see you*, the man's expression indicated it was not to be taken as a request. "Gimme yours." He held out his hand, wiggled his fingers.

Bolan exchanged the keys to the Nova with those to the Cherokee, then shrugged into his heavy leather jacket, turning the fleece collar up against the cold. "Good luck, fellas."

The one who gave him the keys sneered. "This is why we get paid the big bucks. Am I right, Stu?"

The one in the baseball cap snickered as he placed the leather case atop the end table next to Phil's bed. "Yeah, right." He opened the case (which looked like a briefcase to Bolan, but much deeper) and pulled out a large roll of plastic wrap. "It's the job I always dreamed about when I was a kid." He laughed roughly, and then proceeded to spread the plastic out onto the floor next to the bed.

"Well, I'll leave you to it," Bolan said, and headed for the door, concealing the .357 under his jacket as he went.

"Happy New Year," the balding man with the beard said cheerfully, and then kicked the door shut with a bang.

2.

He made it to Vincent's in just over three hours, using the GPS on his phone to navigate through the snow and avoid any traffic issues that would make this day drag on any longer than necessary. When he finally arrived, it was just after noon.

"You have an appointment?" the guard asked through the little shack's open window. He was positioned just outside the big wrought-iron gate. Vincent's house loomed in the distance, perched atop a hill covered in snowy pines like some huge bird of prey watching over its territory. *Place like this must cost millions.*

"Vincent is expecting me," Bolan said from behind the Cherokee's wheel. He had the heater going full blast and the wind cutting through the rolled-down window made it feel like he was driving around in a deep-freeze.

The guard was wearing a dark blue security uniform, complete with a bulletproof vest. He looked bored as he picked up the phone and punched in a few numbers. Bolan waited, hand on the steering wheel, fighting the urge to roll up the window against the cold.

"Okay, boss. No problem. I'll send him right up." He hung up, then pressed a button inside the shack and the gate started to roll aside with an electronic rattle. "They're waitin for ya," he said to Bolan as he hung up the receiver.

"Thanks," Bolan said, and he put the Jeep in gear.

Vincent's house was no Playboy Mansion, but it was situated on a patch of land that seemed to go for as far as the eye could see. As Bolan pulled up to the front he was impressed, to say the least. What he was looking at was something he would've imagined out west somewhere—like Wyoming or Montana. The house was a gargantuan structure of stone and darkly-stained timber with huge windows and buttresses and a wraparound porch wide enough to park a car on. When he knocked on the huge mahogany double-doors, he thought the house might be too big for anyone inside to hear him.

He was wrong.

The door opened within a few seconds and an older man in a large red sweater and brown slacks greeted him. It took him a moment to recognize Vincent's uncle, Lou, without the leather coat and driver's cap.

"Come in," the old man grunted dourly when he saw who it was. "He's in his office."

Bolan stepped into the foyer and shook the snow off, amazed at the size of the place. Everything was wide open, and there was a loft on the second floor that allowed him to see right up into some of the rooms. Sky lights allowed shafts of grayish sunlight to fall down into the living room in bright slants. Two brown leather sectionals were positioned around a TV with an eighty-inch flatscreen hanging on the wall above them. In front of the sectionals, a great white fur rug covered the rich vinyl floor. It looked like someone had ripped it right off the back of a polar bear. *Knowing this piece of shit, someone probably did.* Topping everything off was a monstrous fireplace built of rough-cut stone with a heavy, oak-beam mantel. A collection of mounted elk and deer heads fixed to lacquered plaques gazed down on Bolan with bright, dead eyes.

"Hell of a house," Bolan said with a little whistle. Lou just looked at him and grunted something unintelligible, gestured for him to follow. Bolan did.

Vincent's office was straight through the living room and located at the back of the first floor. Bolan made a mental note of this and archived it. When they reached the open door, Lou took his leave with a roll of his eyes and left him standing there. Vincent was inside behind a large desk, talking on his phone and popping cashews he was scooping out of a glass bowl into his mouth and crunching them loudly.

"That's fine, that's fine. Just send me the paperwork and I'll see what my finance guy has to say. Okay? Okay, then. Sounds good. You have a Happy New Year. Thanks." His eyes found Bolan standing in the doorway as he placed his phone face-down on the blotter in front of him. He grinned hugely.

"Still in one piece, I see," he said with a laugh. He leaned back in his chair and rested his huge feet on top of the desk. To Bolan's surprise, he was wearing moccasins, complete with the little tassels on the sides. Vincent gestured towards one of the chairs. "Have a seat. Any trouble finding the place?"

Bolan sat. "Not at all." He joked, "I could see it from the

interstate."

Vincent seemed amused by this. "My father built this house for me as a wedding gift. Twenty years ago, now."

"Wow."

Vincent nodded. "Indeed. Too bad the marriage didn't last very long. The bitch and I divorced two years later."

"Sorry to hear that." Bolan had no clue what to say to something like that.

"Don't be. Best thing that ever happened to me." He removed his feet from the top of his desk and folded his hands on the blotter in front of him. "Twenty years is a long fuckin time to be in a cage."

Bolan assumed the subject had been changed, and that they were no longer speaking about Vincent's house or failed marriage. "A lifetime," he agreed.

Vincent laughed. "I'd say. How's it feel?"

"How does *what* feel?"

Vincent indicated the air around him, using both hands in a big sweeping gesture. "The world, after all that time. It's gotta be like you stepped out of a time machine or something."

Bolan couldn't have explained it any better than that. "It's something, that's for sure."

Vincent offered him the bowl of cashews. "I love 'em," he said when Bolan shook his head. "Doctor says they're bad for my cholesterol, but what the fuck. So is booze and women, am I right?"

"Sure."

I could kill him right now, he thought suddenly. But there was no way to know how many armed men Vincent had roaming the place. He had a hunch that there was probably a little dark room hidden somewhere in the house, where some serious-faced men were, even now, watching his every move on a set of computer screens. Killing Vincent now would be suicide.

"So how does someone go from doing five years for aggravated assault to twenty years for manslaughter?" Vincent asked.

As if you don't already know. "Like I told you when we met. I did what I had to do."

"From what I read, those assholes came at you three-on-one," Vincent continued, confirming Bolan's assumption that he already knew everything about it. "Pretty impressive, the way you fought them off and even managed to kill one of them. That takes a certain type of man, to be able to keep your head and handle your shit like that."

Bolan shrugged, said nothing.

"That's also the kind of man a boss like me needs in his organization."

"Are you offering me a job?"

"You *need* a job?"

"I could use the money," Bolan admitted.

"Yeah, those fines and court costs can eat a man alive." Vincent turned to his computer, typed in something real quick on the keyboard, then gave a little whistle. "Says here you owe ten grand to the state and almost twenty grand to this Marcus Baxter cat. Who's he? The guy you put in the wheelchair?"

He was looking at Bolan with a mildly curious, shrewd expression. Bolan nodded, unperturbed. After all, everything about his time in prison was public record. "That's him, yeah."

Vincent flashed him a vicious grin. "What'd he do, to get you to wreck his shit like that?"

"He put his hands on my girlfriend, back in the day. Stupid kid stuff."

Vincent laughed. "Kid stuff? Giving the guy a black eye is *kid stuff*. You went to work on him like a fuckin champ."

"Like I said, I did what I had to do. No different than you, I guess."

Vincent frowned, then nodded. "You mean Phil. That fuckin rat got what was coming to him. And believe me, it was a *long* time coming."

"What're you going to do with him?" He suddenly got an image of Phil—glassy eyes and pale, ashen skin—being rolled up in plastic and dumped into the trunk of a car just before it was driven into a frozen lake.

"I'd *like* to run his ass through a wood chipper and fertilize my lawn with his mulch," Vincent said without a trace of humor. "But I suppose he'll wind up in a barrel of acid somewhere. Stu and Rocco know what they're doing. And I don't usually ask how the sausage is made, if you get my meaning." He scowled. "Anyway, whatever they do, it's better than he deserves."

"Aren't you afraid the Feds will come sniffing around looking for him?" Bolan said.

"Sure they will. But they can't find what isn't there, now can they? Same goes for your car. Hope you weren't sentimental about it."

Bolan actually was, but he shook his head. "Not at all."

"Good. Because in a few hours it will be crushed into a cube about this big." He spread his meaty arms about three feet apart, and laughed.

Vincent's phone rang. He stopped laughing, looked at the caller ID, and then picked it up. "One sec," he said, tapping the screen to answer it. "Yeah?" Bolan could hear a voice prattling away on the other end, but couldn't make out any of the words the person was saying. After listening with a mildly bored expression for about twenty seconds, Vincent cut the man off abruptly. "No. I fuckin told you I would take care of it." Vincent paused, listening, and then he looked at Bolan and rolled his eyes dramatically. *You believe this shit?* that look said.

Meanwhile, Bolan sat there waiting patiently. He heard Lou moving through the house behind him, and then a dog barking. Vincent was facing the large window behind his desk now, speaking into the phone in a lower tone, so Bolan turned in his chair. Lou was standing out near the doorway leading into the kitchen, feeding a raw T-bone steak to the biggest Rottweiler Bolan had ever seen. The dog let out a thunderous bark and then snatched the steak out of the older man's hand, devouring everything but the bone in a matter of seconds. For a moment Lou smiled down at the beast, and then his eye caught Bolan watching and his expression soured. He moved off into the kitchen and out of sight.

Big hungry dog. Noted.

Vincent hung up the phone. "Fucking retard. Hard to find people with real problem-solving skills these days. This generation, I swear. Bunch of entitled, lazy mama's boys who want you do everything for 'em. When we're gone, O'Brien, I don't think testosterone is gonna exist anymore." It was clearly a joke, and Bolan expected Vincent to laugh at it, but he just kept shaking his head in that sad, disbelieving way. He looked like a giant child who'd just been told that Santa Clause wasn't real after all.

"So how is it that you know Benny?" he asked once he calmed down from his phone conversation. "You don't seem like the kind of guy that would find a friend in someone like him."

Careful now. You and Benny never really got your stories straight. Walking a fine line here.

"One of my cell mates in the joint dropped his name, said he was someone I could look up if I needed to make some money." Bolan shrugged. "Figured it couldn't hurt."

"Being a barber's lackey doesn't pay much, does it?" Vincent's eyes were like little bright chips of stone.

"No, it doesn't." *He does his homework.*

As if he'd read his mind, Vincent said, "I check out everyone who wants to work for me, O'Brien. It's nothin personal."

If he knows about Rick and the barber shop, he might know about Sara.

And Samantha.

And Roger.

Keep it cool. "I get it. A guy like you can't be too careful."

"Got that right. Benny's an earner, that's for sure. But you gotta be careful dealing with him. He seems harmless enough, maybe even moronic, but he's got a dangerous streak in him."

"I'll be sure to be careful."

Vincent considered this, nodded. "Anyway, if you want to do more than just make a little pocket change, I might have an offer for you. That job we talked about earlier?"

"I'm definitely interested."

"You haven't even asked what it is we do," Vincent said.

"I don't like asking people too much about their business. That can get you into trouble in prison."

"That's a good mindset to have. It'll help you live longer." Vincent laughed, but it was a tired sound. He got up and pushed his chair in under his desk and stood at the big picture window with his hands together behind his back, looking out over the backside of his estate. "We run a very lucrative distribution company called Express Continental. You might've seen our commercials on TV." He chuckled, shaking his head as if the very thought of it all amused him. "My father is nearing eighty now. He's basically handed the business off to me, though it hasn't been made official yet. His father — my grandfather—built this business back during Prohibition, making his money running whiskey between Detroit and Kentucky. When the government legalized liquor in December of 1933, granddad took the money he'd saved and invested in a fleet of trucks and started a legitimate company, shipping everything from auto parts to produce to retail goods from coast to coast. Problem was my father, bless his wicked old soul, didn't like Uncle Sam dipping his fucking hands into our pie, so he started to use the trucks granddad bought to transport a lot of things the government couldn't tax. Long story short, he got into the guns and drug business, which eventually led to a partnership with the cartels south of the border. So that's what we do: we run distribution for the cartels here in the United States, and we make hundreds of millions doing it. They have product they want to sell on this side of the border, we make sure it gets into the hands of the people who have the money to pay for it. Simple and profitable. Understand?"

Bolan said that he did.

"Good. Now, about this job I'm offering you. I need a man like you who can handle himself and follow my orders without question. You'd have to get your hands dirty, of course, but that doesn't seem to be a problem for you, am I right?"

He we go. Show time. "Not at all," Bolan said. "I can do whatever you need."

Vincent's eyes were shark-like. "Kill someone? If it came to that?"

Bolan did not hesitate. "If that's what you want."

Vincent paused, thinking. Then he waved his hand toward the door in a dismissive gesture. "I want you to wait in the parlor while take a shower. Have a drink at the bar, anything you want. When I'm done, we'll have us a steak dinner at my favorite place and talk about what I need you to do. That sound good to you?"

Bolan stood, keeping his face as blank as possible. "Sounds good."

Vincent came around the desk and clapped him on the back, led him out of the office. "Alright, then. I'll see you in a few minutes."

CHAPTER FOURTEEN

1.

Benny called him a week later. He sounded nervous.

"What's the matter?" Bolan asked.

"Vincent has me goin along on this thing."

"So?"

"So, I don't like this shit. It's too risky."

"Why are you going, then?"

Benny sighed. "Vincent says since I vouched for you, it's my responsibility to make sure you don't screw anything up. Seriously, O'Brien, it's *my* ass on the line here."

Mine too. "You know what the job is?"

"Yeah." He didn't sound too enthused.

"What is it?"

"There's this other outfit from Chicago—the Murphys—that's been tryin to knock Vince and his family outta the game for years now. Real bad asses from what I hear. Apparently, they got a truckload of guns heading straight through Vince's territory on its way south to the Keys."

"Okay."

"We're gonna hit it and take their shit. You up for that?"

"I'm up for anything."

"Well, this ain't gonna be just a robbery, you dig? Vincent wants to make an example of these guys. Wants to send a message back to old Jack Murphy and let 'em know he's fuckin with the wrong cat. He wants this done bloody."

"I can handle it," Bolan said.

"Yeah, well, I don't know if *I* can."

"You'll be fine. Anything else I need to know?"

"Wear black and bring a gun. I seem to remember you had a rifle the night we met." He still sounded a little salty about that. It made Bolan smile. "Best bring it."

"What about the other two we talked about? The ones who shot Samantha."

"I still don't know who Vincent used to kill your girl and her husband, but I'm gettin close."

Bolan's voice was cold. "How close?"

"I found out he used some hitters from up north."

"Where?"

"Duluth, I think."

Bolan frowned. "Minnesota?"

"If that's where Duluth is, then yeah—Minne-fuckin-sota."

"Watch how you talk to me, Benny," Bolan warned. He could feel the small hairs on the back of his bull neck bristle. "Remember our deal. I hold your ticket, my friend. You don't get to treat me like some dog shit stuck to the bottom of your shoe. You don't help me, you die with the rest of them. Got that?" *Actually, you'll die anyway. It's just a matter now whether you go out quick and quiet, or screaming.*

"I got it, man. Sorry."

"I want those names, Benny."

"I said I got it. Sheesh."

"You have one more week," Bolan told him. "I don't have their names by then, I kill you instead and call it even."

"Alright, *damn!*"

Bolan waited, letting it all sink in. Then, "When do we meet?"

"Tonight. I'll call you with the meeting place once I find out where the hell it is."

"Alright." Bolan hung up.

Here we go.

2.

They met at a rest stop off the interstate. Benny was already there with the rest of them when Bolan pulled in and killed the Cherokee's engine.

He counted four men besides himself and Benny. All of them were dressed in black from head to heel and wore what looked like military vests with spare ammo pouches strapped to the front. They were also carrying military-grade rifles.

"This him?" one of them asked Benny as Bolan walked up.

"Yeah, that's him," Benny said. "Name's O'Brien."

"Don't give a shit what his name is," the guy said, eyeballing Bolan. "As long as you follow orders."

Bolan looked at him, stone-faced. "You're the boss, then?"

"That's right," the guy said. His breath smoked in the dark. "Do everything I say, and this'll go as slick as shit through a goose."

Bolan sized the guy up in a single glance, saw nothing impressive. Five-foot-eight, maybe nine. Asian decent. His hair was slicked back, shiny with some kind of Brylcreem or something. He had a spider tattooed on the right side of his neck that looked as if it was crawling when he moved his head around.

"What's your name?" Bolan asked.

"What does it matter?"

"So I know what to call you."

"Lee. That's all you need to know."

Bolan smirked. "A bit on the nose, isn't it?"

Lee frowned and the color rushed into his cheeks in bright blooms. "Why? Because I'm Asian? You some kind of racist asshole?"

"Aren't we all?"

"Hey, hey," Benny said, stepping in between them. He didn't like the way Lee had suddenly tightened his grip on his M4. "He's just blowing off steam before the big show." Benny turned and fixed Bolan with a hard look. "Ain't that right?"

Bolan nodded. "Yeah, man. Nothing personal. You're in charge."

The other three had been watching this exchange with some amusement, but didn't say anything. They were all dressed in black military dress and carrying the same M4 as Lee, though each one was fitted a little differently, depending on the man carrying it.

Vincent doesn't want any mistakes on this one, he thought.

"Alright, listen up!" Lee announced. "Benny, you ride with James, Colin, and Kirk." He turned and looked at Bolan with a sour expression. "I'll take the new guy. You all know what to do, so no fuck-ups on this." The other three men nodded and climbed into a black van parked next to the rest stop's bathroom entrances. Benny gave Bolan one final look of anxiety, and then disappeared through the side door of the van.

"You and me now, rookie," Lee said, and then he jumped into the Cherokee's passenger seat.

Bolan watched as the van's engine started, lighting up the taillights a bright nuclear red in the cold darkness, and then slid in behind the wheel of the Jeep.

3.

Lee directed him to follow the van.

"Stay two car lengths behind," he instructed curtly, his weapon resting in his lap.

"Not a problem," Bolan assured him, tapping the breaks to allow the van to increase its lead.

About two miles up the road, Lee told him to take the 308 exit and stay behind the van. This took them down to a two-lane highway, where they continued in a northwesterly direction. A short time later, Lee tapped the earpiece he was wearing, said, "Time to set up shop. Target should be visible in about five minutes." He listened to whoever was on the other end, then nodded. "Copy that." He turned and looked at Bolan, nodding towards the road ahead. "Just follow James and do exactly what he does."

"How do you know they're coming?" Bolan asked.

Lee gave him a contemptuous grin. "Modern technology,

convict." He said the word *convict* like he wanted to spit. "We have a guy inside their organization. He owes a lot of money to one of our casino boats down south. I offered him five grand to plant an Apple AirTag inside the back of the truck." He held up his iPhone. Bolan could see what looked like a GPS map with a small blue dot moving slowly along a gray line representing the highway on which they were now sitting. "I can follow it anywhere they go with this baby."

Bolan didn't say anything. He turned his attention back to the van in front of him. His heart was hammering, and he could feel the sudden surge of adrenaline dumping into his bloodstream. *I'm really going to do this,* he thought to himself with sudden sick wonder.

He followed the van until its driver (James) braked and did a quick turn, so that he was completely blocking the right-hand lane.

"Take the left," Lee told him, pointing.

"Got it." Bolan turned left and parked the Jeep in line with the van, so that their bumpers were almost touching. When he turned the engine off, there was no way for anyone coming from either direction to pass without driving off the side of the road.

"Show time," Lee said excitedly, and got out of the Cherokee. Bolan reached behind him, snatched up the M16 from under the backseat, and followed him out.

4.

They stood in a line across the road, shoulder-to-shoulder, six armed men facing south in a modern day version of the Spartan Phalanx.

Benny stood on Bolan's left, holding his Glock. His head and face was covered in a black ski mask.

"What's with the mask?"

Benny shrugged. "I ain't takin any chances. You don't know the Murphys. They ain't gonna take this shit lyin down, and if there's even a slight chance one of these pricks gets away, I don't want those crazy Irish bastards kicking in my door."

Bolan frowned, thinking maybe he should've worn a mask, too. *Too late for that now.*

Lee shouted, *"Here it comes!"* and the rest of his men suddenly put their game faces on.

Bolan and Benny looked up and saw headlights coming straight at them. Bolan set his long legs and braced the stock of the M16 against his shoulder, ready to go. The rifle suddenly felt like it gained ten pounds in his hands.

"Wait until it stops!" Lee shouted to his right and left. *"Nobody shoots until I give the word!"*

The truck was one of those big box trucks you might see FedEx or a moving company use. It was big and white all over, without any logos or signs painted on the sides. It began to slow as it approached, and then the driver saw what was waiting for them in the headlights and stomped on the gas. Bolan could hear the diesel engine roar as the lumbering truck began to pick up speed. He waited for Lee to give the order as the monstrosity began to bear down on them, and then couldn't wait any longer. He leveled the M16 with the truck's windshield and squeezed off a barrage. The rifle barked thunderously and the bullets passed through the windshield, chewing the glass into tiny, hot little fragments before striking the driver. His chest erupted in a burst of shredded meat. Bolan saw the man suddenly start flopping behind the wheel like a rag doll, and then the truck veered off and smashed full-force into the metal guardrail on the side of the highway, coming to a smoking, hissing stop.

Then it was massacre.

Lee was screaming and the shooting started. The guy in the passenger's seat kicked his door open and dropped down onto the frozen gravel shoulder next to the road, raising his automatic. It looked like an AK-47, but it was hard for Bolan to know for sure. And it didn't matter, anyway. With a fierce grin of murderous intent pasted to his face, the passenger only managed to squeeze off a few rounds that went nowhere before one of Lee's men opened up on him with his rifle, turning the poor bastard into a flailing doll, spraying blood and brains in a bright burst before he crumpled to the ground and rolled lifelessly into the snow.

With the two in the front taken down, Bolan and Lee and the rest fanned out and surrounded the back of the truck in a wide semi-circle, their breath and barrels smoking in the freezing cold. Lee shot Bolan an ugly look of rage for not waiting for his order, but quickly turned his full attention on the rear of the truck.

"You in the back! Come out with your hands in the air! None of

you have to die like these two out here! Do it now!"

There was a long pause of silence. Bolan and Benny exchanged looks, and then they could hear someone inside the box trailer moving around. Lee opened his mouth to repeat his orders when they heard the rapid-fire of an automatic weapon—from *inside* the truck —and holes suddenly appeared in the metal paneling as the bullets punched through and whizzed past them in the dark. Bolan and Benny ducked for cover, while Lee and his men returned fire, spraying every inch of that trailer with hot lead. No one stopped firing until they had to reload. When they did, the truck was a mass of pitted and shredded metal.

"Hold your fire!" Lee held up his hand, waving it around wildly. The gunfire stopped and the silence of the night swept in. There was no sound coming from inside the truck now. Only the hiss and tick of the truck's dying engine as it poured coolant and diesel fuel onto the asphalt from countless wounds.

"Colin, get the door," Lee ordered, raising his M4.

Colin approached with his rifle up and had to jerk on the door to get it to open. It finally moved with an ear-splitting screech. "I need a light!"

Lee stepped up and clicked on the flashlight fixed to the side of his barrel. Bolan approached the back of the smoking truck. It looked like the entire inside of the trailer had been painted with blood and brains. Four men lay in crumpled, shredded heaps in front of a stack of dull green metal crates. They lay twisted and piled atop one another, some of them with their faces completely obliterated. The one closest to Bolan, near the door, had one of his arms completely torn from his shoulder during the exchange. Bolan could see the bright pink meat of his bullet-chewed stump as it continued to pump blood out onto the floor of the truck. Only the poor fool who'd started shooting earlier had had a chance to fire his weapon; the rest of them looked like someone had tossed them into a wood chipper before they knew what was happening.

"I think I'm gonna be sick," Benny wheezed, and then he turned, ripped the mask from his face, and heaved his supper up onto the shoulder of the road.

Lee wheeled on Bolan. "What the fuck was that?" He gave Bolan a hard shove. It might've sent a lesser man stumbling. Bolan simply looked at him, as unmovable as a statue. "You were supposed to wait for my orders! Fucking *rookie!*" He spat angrily into the snow.

"The truck wasn't stopping," Bolan said coolly. "I stopped it."

"That wasn't what I told you to do!"

Bolan's eyes lit up. "I don't need your fucking permission to save my own life, asshole."

Lee stared at him, eyes wide, mouth half-open. "What'd you just say to me?" he said softly.

Bolan bared his teeth like a dog. "You heard me. You put my life in danger, *asshole.*"

And then Lee did something no one standing there expected. He reached out and slapped Bolan, hard, across the face. It happened so suddenly that Bolan just stood there for a second and blinked. Benny made a small, regretful groaning sound in the back of his throat, and the three guys under Lee's command sucked in their breath through their teeth, shaking their heads.

"Got anything to say about *that?*" Lee wanted to know.

Bolan's answer was just as swift and unexpected as Lee's, only his movement was almost too quick for the eye to follow. His sledge-like fist crunched with a terrible impact against Lee's jaw, and the man catapulted through the air and fell in a crumpled heap near the back of the bloody box truck.

Bolan turned to the others, who had made as if they were going to raise their weapons. But for a slumbering glitter in his pale blue eyes, his manner was the same as it had been when Lee slapped him.

"What the fuck did you just do?" Benny cried. He knelt and examined Lee's prostrate form. The man wasn't moving; his broken jaw hung open, his head was bent at a strange angle. But it was his eyes that sent a chill running down Benny's back. They were open and staring sightlessly up into the night.

Benny turned slowly with a dawning look of horror on his lean, white face. "You killed him," he said in a whisper. "You broke his neck. He's fuckin dead."

Bolan noticed the other three were now inching closer to get a good look at Lee. The expressions on their faces darkened when they realized Benny was right; their heads began to slowly turn towards Bolan even as their hands closed around the grips of their weapons.

Nothing for it now, Bolan thought, and then he raised the M16 and shot all three of them at nearly pointblank range, his 5.56 rounds tearing through their bodies and sending them dancing along the gravel shoulder as blood and brains flew from their wounds in thick, ropy streamers. When he finally released the trigger, all three men were as dead as Lee and the others inside the truck.

Benny had been screaming the whole time, though Bolan hadn't been aware of it. Now, as smoke drooled from the barrel of Bolan's rifle, Benny was hysterical, jumping up and down and waving his arms like a man in desperate need of a toilet.

"What the fuck, Bolan!" he shouted, putting his hands to the sides of his head, like his skull was coming apart and he was trying to push it back together. His eyes were bright balls of glass. "Do you know what you just fuckin *did?*"

Bolan shouldered his rifle and went about gathering up their guns. "I know exactly what I did, Benny. The same thing I'm going to do to Vincent and the other two." He stopped and gave Benny a hard look. "You, too, if I don't get their names."

Benny looked at him, blinking. "You're fuckin crazy, man. This is *crazy!*" He indicated the four bodies outside the truck with a wide sweep of his arm.

"What did you think I was here for?" Bolan asked as he dumped the weapons into the backseat of the Cherokee and covered them with an old blanket he found in the back hatch. "Did you think I was really going to work for these assholes permanently?"

Benny's mouth was moving, but nothing was coming out.

"No, Benny," Bolan went on to explain, "I'm here for one purpose: to kill those responsible for the murder of my daughter and her husband. *That's* what this is all about. You got that?"

Benny nodded his head numbly. "Sure, man, sure. I got it." He was giving Bolan the same look he might give a tiger suddenly let out of its cage.

Bolan pointed at the four dead men. "Don't you *dare* feel sorry for these cocksuckers. They got what was always coming to them, in the end. More than likely, one of them might've been ordered to kill *you* sometime down the road, once you were no longer useful to Vincent. That's what guys like him do, Benny. They use you up, and then, when you have nothing more they need, they discard you like an old pair of underwear."

"But you can't . . ."

"I just did."

"I mean, they're gonna *know*," Benny said, "and it won't take Vincent long to figure it out, either."

"They'll only know what we tell them," Bolan said coldly. He looked around at the empty highway and the trees standing like snowy shadows in the dark. "You see anyone else?"

Benny gave him a frightened look. "This is crazy," he repeated.

Bolan looked around at the bodies on the road and the shot-to-hell truck, and shrugged. "Seems to me like someone got here first. You and me? We were running late."

When Benny didn't answer, Bolan hung the M16 on his shoulder, thumbing the strap. "These guys were dead when we got here. Lee told you and me to wait at the rest stop, said he didn't trust a couple of rookies. Only he and his crew never came back. We waited for a long time, but no word. We even tried to call them on the radio, but no one answered. So we got in the car and started to look for them, and that's when we found the truck and the bodies." He swept the scene with his eyes, cocking his eyebrow when he looked back at Benny. "They were all dead, every one of them. Nothing we could do. Am I right?"

Realization dawned on Benny's face. "Yeah, yeah, okay," he was saying as he slowly paced around the crime scene, playing it all out in his head. His face was bright with sweat. He nodded as he took in the scene around him, filtering it through this new narrative. "I think it could work."

"Alright, then. That's what we tell Vincent."

"It's perfect," Benny said, more to himself than to Bolan. "There's no way for anyone to know any different."

"Nope," Bolan agreed. "That being said, we need to go. Before some Good Samaritan drives by and decides to call the cops."

Benny looked at the truck "What about the guns?"

Bolan followed his gaze. "What about them?"

"Might come in handy later."

Bolan nodded. "Help me get them into the Jeep." He cautiously climbed up into the back of the trailer, careful not to slip on the blood now soaking the floor and running down through the cracks onto the highway. He broke the lock and opened one of the crates. It was a full-blown arsenal inside, neatly packed with dozens of automatic rifles, pistols, shotguns, and what looked like hand grenades.

"You got someplace for 'em?" Benny asked as he looked them over.

Bolan closed the lid and pushed the first crate to the edge of the trailer. It was damn heavy. "I have a place," he said with a grunt. He was thinking of Rick's barn. "There's three more of these back here. Let's hurry it up and get gone."

When they were done, both of them had turned towards the Jeep when Benny suddenly stopped him. "We should burn the truck," he said.

"Why?"

"Evidence," Benny said. "State police will be all over this shit;

probably the FBI and ATF, too."

Bolan agreed. There was a red gas can inside the van James had been driving. He took it, emptied half of it out inside the cab and poured the rest over the bodies, and then used Benny's cigarette lighter to turn it into a roaring fireball in a matter of a few seconds. Bolan could see the light of it in the rearview mirror for two miles before it vanished out of sight. It put it a big, stupid smile on his face.

CHAPTER FIFTEEN

1.

The argument was getting pretty heated between Vincent and Lou. Bolan and Benny were sitting in front of Vincent's desk, stuck dead in the middle of it.

For over an hour now, Vincent and Lou had taken turns grilling the two of them about their story, asking the same questions in twelve different ways, making sure they understood everything down to the minutest detail. Bolan could see Vincent was studying them both, looking for any discrepancies or signs they might be lying. After all, an all-out war with the Murphys was now brewing on the horizon because of what happened to that truck. And then there were the Feds. Benny had been right about the FBI and the ATF, but neither of them had thought about Homeland Security sticking *their* noses into it. Uniforms from all three agencies had descended like locusts on Vincent's trucking company and his private home, going scorched earth, leaving no stone unturned. They confiscated everything that wasn't nailed down, including Vincent's phone and laptops, and a large group of his warehouse workers were rounded up and brought in for a fifteen-hour marathon of questioning that would've broken any one of them if they'd *actually* knew anything.

In the end, nobody said anything and the Feds were right back where they started. Vincent had the house and the Express Continental offices scanned for bugs, and there were armed guards at every entrance into Vincent's home, checking everyone who arrived for weapons and wires. It was turning into a shit storm of apocalyptic proportions, and Vincent was seething.

Now, Lou was standing on the other side of the desk, fuming at his nephew and seemingly willing to make things worse.

"This isn't *my* fuck up, boy," he grated. "*My* guys were professionals. Every one of 'em."

Vincent laughed bitterly at that. "Yeah, they're professionals, alright. Good enough to get their asses shot and barbecued."

Lou's face reddened. "Go fuck yerself! I been doin this type of shit since you was just a tadpole in your daddy's sack!" His eyes slid over to Bolan and Benny beneath his bristling white brows. "You wanna blame somebody?" He tossed a contemptuous nod at Bolan. "Try this one here. He was supposed to be there with 'em. And what does he do? He's sittin at a rest stop, twiddlin his fuckin thumbs while my guys are bein *slaughtered!*"

Bolan felt the heat rise in his face, but he refused to take the bait. He just sat there, coolly returning Lou's gaze while Vincent paced at the window with his huge hands folded behind his back. It was two weeks into the new year and the snow gave no sign of letting up. It was blowing outside with a vengeance, driven by a wind that sounded like a mother in mourning.

"Look," Vincent said finally, letting the words out on a heavy sigh. "Fact is, *somebody* hit that fuckin truck, and Jack Murphy is gonna want blood. If it wasn't us, and it wasn't them, then who the fuck are we talkin about here?"

Lou was quiet, thinking it over. Finally, he said, "So, whaddya thinkin? New player in town?"

"Gotta be," Vincent said ominously. "Whoever it is, they not only knew what was in it, they knew where *we'd* be hittin it." He bared his teeth in a savage frown. There was no way of knowing what he was thinking, but Bolan could see dangerous thunderheads gathering on his brow.

"Who the fuck would have the balls and the know-how to pull off somethin like this, though?" Lou wanted to know.

Vincent gave him a chilling look. "The Feds, maybe. Tryin to send us a message. I dunno. No tellin how deeply they've embedded themselves up our ass, after Phil."

The old man stiffened at the mention of his traitor son's name. It was subtle, but it was there. He caught Bolan's eye, scowled, and then said, "So, what're we doin about it?"

Vincent reached down into an ashtray sitting near the corner of his desk and picked up the stub of a cigar, lit it with a snap-lighter from his pocket. He sat behind his desk, smoked and thought it over. Bolan and the rest just sat there watching him, no one saying a word. At last, Vincent looked from Benny to Bolan, and back to Benny.

"I want you and your big-muscled friend here to pound the pavement," he said, sucking on the cigar until the snarled tip burned a bright angry red. Bolan could see the reflection of the cherry burning in his eyes like tiny windows into hell. "Start askin questions. Twist some arms. Hell, break 'em if you gotta. I want to know if any of our guys could've done this."

"Vince, yer not serious," Lou complained. He was also looking from Bolan to Benny, his face twisted into a scowl. "These two turds?"

Vincent silenced him with a single look. Lou might've been the elder, but it was Vincent who wore the crown. And Bolan could see in the way the old man fidgeted and fell silent that *Lou* knew it, too.

"It's their fuckin mess, they can help clean it up," Vincent stated with deadly patience. He turned his eyes back to Bolan. "You think you can handle that, O'Brien?"

"Sure, Vincent. We can handle it."

This was the last thing Benny wanted to hear, but he smiled and nodded like a good little toadie. "Sure thing, Vince."

Lou said, "Nephew, please tell me you're not putting these dipshits on this."

Vincent's head swiveled up to him. "You gotta better idea, I'm all ears."

Lou opened his mouth, then snapped it shut.

He doesn't believe my story, Bolan thought. *But he can't prove me wrong, either. He doesn't want to risk looking like an old fool who's time has long past. Which is exactly what he is.*

This tension between Vincent and his uncle, it wasn't just a family thing, Bolan realized. There were two different ideas at war here: the way things *used* to be done, and the way things are done *now.*

Maybe I can use that to my advantage.

At last, Vincent crushed out the cigar and waved the trailing smoke out of his face. "You fellas get outta here. Me and my uncle have some things we need to discuss. And Benny?"

He and Bolan were rising from their chairs at the same time. Benny froze, his skinny ass hovering over the cushion as he looked into Vincent's angry, suspicious eyes. "Yeah, Vince?"

"Don't you screw this up," Vincent warned him. There was no need for him to explain what would happen if he did.

Benny got the message. "I won't, Vince. I give you my word."

"I don't want your word. I want answers." He pointed at the door behind them. "Now get the fuck outta here, both of ya."

Bolan followed Benny out of the office into the hall. The door slammed shut behind them, and instantly he could hear Lou raising his voice, mounting a furious argument now that he and his nephew were alone. Bolan grinned to himself.

"You think they bought that bullshit?" Benny asked as they walked past two men armed with automatic weapons and made their way to Bolan's Jeep.

"I don't know. We'd probably be dead right now if they didn't."

"What're we gonna do?"

Bolan opened the driver's side door and looked at Benny across the top of the roof. "We need to give him someone."

"Got anyone in mind?"

"How about Uncle Lou?"

"Oh, I gotta hear this!" Benny chuckled and got into the car.

2.

They decided to grab a bite to eat at a small diner outside of Cambridge. While they were waiting for their drinks, Benny told him he had a line on the two men who killed Samantha and Roger.

"I was right about them bein from Duluth," he was saying when the waitress brought them their sodas. "I guess they're private contractors or something. Guys like Vincent use them when they need someone from outta town to do the job."

"So it can't be traced back to him," Bolan figured. He took a sip of his Pepsi. "What's their names?"

Benny grinned wolfishly. "I got better'n that." He took out his smartphone and laid it on the table between them. Bolan leaned in, scanned the photo of two men raising their drinks at what looked like some kind of party. There was a bar and big flatscreen TV on the wall in the background and dozens of other people. Might've been a Super Bowl party or something. The one on the right was a large white guy with long hair and a beard. He looked like a biker. He had a tattoo of a burnt American flag on the side of his neck. His partner was shorter, black, head shaved with a beard cut close to the face. Both men were grinning like fools.

"So who are they?"

"The white dude's name is Jake Langston. His partner is Henry Cooper. They're the real deal, man."

Bolan's eyes lifted up to meet Benny's, causing the bookie to recoil from him a little. "So am I."

"Sure, man, I know that. But these sick fucks have killed more people throughout the Midwest than heart disease. Most shooters have a code—no women or children, that sort of thing—but not these pricks. They'll kill women and children, they don't care. Trust me when I tell you that you'd be doin the world a fuckin favor takin out these shit bags."

Bolan studied their faces a little longer, then used Benny's phone to send the picture to himself. "How do I find them?" he asked, putting his phone back into his jacket pocket.

"Still workin on that one. But I know they're from Duluth, for sure."

"That doesn't help me, Benny. Duluth is like six hundred miles from here."

"I said I'm workin on it. Give me another couple days, maybe a week, and I'll have somethin you can use."

The waitress returned, plunked their plates full of food down in front of them, flashed Bolan a lusty smile and a wink, and then told them to enjoy their meal. When she was gone, Bolan took the top off his tenderloin and smothered it in ketchup and mustard.

"So what's yer plan for Lou?" Benny asked around a mouthful of food.

Bolan took a bite from his sandwich and cleaned his fingers on a napkin. "I was hoping you'd tell me."

"What're you talkin about?"

"You gave me the idea," Bolan said, "when you said we should take the guns, that we could use them later. I figure we find a way to plant them on Lou, make it look like he was behind the hit on that truck."

Benny nodded. "That's a good idea. Meanwhile, we should make some noise, rattle some cages. It'll show Vincent we're trying to smoke out the rat."

"But how the hell do we make it look like Lou stole them?" Bolan asked. He had a sneaking feeling Benny was much better at this sort of thing than he let on. *Better keep a close eye on him.*

"First, we need some dirt on the old man," Benny said.

"Like what?"

Benny thought it over while he chewed. "I got a place we can start."

"Yeah?"

"Oh yeah," Benny said. "I got just the cocksucker we can talk to."

"One of Vincent's guys?"

Benny placed what was left of his sandwich on his plate and wiped his mouth on a napkin. "The guy's name is Diego. I don't know if that's his first name or his last, don't wanna know. A while back, I needed to make a run down to Tennessee to collect on a debt from this poor bastard outside of Memphis. I was nervous about goin alone, so Vincent suggested I take this Diego prick along."

"What's he do?" Bolan asked.

"He runs a body shop right here in Cambridge. Chops up cars and reworks them so Vincent can transport shit across the border without getting caught. That sorta shit. Anyway, I take the guy with me and we go to Memphis. Guy who owes me doesn't have the money, so Diego uses a pair of pliers and breaks three of his fingers, one by one, like he was crackin walnuts." He stopped, looked down at his own fingers, and shuddered.

"He just broke the guy's fingers?"

Benny nodded. "Just like that. Anyway, we got the money and headed home, but it was getting late, so we had to stop over at a motel for the night. All we could get was one room with two beds. I thought that was cool at first, and then I told this dude I was makin a run to the liquor store. He said cool, that he saw a lot lizard hanging out by the office and that he wanted to try and get a blowjob or something. I said whatever, I'll be back in a bit. So I drove into town a few miles up the road, got a small bottle of some good vodka, and came back." He sat forward, resting his elbows on the table. "I wasn't gone more than thirty minutes, Bolan—forty *tops*—and I come into the room and find the girl naked on the bed with her face all beat to hell. *He* was naked, too, and standing over her, his fuckin knuckles all tore up and bloody." He paused, looked at Bolan with a haunted expression. "The chic was dead, man. Her nose was smashed in, and her mouth just fuckin *wrecked.* I swear, there was blood from her face on the fuckin walls behind the bed. He killed her, dude. And for nothin." He gave his head a regretful shake.

Bolan studied his face, feeling zero sympathy for any of the actors in this sordid little play, least of all for Benny. "What did you do then?" he asked slowly, not really sure he wanted to hear the rest of it.

"I fuckin told him that shit wasn't cool. I took my vodka, jumped in my car, and got the hell outta there."

"You just left him there?"

"Damn right I did."

"With the dead girl?"

Benny flashed a small, wicked grin. "Well, I didn't leave right away."

"What does that mean?"

Benny glanced around at the patrons in the other booths, as if to make sure none of them were listening in, and then he said, "I waited in my car across the street from the motel for a few hours. I had this feelin, you know? And sure as shit, around midnight or so, Diego comes outta the room with the girl wrapped in a sheet. He must've called someone, because this utility van shows up and parks in front of his room. He and the driver puts the hooker in the back and I follow 'em out to this back road in the hills and the two of 'em bury her in a shallow grave."

Bolan was intrigued in spite of the fact that this story made him feel a little ill. "You just wanted to watch them bury a body?"

"No. Pay attention, O'Brien. You wanna make it in this world, you gotta learn how to leverage power, my friend."

Unimpressed, Bolan said, "Go on."

"So I called the guy whose fingers Diego broke, asked him if he wanted some payback. He says, Sure, what's the catch? I say, You gotta help me transport a body." Benny chuckled. "I can only imagine the look on this poor shitbag's face when I said *that!*"

Bolan didn't find any part of this story funny. "Get to the point."

Benny saw the blank expression on his face and the laughter dried up pretty quickly. "No sense of humor in you, man," he said glumly. "Anyway, I had him follow me out to where the dead girl was buried and made him dig her back up."

"You still have her body?" Oddly, this didn't really surprise him.

Benny nodded. "Yep. In a deep freezer, wrapped in plastic. No one's gonna find her until I'm good and ready. And she's got *plenty* of Diego's DNA all over her, too." He made a gross face, and then pretended to shiver.

Bolan didn't know what to say to any of that. He just looked at him the way someone might study a particularly vile species of cockroach and said, "You're a real classy dude, Benny."

"Guy's a fuckin psycho," Benny replied, as if this was all the justification that was needed.

"I don't see how this helps us," Bolan said.

"Diego has no idea anyone knows about the dead hooker," Benny explained. He said it like he was explaining how two plus two equals four. "I can use that to get the prick to tell us anything about Lou we wanna know."

Bolan was skeptical, but it was all they had to work with, so he nodded. "Okay. But he can't be too happy you left him down in Memphis, though. That going to be a problem?"

Benny shook his head. "Nah, it's fine. We worked it out. I even paid him a little more than his cut to smooth things over."

Bolan was doubtful, but didn't push it any further. "This shop he runs—how many guys does he have?"

"Skeleton crew," Benny said. "No more'n four or five work for him. Mostly half-starved illegals payin off their debts to some Mexican coyote. Diego basically uses them for slave labor."

Bolan took a moment to mull this over. "You think he might have something against Lou we can use?"

Benny shrugged. "I don't know. Probably."

"You don't sound too sure."

"It's hard to say, man. Diego has his hands in all kinds of shit. Lou uses him on the side for his personal business sometimes, like when he needs to move something without drawing the attention of the cops. I say we start with him."

"Good a place as any," Bolan agreed.

Benny drank down a mouthful of his Diet Pepsi and burped loudly. An old woman in the next booth turned and shot him an ugly look. Benny smiled at her, and then flipped the middle finger at the back of her head when she turned back around.

Bolan gave him a distasteful frown. "You're a fucking pig, you know that?"

Benny looked affronted. "What did I do?"

Bolan shook his head. "So where's this shop?"

"North side, Broadway and Fifth." Benny took another long pull on his Diet Pepsi, washing down the rest of his tenderloin.

Bolan got out of the booth, dropped his napkin on his plate. "Grab the check and let's go."

Benny looked at him. "Seriously?"

"Now, Benny."

"Asshole," he heard Benny mutter as he made his way to the door and stepped out into the cold.

3.

From the outside, Diego's shop looked like an abandoned junkyard. It was a big sheet metal building surrounded by a high privacy fence in badly need of a paint job. Busted cars and trucks sat in rotting heaps in all directions, some of them stacked high enough to see them over the shoddy-looking fence.

When Bolan and Benny pulled up and got out of the Jeep, a monstrous gray pit bull came lumbering out of an open door wearing a heavy log chain connected to a studded leather collar around its neck. The dog was a beast, heavily muscled, and looking like it might've teethed itself on tractor tires when it was a pup. As Bolan walked up to the office door, the dog let out a single, nerve-shattering bark, watching them both with murder in its small, glittering brown eyes.

"You got that Magnum on ya?" Benny said, nervously eyeing the growling dog.

"Yep." It was concealed under Bolan's jacket.

"If we you have to shoot anyone, kill the mutt first."

"You think we'll have to shoot someone?"

Benny wasn't taking his eyes off the dog. He shrugged. "Always a possibility."

The dog seemed to be looking right at Benny when it began barking furiously. Benny's hand slowly rested on the butt of his Glock.

"Shut the hell up, ya fuckin mutt!"

A man fitting Benny's description of Diego stepped out from the dark interior of the inner shop wearing blue, grease-stained overalls. He was an inch or two shorter than Bolan, but well-built, with black hair shaved to the scalp and about three weeks' worth of stubble. Various jailhouse tattoos reached up the side of his neck from under his collar.

"How many times I gotta tell you to keep your mouth shut, huh?" His question was directed at the dog. He reached down and gave the animal's head an affectionate, violent shake. He seemed not to even notice Bolan and Benny standing there. "Now get your ass back inside and lay down. Go on!"

The dog huffed, but it obeyed—to Benny's visible relief. When the dog was gone, Benny removed his hand from his gun and stepped up to Bolan's side, smiling crookedly as Diego rose to his full height and zeroed in on him.

"Fuckin Benny." He spat the words out like an ancient curse. "Vincent's little *cabrón* bootlicker. What the fuck you want here, *puta?*" His eyes slid to Bolan, sizing him up and down. "And who's this? Your jolly fuckin giant?"

"We're here on business, Diego," Benny said. He motioned toward the door. "Let's go inside."

Diego looked from Benny to Bolan, then back again. "Whatever the fuck it is, we can talk right here. I still ain't forgot what you did down in Memphis, homie."

"It's freezing balls out here," Benny insisted. "What we need to talk about ain't for the whole world to hear, you dig?"

Diego considered this, passing another glance over Bolan. Finally, he nodded gloomily. "Alright. Let's go into the shop."

He led them through an open area where three different cars were up on lifts in various stages of repair. As they passed, faces dark with grease and dirt peered up at them from the pits, watching them with curious expressions.

At the back of the shop they stopped in front of a bench piled with tools and engine parts. Chains with large hooks hung from pulleys connected to heavy metal frames in the gloom all around them. A few feet away, a man was busy welding what Bolan thought was a gas tank, throwing a shower of blue and white sparks in a rooster tail as he moved his torch slowly along the seam.

"So what the fuck you want?" Diego asked. "I told Vincent he'd have his wagon ready in another couple of days. I'm right on schedule, just like I said."

"This isn't about that," Benny said.

Diego frowned. "Well, *what*, then?"

"You heard about Lee and his crew?"

Diego nodded. "Heard they got *got*."

"They did," Benny agreed. "Someone ambushed them on the road and stole everything in the truck."

"That ain't got nothin to do with me, homie." Diego uncrossed his arms and let them dangle at his sides. His eyes kept shifting from Benny to Bolan. "I been here all week, workin like a Hebrew slave to get Vince's rig done for next week."

"So, if we were to take a look around, we wouldn't find anything from that truck in your shop?" Bolan asked. He was watching Diego's hand creep slowly to the bench behind him, searching for something to grab hold of and use for a weapon. *He's going to make this hard.*

"You can *try*, puta," Diego shot back. Now his hand closed around the rigid grip of a large socket wrench. "But I'll bust yer fuckin head before ya do!" He brought the wrench up in front of him, pointing it squarely at Bolan. "Take one step, see if I'm playin!"

Bolan called his bluff, and when Diego raised the wrench, he smashed his elbow against the bridge of the man's nose, causing it to explode like a tomato being hit with a hammer. There was a dull crunch as the cartilage pulverized, and Diego let out a muffled howl as the force of the blow sent him flying into the bench behind him, scattering tools and parts with a loud clatter.

"Son of a *bitch!*" Before he could recover, Bolan shoved him back against the bench and pinned him down with a hand locked around his throat. The arm that held him was thick with corded muscle and strong as iron. Diego's nose looked like a bloody, deflated balloon, and both his eyes were black and starting to swell.

"Any more of that, and I'll blow the top of your head off," Bolan warned as he drew the .357 and placed the barrel up under Diego's chin. He pulled the hammer back to full-cock, taking a mean little pleasure in seeing Diego flinch at the sound.

"Alright, *alright!*" The tension went out of him like air from a punctured tire; everything sagged at once. "Look, homie, I don't know *shit* about no truck or some fools gettin smoked! I swear on my daughter's eyes, man!"

Bolan gave his throat a little squeeze. "Then who did?"

"I don't know, man. All I do is make it so Vincent can transport his shit across the border without the Feds finding anything. *That's* what I do. I don't do wetwork or *none* of that shit!"

Bolan sensed movement behind him. Tightening his grip on Diego's throat (the man made a comical *urk* sound as the air was suddenly cut off), he turned and saw three men in dirty overalls standing about twenty feet away, all of them holding some kind of tool in their hands with frightened, uncertain expressions on their faces. None of them looked as if they understood English very well.

"Tell them to back off, or I'll take your head apart right now." He pressed the Magnum's barrel up into the soft flesh of Diego's under-chin to illustrate his point.

Diego nodded. Bolan loosened his grip on his throat to allow him to speak. He said something to the three men in Spanish. They exchanged looks, and then one of them shrugged and turned back to one of the cars hoisted up on its hydraulic lift and resumed whatever work he'd been doing to the vehicle's brakes. The other two quickly lost interest and descended back down into the grease pit below the floor.

Bolan released Diego and took a step back to give the man some breathing room. "Last chance to tell us what we want to know."

Diego sat up, rubbing at the front of his throat. "I told you already. I don't know *shit!*"

"I believe him," Benny said cheerfully. He'd been watching the whole time with a huge, mean-spirited grin plastered across his face. "I guess maybe we should bark up another tree, huh?"

Diego nodded. Blood fell to the dirty concrete floor with big, thick, wet splats. "Fuckin right, you should, stupid *puta!* I told you from the start I have no idea what yer talkin about."

Bolan still had the gun in his hand. He pressed the tip of the barrel against the hard ball of Diego's left kneecap, trying not to grin when the man let out a girlish little whimper of fear. "What do you know about Lou Manga?"

Diego was trembling, but he was aware that the eyes of the men in the pits were still watching him. He had a reputation to uphold, and so he took a deep breath and powered through it. "The old man?"

"That's him."

"Whaddya wanna know?"

"Anything. He ever branch out, do his own thing?"

"You mean behind Vincent's back?"

"That's exactly what I mean."

Diego grew quiet. He was thinking. Bolan let him. After a full minute or so, he looked up and gave them both a nod. "Might be I got somethin."

"What is it?"

Diego licked his lips. "I ain't no fuckin snitch, but if I was . . ." He trailed off, grabbing his nose with his fingers. Turning his head, he blew out a fat wad of blood and snot. It splatted wetly on the floor near Benny's feet. Benny looked down at the mess, frowned distastefully, and took a step back from it.

"You were saying?" Bolan urged.

"Maybe go down to that storage place over near Union Center," Diego said. His voice was muffled; his breath whistled wetly through his broken nose.

Benny asked, "What will we find there?"

Diego shrugged. "Dunno. But Lou's gotta deal goin with some bangers outta New York. Some real hardcore niggas."

Benny frowned. "What kind of deal?"

"I did some work for the old man here and there, over the years. Fixed up a couple of cars with some armored plating and shit. Lou asked me if I could modify one of those big rigs a few weeks back, said he had some cargo he needed to ship out to New York. Flashed me a few grand, told me to keep it out of Vince's ear, ya know? Anyhow, I got a good look inside some of those containers he was sendin off to the Big Apple." He whistled. "It was full of fentanyl and shit. Enough to kill a pack of rhinos."

Bolan and Benny exchanged looks. "And Vincent doesn't know about it?" Benny asked.

Diego looked at him like he was retarded. "I told you he didn't want the boss to find out, didn't I? Ask me, Vince don't know *half* of what that old lizard be up to these days. Lou's been bringin that shit up from the border for over year now."

Bolan concealed the Magnum back under his jacket, noting a visible sigh of relief escape Diego when he did so. "Sorry about the nose," he lied.

Diego scowled. "Yeah," was all he said about it.

Bolan suddenly had an idea. He looked at Benny. "Suppose there were *guns* in one of those storage units," he suggested. "Like the ones stolen from that truck the other night."

Benny grinned. "Yeah. Vincent might be pretty pissed about that."

Bolan grinned back, nodding. "He would."

"Look, man, I *told* you!" Diego piped in. "I don't know *shit* about no guns!"

"Oh, but you do, Diego," Benny corrected.

Diego just gave him a confused look. "Huh?"

"Anyone asks, especially Vincent, you're gonna tell 'em about Lou selling some guns to those bangers from New York," Benny said.

"Why the fuck would I do that?"

Benny stepped closer, took a sinister pleasure in the way Diego suddenly recoiled from him. "Because if you don't, the Tennessee State Police might get an anonymous call about where they can find a murdered whore. A murdered whore with *your* DNA all up inside of her. You dig?"

Realization dawned on Diego's mongrel face then. A mean, murderous twinkle suddenly sparked far back in his dark eyes. "You muthafucka."

Benny's grin almost reached his ears. He nodded. "That's right. I happen to know where she is; and all I have to do is make one call and the cops will find her body within an hour. And don't bother having one of your illegals here go down to Tennessee and dig her up. I already did that for you."

Diego was shaking now, and Bolan was pretty sure it wasn't from fear. "You a sick fuck," he hissed.

"Says the man who killed her with his bare hands," Benny shot back. "You do as I tell you, and no one ever finds her. You don't . . ." He let the implication hang in the air between them.

Diego wrestled with this for a moment, but even someone as depraved as him understood he wasn't coming out of this one on the winning side. He nodded. "Alright, man. Whatever you say."

"Union Center, was it?"

"That's right," Diego said slowly, his voice thick with loathing. *I can relate,* Bolan thought. "Lou owns the place. He's been movin shit in and outta there for years. He's supposed to be meetin with those cats over there in a few days, too."

Benny gave him one final, malicious grin. "Better get that nose looked at, friend," he said with a laugh, and then turned and followed Bolan back through to the front of the shop.

"Go fuck yourself!" Diego shouted back. His voice was thick and clotted. *"Hope ya die in a fire, ya piece of shit!"*

Benny, in response, flipped him the middle finger over his shoulder, and then stepped into the parking lot.

CHAPTER SIXTEEN

1.

Diego had told them the truth, to Bolan's complete surprise. Lou actually did have a meeting planned with someone at the storage unit the very next night. A guy working inside Vincent's home who owed Benny a couple of grand tipped him off that the old man had made some calls (all very hush-hush) and that he was planning on leaving around midnight, driving a black Audi. Benny called Bolan and told him what he'd heard, and the two of them immediately went back out to Rick's and loaded the guns into Benny's Denali and parked a block away from the storage place.

"We go on foot from here," Bolan said when Benny killed the engine.

Benny said, "Let's just get this shit over with."

"Come on."

They hit the pavement running, staying low and crossing through a snowy, park-like patch of grass where they stopped and hunkered down behind a screen of dead bushes. Their position was a good one, slightly elevated above the storage units below, giving them an unobstructed view of the area.

From here, Bolan could see the main gate with its little number pad that would open the fence and allow the visitor to proceed into the lot once the proper code was punched in. There were four rows of concrete units, each topped with blue, sloping metal roofs. He counted twenty individual units on each side. In the last isle, a semi truck with a trailer with the Express Continental logo on the side sat off by itself. No one was behind the wheel, and the running lights were off.

That has to be the truck Diego rigged up for Lou, Bolan thought. The rest of the place was empty at the moment. The halogen security lights placed at strategic intervals around the lot lit the entire complex up as bright as day. No one would be able to get in or out without him seeing them.

After some time had passed, Benny said, "So where the hell are they? I'm freezin my balls off here."

Bolan was propped up on his elbows. The wet and cold was slowly creeping through his jeans; his legs felt like a pair of Popsicles. "It was your guy who told us about it. Ask him."

"Ansen's a good dude," Benny said. "Owes me two grand. I told him I'd call it even if he gave me some good intel on Lou's comin and goin. We can trust him."

I don't trust any of you shit bags as far as I can throw you. "I hope you're right."

They stayed that way for a long time. After about an hour or so, Bolan was ready to call it for the night when Benny grabbed his arm and then nodded down the hill. A black Audi was pulling up to the gate. The driver's side window rolled down and an arm encased in black leather reached out and punched a few buttons on the keypad and the gate buzzed and began to roll back on its wheels. Bolan tried to get a look at Lou through the window, but the Audi's roof was blocking him from seeing any more than the left arm and the shoulder to which it was attached.

After the gate stopped, the Audi's taillights flared and Lou drove into the unit and made his way along the main track, slowly turning left. He was in the next aisle now, so that he was facing the spot where Bolan and Benny were hiding. The Audi's engine cut off and Lou just sat there behind the wheel, waiting.

Bolan opened the camera app on his phone, switched it to video, and started to record. He zoomed in as much as his phone would allow, trying to keep it steady on the Audi's windshield. Lou wasn't alone in the car. There was another guy sitting in the passenger's seat, though Bolan couldn't tell who he was.

"You recording?" he asked Benny.

"On it," Benny said. "Looks like he's got Patrick with him."

"Who's that?"

"Patrick Manga," Benny answered with open distaste. "Lou's grandson. He's a psychopath in training, from what I hear."

"It's a family affair."

"Has been for the last hundred years or so," Benny agreed. "Remember that guy, Phil, who Vincent had smoked in Detroit? Well, Patrick's his son."

They both fell silent and waited. Another twenty minutes crawled by and a big blue Chevy Suburban pulled through the gate. They didn't stop, just passed through and immediately turned left so that when they pulled into Lou's aisle, the two vehicles were facing each other.

"Here we go," Bolan said. He could feel his heart begin to pound with excitement. All he needed was a video of Lou speaking with the guys from New York, nothing more.

Lou and Patrick exited the Audi and walked around to the front bumper. Four men got out of the Suburban and joined them, shaking hands. Heads were nodding back and forth, and Bolan thought he could faintly hear someone laugh, but it was hard to tell. By this point his balls felt like they'd shrunk to the size of peanuts, and he was pretty sure his legs were completely numb. The skin of his face was red and raw, and the muscles in his jaw felt stiff and rusted shut.

The meeting went on for about fifteen minutes. Lou was having a robust conversation with the leader of the bangers, when one of them opened the back of the Suburban and produced a large black suitcase and dropped it down on top of the Chevy's hood. Bolan kept the video going, zooming in on the suitcase as Lou opened it, studied what was in it for a second, then closed it and handed it back to Patrick, who then walked it to the back passenger door and placed it carefully in the backseat. Once the money was secure in the car, Patrick took a set of keys from his pocket and went to one of the units and opened the lock. The door rose with a metallic shiver, and all six men went inside.

"They're moving the dope," Benny said under his breath.

Bolan didn't say anything. He watched as all six men eventually came back out. Two of the four from New York were carrying what looked like a blue plastic barrel sealed with a black metal ring. And it looked heavy. The two men carrying it, neither of which appeared to be physically small in size, were struggling to hump it over to the back of the semi trailer.

Lou climbed up into the truck and started it up. The headlights and runners came on in a bright flash. Patrick went around the back, opened the trailer, and then helped the two men place the blue barrel inside, closing the trailer doors with a bang when they were finished. All of this only took about five minutes, but to Bolan it felt like an hour. He was seriously freezing now, trying to keep his teeth from chattering while he held his phone steady in hands that kept wanting to shake.

Another five minutes of small talk and two of the bangers jumped up into the semi truck, while the other two piled back into their Suburban. Eventually they all left, the semi following the Chevy, leaving Lou and Patrick alone.

"Diego wasn't lying," Benny said, a little surprised. "I would've bet good money he was jerkin us around."

Bolan had had enough of the waiting and the cold. "Doesn't matter," he said. "I don't give a shit about that. Soon as they leave, we plant the guns, take some pictures, and then get the hell out of here."

After another few minutes or so, Lou and Patrick finally got into the Audi and left.

"Shit," Bolan said, half-rising from the frozen ground once their taillights disappeared down the street.

"What is it?" Benny asked.

"The code," Bolan said, nodding down towards the front gate.

"No worries," Benny told him. "I got the code when he punched it in." He held up his iPhone, gave it a little shake.

Bolan looked at him, impressed. "My phone didn't zoom in that far."

"I've been meaning to tell you," Benny said, getting to his feet. "You need to drop that prepaid shit and get a *real* phone." He laughed.

"Let's go," Bolan said. He didn't wait for Benny.

2.

Vincent was in a foul mood.

They met him at the Express Continental offices off the highway north of Cambridge. It was a large compound with three main buildings: the personnel office, the repair shop for the trucks to get their routine maintenance done while they waited for their trailers to be loaded, and a warehouse stacked to the rafters with various goods. The entire place was surrounded by a high security fence, and trucks of all shapes and sizes with the Express Continental logo brightly painted on the sides came and went, nonstop. It was like a gigantic, mechanical beehive of activity around the clock. Most of the low-paid workers knew nothing about their boss's *real* business with the cartel, which is what saved them from being arrested when the Feds swooped in; they were just your average, every day men and women trying to make ends meet, all of them dressed in blue overalls with the company logo sewn on the breast in bright orange.

"I told you to find me the assholes who hit my truck, and you bring me *this?*" Bolan's phone looked like a tiny kid's toy in Vincent's huge hands. They were in his office on the second floor, overlooking the truck yard. Bolan could hear the guttural rumble of big diesel engines idling in their docks, and the incessant beeping of forklifts traveling in reverse. "What the fuck am I even lookin at here?"

Bolan was standing near the door, where two men in heavy leather jackets and jeans were guarding the exit with cradled AR-15s. Benny was seated in a chair in front of the desk, watching Vincent with a wary expression.

"We got a tip from your guy, Diego, and we followed up on it," Bolan said reasonably. "I think the video speaks for itself."

Vincent raised his eyes from the phone and glared at him across the room. A lesser man would've wilted beneath that gaze, but Bolan had seen it all before, and from much bigger monsters than Vincent Manga. People like to think they know what tough is, but in Bolan's experience, the majority of the population walking around had no idea.

"So Lou has a little something on the side," Vincent said with a dismissive shrug. "So what? It's not against the rules. I don't mind if my men make a little extra scratch now and then, as long as it don't interfere with the family business."

Benny cleared his throat. Vincent's attention immediately swung in his direction like a fog lamp. Benny fidgeted beneath his gaze. "All due respect, Vince, stealin your shit is the *definition* of interfering with your business."

A single bead of sweat rolled from Vincent's scalp and made a trail down his left cheek. He uttered a small, jagged laugh, but there was no humor in it. "I'd believe it was *you* who hit that truck before I looked at my uncle," he said. Benny blinked at that, but only Bolan noticed. "Doesn't make any sense."

"The camera doesn't lie," Bolan said flatly.

"All I see is a suitcase full of money in this video," Vincent barked back. "Where's the fuckin guns?"

Bolan met his eye across the room. "Keep going."

Vincent frowned, looked down at the phone. He used his big,

blunted thumb to swipe the screen to a photo of one of the units standing open. In it, Benny was photographed shining his phone light on an open metal crate of military-grade hardware. Vincent swiped several times, saw more pictures with more guns from different angles. At one point he squinted and brought the phone closer to his face as something caught his eye.

"That blood there?" he asked.

Bolan nodded, but said nothing.

Vincent stared at the images for a long time. At last, he put the phone down on the desk, stood, and turned toward the window. A big Peterbilt was being loaded with engine parts bound for Oklahoma just below, with a team of forklifts zipping in and out of the trailer like big, motorized ants.

"If I accuse my uncle of something like this and I'm wrong, all trust will be broken." He turned and regarded both of them with a black look. "And he'll kill the both of you, make no mistake."

"Who're you gonna believe, Vince?" Benny piped up. "Lou, or yer lyin eyes?"

Vincent sighed heavily and dropped into his chair behind the desk. He looked tired and angry. His eyes were hooded, and the flesh around them dark and puffy, like he hadn't slept in days. He was choosing his next words very carefully, Bolan decided. When he looked up, there was a pained expression in his red-shot eyes.

"I ring this bell, it can't be unrung," he gloomily. "You

understand that?"

Both Bolan and Benny nodded that they did.

Vincent placed his hands on the desk and heaved his vast bulk up onto his feet. "Let's go. I wanna see this shit for myself. We'll take my car." He looked at the two men standing on either side of the door. "I want the two of you in another car, right on my ass. Got it?"

The two men nodded. "Copy that," one of them said, then he opened the door for his boss.

3.

It was dusk by the time they arrived at the U-Store facility. Like before, no one was here. Vincent had to punch in the code to open the gate.

Bolan showed him which unit. Vincent parked his Cadillac in front of it, killed the engine. His guards pulled up behind him, got out and took up positions near the entrance.

Vincent looked at Bolan. "You'd better be right about this. But I hope to God you're wrong."

The three of them got out. Bolan and Benny hung back by the Escalade while Vincent took a ring of keys from his pocket. They exchanged looks. Benny was nervous. Bolan was nervous, too. Neither man spoke.

Vincent unlocked the door and pulled it up with a rattle and bang as it came to a sudden stop on its track, revealing the small, cinder block room in which, not twelve hours ago, Bolan and Benny had stashed the guns. Bolan had arranged them in the center of the floor, placed side by side in neat rows to make it look like they were ready to ship out. He hoped it would be enough to convince Vincent that Lou was a traitor. If it wasn't, then they would all die right here, right now.

At first Vincent just stood there. He was speechless. Bolan gave him a sideways glance and took a sinister joy in seeing the man's mouth twitch as he tried to speak, his eyes wide as dinner plates as they jumped from crate to crate, his brain unable to process belief in what he was seeing.

After about two full minutes, he made this little growling sound deep in his throat and his eyes narrowed to angry slits. Storm clouds gathered on his big, sloping brow as he walked over and began looking through the dozens upon dozens of AK-47s, M4s, 9mms, .45 autos, military shotguns, scoped rifles, frag grenades, flashbang grenades, stacks of military plate-carriers, and more than a dozen flak jackets; it was enough to outfit a small army.

Bolan remained with Benny at the entrance to the unit, looking from Vincent to the crates, and back to Vincent.

"Lou," Vincent finally said in a small, hurt voice. "Lou, what the fuck? First that rat-fuck Phil, and now you." He looked like a man lost and confused, shaking his head slowly from side to side. "What the fuck did you do?" When he finally turned around, Bolan could see in Vincent's eyes that Lou's fate had already been decided. "I never would've believed it."

Bolan said nothing.

Vincent was standing in front of him now, smelling like sweat and rage. His eyes were wide and wild, but not crazy. He was in full control of himself, even if his brain was boiling inside his huge, knuckle-dragging skull.

"You did good." It came out like a whisper to a midnight lover. "You did real good." He placed a huge hand on Bolan's shoulder and gave it a gentle squeeze. "Now I want you to grab that cocksucker and bring him to me."

Bolan wanted to shrug the hand away, but fought the urge. "Where do we find him?"

Vincent looked half-drunk. He was beside himself with hurt, disbelief, and raw anger. "He, uh . . . he's having dinner with Patrick and his girl tonight. Knowin Lou, they'll eat late. Probably around eight or nine. You grab him and take him out to the barn. Where we met that one night?"

Bolan remembered. "Alright."

A mean light sparkled in Vincent's eye. "I don't want you to harm a single hair on his old fuckin head. You get him to the barn and leave the rest to me."

CHAPTER SEVENTEEN

1.

According to Vincent, his uncle's favorite eatery was a barbecue joint called the Fire Pit. Lou was particularly fond of their Baby Back Ribs with a tall glass of Guinness to wash it all down. The Fire Pit was located in downtown Cambridge, where all the fine dining and shopping one could want was located on both sides of the main strip. Bolan and Benny parked out front with a slew of other cars and waited.

Bolan was watching the front of the place. It had large plate glass windows with scarlet curtains trimmed in gold and the establishment's name painted in flames on a sign hanging above the door next to a cartoon pig holding a meat fork.

"Think he's in there?" he said. The light spilling through the restaurant's windows was soft and warm, pooling on the snowy sidewalk out front like phantom gold. He could see dozens of bobbing heads inside, laughing and talking and stuffing their faces.

"Vincent wants him dead, so yeah, I think so," Benny replied. "This is going to be the end of an era, for sure."

Bolan turned and looked at him. "What does that mean?"

Benny shrugged. "This guy's killed more people than polio, if you believe the stories."

Bolan turned his attention back to the front of the restaurant. "I've seen worse." He personally knew an inmate who was serving a hundred and fifty years for killing his own mother and cooking her brain in a skillet before eating it.

"I'm just sayin. This is *big*, man."

Bolan shook his head. He wasn't impressed. "I saw a lot of old guys like Lou in the joint," he said, remembering faces he hadn't seen in a long time—faces he never wanted to see again as long as he lived. "They're over the hill, coasting on their scary reputation from their youth to earn them respect with the younger generation. Truth is, that reputation is more than likely bullshit, spread around by starry-eyed punks with daddy issues who need a hero to look up to. Lou, Vincent, all the rest—they're not heroes, Benny; they're just bitter, twisted old men who put zero value on human life. They're lower than scum. Push comes to shove, their scary reputations won't save them when another wolf comes along who's bigger and badder."

Benny was looking at him with a mildly amused expression. "Tell me the truth, O'Brien: who hurt you?"

Bolan laughed. "Shut up."

"Seriously, you really believe all that shit you just said?"

"I do. Time-tested, too. In prison, the *really* scary people don't go around talking about how scary they are, or the evil things they used to do."

"I think you're wrong about Lou, though," Benny argued. "That old man is dangerous, no matter how old me might be. We need to be careful, is all I'm sayin.'"

"We will be."

They sat out in the cold for over an hour and a half. At one point Benny insisted Bolan turn the car on and crank up the heat. They could see their breath inside the Jeep. Bolan complied, starting the engine just as the door to the Fire Pit opened and three people walked down the front steps and stood in the snow on the sidewalk.

"That him?"

Benny leaned forward with a creak of leather. "Hard to tell. Maybe the one in the middle."

Bolan squinted through the glass of the driver's side window. The light shining out of the restaurant's big plate windows cast the three figures into silhouettes, making it nearly impossible to see their faces.

"I can't tell," he said.

"Let's just see what they do."

They sat and watched as the three figures on the sidewalk chitchatted among themselves, and then one of them walked up to a silver Lincoln Town Car and opened the passenger side door, taking a step back to allow one of the others to get in. The one getting into the car was definitely a woman, Bolan was sure of that; then the other two embraced with a hug, and one of them broke away and opened the driver's side and slid in behind the wheel, leaving only the one person standing on the sidewalk. After a few more pleasantries between this person and the two now inside the car, the Lincoln started up and pulled away from the curb. The man left standing on the sidewalk watched the Lincoln's taillights vanish down the street, and then turned the collar up on his jacket and started to walk.

And he was alone.

"That's Lou," Benny said.

"You sure?"

Benny nodded. "Oh, I'm sure."

Bolan watched as the man slowly made his way along the sidewalk. He expected Lou to get into a car at some point, but he just kept going until he finally turned the corner at the end of the street and disappeared from view.

"Keep your phone on you," Bolan said, opening the driver's door.

"Whaddya doin?"

"I'm going to follow him. Get behind the wheel and be ready to move when I call."

"Wait!" But Bolan wasn't waiting. He left the door wide open

and trotted across the street. Benny watched him go to the end of the sidewalk where he was certain Lou had gone, and saw Bolan disappear around the corner before muttering a curse under his breath and sliding over into the driver's seat.

2.

Benny had been right. It was definitely Lou. Why the old man chose to walk alone in the cold on a night like this, Bolan couldn't say, but he was elated that he had. It would make grabbing him that much easier.

He followed him for about three blocks, until Lou stopped at a crosswalk and made his way to the other side of the street. Bolan hung back in the shadow of a darkened doorway to wait for him to gain some distance, and then followed him for another two or three minutes.

Lou broke off and cut through the parking lot of a liquor store. The bright neon-yellow sign out front said it had the best deals in town on bottles of Wild Turkey and Dark Eyes vodka; Lou went inside.

Taking out his phone, Bolan dialed Benny and said, "He's at the Marathon Wine and Spirits. Get your ass over here and park around back." The rest of the parking lot was empty and cloaked in shadow, with only the single light from the street shining on a set of steel dumpsters sitting against the side of the brick building.

"I'm on it," Benny said, and hung up.

Bolan crossed the street and positioned himself next to the dumpsters, watching the front door of the store. A minute or two later, Benny pulled into the lot behind him and killed the lights.

After what felt like an hour, Lou came out of the store with a bag in his hand and began to walk back towards the Fire Pit. That's when Bolan drew the large combat knife from his belt and stepped out from between the dumpsters. The glare from the streetlight flashed coldly on the long, broad blade in his hand, forcing Lou to a stop with a hiss of breath through his teeth.

"Get the fuck outta here, tweaker," the old man said with a startled grunt. His hand still held the paper-wrapped bottle by the neck. His nose and cheeks were red, and his eyes were watering from the cold beneath his thick, wool driver's cap. He was wearing the same leather jacket he'd worn the night Bolan met him in the barn. "You don't wanna fuck with me tonight, sonny."

Bolan realized the old man couldn't see his face. The light from the street lamp was falling on his back, making him nothing more than a imposing, featureless shadow to Lou's eyes. He tightened his grip around the haft of the big knife, looming over him, ghoul-like, in the dark.

"I need you to come with me," he said in a low tone, hoping Lou wouldn't recognize his voice just yet.

Lou laughed, expelling a cloud of smoky breath into the thin, icy air. "Go fuck yourself, chief. Run along before I blow your junkie head off." He put his hand inside his jacket pocket to make it look like he had a gun, but Bolan knew a guy like Lou Manga—if he'd actually been carrying one—would've pulled his piece the moment he sensed a threat.

Big mistake, old man.

"I'm not going to tell you again. You're coming with me." Bolan began to slowly walk towards him, forcing the old man back on his heels. A mixture of concern and confusion dawned on Lou's deeply-lined face now.

"I don't know who the fuck you are, but you obviously don't know who *I* am," Lou said shakily, trying to sound tough and defiant, but it was obvious he was suddenly afraid for his own life.

So much for your scary reputation.

"I know who you are," Bolan told him. "That's why you're coming with me." He took another few steps when Lou suddenly flung the bottle at him, then turned and took off running across the parking lot towards a stand of bushes that separated the liquor store from a small, crooked alley running between a row of tall, brick buildings on each side. It was at this point that Benny, still waiting behind the wheel of Bolan's Jeep, flashed on his lights and revved the engine, nearly running the old man over as he brought the Cherokee to a sudden dead stop.

There was a loud shriek of rubber on asphalt; Lou let out a yelp in a cracked voice as he struck the hood with a weighted *thud* and rebounded off the Jeep's front end, hitting the pavement with his arms pinwheeling around him as he went down. Before he could get back to his feet, however, Bolan was on top of him, scooping him up like a sack of wheat and throwing him over his shoulder. He was surprised at how little Lou weighed as he went around to the back of the Jeep. Opening the hatch, he tossed the old man inside, slammed it closed, and then walked to the front of the car and yanked Benny from behind the wheel with an arm like iron, sending him spinning into the parking lot.

"Get back there and watch him!" Bolan barked at him.

"What the fuck am I supposed to do with him?" Benny cried, throwing his hands up into the air.

"Keep your gun on him." Bolan pulled the driver's side door shut, cutting off any further discussion on the matter.

"*Fuck!*" Benny stomped his foot like a child throwing a tantrum, and then drew his Glock and climbed into the back with Lou. The geezer was starting to groan with pain. There was blood running from a gash on his upper left cheek; a spot of raw road-rash burned an angry red on his forehead where his face had suddenly been introduced to the pavement.

Benny said, "I think he's hurt, man!"

"Well, you *did* just hit him with a car," Bolan answered over his shoulder as he put the Jeep in gear and pulled out of the parking lot.

3.

Lou was mostly still and quiet the entire drive north. Bolan kept glancing back at Benny's lean, sweat-slicked face in the rearview mirror, worried the old man might be dead. Benny had clipped him pretty hard.

"He still breathing?"

Benny's face was pale as old bone in the mirror. "Yeah, he's breathin. But I think I really fucked him up, man. Vince ain't gonna like that."

Vincent wanted to hurt Lou himself. He'd been very clear about that. *Maybe he'll hurt Benny, too. Not my problem, either way.* "I don't think Vincent will give two shits, to be honest," he said, trying to keep Benny calm.

Bolan found the barn strictly from memory. He passed the truck stop where he'd first met Vincent that night that seemed so long ago now, and kept going in a northeasterly direction until he found the exit he wanted. The snow out here was deep; it had blown over most of the roads, so that when you looked out across the flat, empty fields it was just a white sheet as far as you could see. Luckily, though, someone had thought to plow the back roads out here, making it much easier to find his way. He turned onto the one he wanted and, within a few minutes, he spotted the barn with its sagging roof and lonely windmill.

Vincent's white Escalade was sitting outside. Bolan pulled the

Cherokee up next to it and killed the engine.

"Grab him and bring him inside," he said.

This was easier said than done. As soon as Bolan's boots hit the snow, he heard Lou come alive with a ruckus. He was screaming and cursing, and Benny was shouting for help. The Jeep was rocking on its wheels from side to side as Lou kicked and thrashed. At one point, Bolan saw Benny's face pancake against the window and he thought for sure Lou had gotten the better of him. But the old man's wounds had taxed his endurance, and he'd underestimated Benny's own survival instinct. Benny threw his weight backwards, knocking Lou down between the front and back seats, and he started punching him repeatedly in the head and face. Bolan ran around to the other side and threw the door open.

"What the fuck are you doing?" He grabbed ahold of Benny's jacket and yanked him off Lou, who was cowering down on the floorboard with his arms up to protect his face. He scowled at Benny. "The hell's the matter with you?"

"Old fuckin lizard!" Benny exploded, scrambling in the snow to get to his feet. Bolan had flung him harder than he'd intended. Benny was beating the snow from his knees and the front of his jacket. There was a trail of blood from his lip to his chin. He spat angrily, wiping it off with the back of his hand. "He's not as hurt as I thought."

"Guess not," Bolan said. He turned back to the Cherokee and found Lou still lodged between the seats. He grabbed the old man by his jacket and hauled him out with a grunt, standing him on his feet. "Take it easy, or I won't be as gentle as Benny," he warned.

This was the first time Lou had gotten a good look at him— Bolan could tell by the way the old man's eyes lit up with surprise (and then anger) when he focused on his face.

"You cocksucker," Lou breathed. He was seething. His face was bruised and there were little pinpoints of blood seeping through the raw flesh where Benny had clipped him with the Jeep. "I don't know what fuckin game you and yer boyfriend over there are playin, but you're a fuckin dead man!"

Bolan grabbed his arm and folded it up behind his back, applying just enough pressure to assure Lou that he would twist it off if he didn't cooperate. "Move."

When Lou saw his nephew's Cadillac, he stiffened his legs like a defiant horse, digging his heels into the snow. "What the fuck is goin on? Vince! *Vince!*" He was shouting towards the barn doors. They were closed. No answer came from within. "Vince, what the fuck is goin on? Vince, you fuckin *answer me!*"

Now the doors swung back on their rusted rollers, opening the front of the barn like a big toothless mouth. When the doors came to a stop, Vincent slowly emerged from the heavy darkness within like some ogre from a dark fantasy story. He was wearing a light brown turtleneck sweater and black slacks with polished, pointed-toed black shoes. A revolver rested in his right hand, a nickle-plated .38. When he saw his uncle, there was a mixture of rage and sadness warring on his big, apish face. Bolan thought he might shoot the old man where he stood; he tensed himself for the shot.

"Take him inside," Vincent said without addressing his uncle's bewilderment. "Strap him down."

Lou's eyes bulged from their sockets like a pair of hard-boiled eggs. "*Vince!* What the fuck is this? What's goin on?"

Vincent was in the middle of turning around to go back inside when he froze. He just stood there a moment, like a man pulling himself together before a big meeting. Finally, he turned back around and his eyes settled on his uncle like the gaze of a vengeful, heathen god. Bolan saw the death sentence written there; Lou wasn't walking away from this.

"What's goin on here, Uncle, is a reckoning," Vincent told him cryptically. He didn't raise his voice. It was low and even, almost monotone. "Like father, like son, eh?"

Lou's mouth opened and began working to form some kind of response, but nothing came out. The look of utter astonishment on his face was priceless. At last, his mouth snapped shut and his expression hardened, though the fear was still there, in his eyes.

"Let's get to it, then," the old man said with such loathing and contempt that Bolan was sure he would spit at his nephew, but he didn't. He relaxed and allowed Bolan to push him into the dark interior of the barn. The doors rolled shut behind them like the clanging door of a dungeon.

4.

Lou never spoke a word as one of Vincent's men zip-tied him to a metal chair they'd bolted into the concrete floor, directly in the center of the barn. Above them, a choir of pigeons cooed and fluttered in the rafters.

Bolan and Benny stood in front of Lou, while the two guards who had followed them from the Express Continental offices stood behind him, stone-faced and immovable as concrete pylons. Both wore their AR-15s strapped to their shoulders.

Lou didn't struggle when they tightened the zips around his wrists and ankles; he just eyeballed Bolan with a murderous look that would've made Charles Manson blush. Bolan returned his gaze, unperturbed, fighting back the urge to laugh in his face.

Maybe now you'll have a little taste of the same fear Samantha and her husband felt when your guys broke into their home and murdered them in cold blood, he thought, bristling inwardly. It was all he could do to keep himself from pulling his knife and cutting the old man's throat down to the spine. *You may not have been the one to give the order, but you knew all about it, didn't you, Lou? Of course you did. I hope they have a nice spot reserved for you in hell.*

"You gonna tell me what the fuck all this is about, Nephew?" Lou said at last.

Vincent held his hand out to Bolan, snapped his fingers. Bolan knew what he wanted. He took his phone and gave it over. Vincent opened it, went to the photos section on the homescreen, scrolled down until he found the video and then leveled the phone in front of Lou and let him watch his meeting with the gangbangers at the storage facility the night before.

At first, Lou watched with mild curiosity, and then he gave a short little laugh and looked up at his nephew. "And? What the fuck is this?"

Vincent handed Bolan back his phone. "That's you making a deal with some lowlifes back east, am I right?"

Lou nodded. He was looking more confident now. His eyes kept darting to Bolan with this glitter in them that said *I'm gonna get you for this, you piece of shit.* "Yeah. So what?"

Vincent looked at him, surprised. "Yer not even gonna deny it?"

"That I sold them some powder? Why should I?"

Vincent flashed him a murderous grin. "There it is," he said, pointing at Lou with the gun.

Lou was genuinely confused. It was almost sad to watch. "There *what* is? Vince, what the hell you talkin about? Get me outta these fuckin things!" He pulled against the zips, trying to break them loose.

"You ambushed that truck, killed my men—*your* men—and then stole the fuckin guns," Vincent accused. "Now that I think about it, yer the only one who could've pulled that off. You get your grandson to help you?" Vincent bared his big, round teeth with a snarl. "You turn little Patrick against me, too, eh?"

Lou's eyes widened. He shook his head. "I have no idea what the fuck yer talkin about, son."

"Don't you call me that!" The sudden outburst of rage made everyone in the room jump. Vincent's face went red and spittle flew from his quivering lips as he pointed at Lou with the barrel of the . 38. "You don't get to do that! You don't get to call me that, you traitorous piece of shit!"

"I don't know what yer talkin about!" Lou shouted back. He tried to stomp his feet, but the zip ties cut into his skinny ankles. "I didn't attack that truck, Vince! Patrick and I had nothin to do with that!"

"Then why are you on video selling those bangers my shit?" Vincent demanded. His chest was heaving.

"What you saw was me and Patrick selling them some dope I had shipped up here from the border," Lou shot back. "I brought it in through Brownsville! Ask Diego, he'll tell you how he outfitted a truck for me!" His eyes were bright and dangerous. "Go on! Ask him!"

Vincent looked to Bolan. Lou's gaze followed.

"Diego's the one who told us you were meeting those bangers to sell them some guns," Bolan said.

Lou's eyes blackened. "Fuckin liar! Yer fuckin *lyin!*"

Bolan shook his head. "I can get him on the phone right now."

"Do it!" Lou spat contemptuously. "Fuckin call him!"

Bolan looked at Vincent. Vincent nodded. Bolan dialed the number.

"Yo, what the fuck you want now, homie?" was Diego's greeting on the other line. He was on speaker. "I done told you everything I know!"

"Diego, this is Vincent."

"Oh, shit. What up, Boss Man? I thought you was someone else."

"Diego, I'm gonna ask you something, and if you lie to me, I will send some guys to your girl's apartment and cut her and your infant daughter into tiny little pieces. You understand me?"

Diego swallowed loudly on the other end. "Y-yeah, Vince. Yeah, I got you."

Bolan felt the little hairs prickle on the back of his neck. *He says the wrong thing, and it'll be me in that chair.*

"Did my uncle pay you to outfit a truck for him?"

"He did, Boss."

"And did he tell you why?"

Lou was watching Bolan's phone with eyes completely devoid of fear. *He thinks Diego will tell him the truth,* Bolan thought. *He's counting on it.*

"He said he had some guns he needed to get rid of, like *ASAP*," Diego was saying. "He asked me if I could—"

"Liar!" Lou exploded. "Fuckin *LIAR!*" He began to thrash against his bonds, trying to rip his wrists and ankles free. All he managed was to cut the skin on his arms and send his heart rate into stroke territory. "I'll fuckin kill you, you lyin piece of *SHIT!* You hear me?"

Bolan and Benny exchanged looks. There was a merry little twinkle in Benny's eye.

Vincent frowned, nodded to one of the men standing behind Lou's chair. The man didn't say a word, simply walked around in front of Lou and slammed his fist into the side of the old man's face, rocking his head back on his neck hard enough that Bolan thought he might've killed him. But then Lou shuddered and groaned, shaking his head, and the barn went quiet.

"You sure about this?" Vincent asked Diego through the phone. "You'd better be sure."

"I'm sure, Boss. I wouldn't lie to you."

Vincent eyed Lou across the barn and nodded. "Alright. We'll talk later." And he hung up.

"There it is, Uncle," he said after a brief pause, tossing Bolan's phone back to him. "Straight from yer own witness' mouth. You sticking with yer story?"

"Vince, I swear to God, I had nothin to do with this. I'm bein set up." His speech was sluggish, his eyes having a hard time focusing. *That last blow might've done it,* Bolan thought.

"I think we've heard enough about it," Vincent said with grim finality. "My only question now is *why?* Why would you do something like this to me? You realize what you've done? Jack Murphy wants to go to war over this, Lou. You're old enough and smart enough to know that war is bad for business." He stopped, and then his face hardened. "Was it because of Phil? Because I had him killed?"

Lou's expression was almost rabid. "Don't you ever speak his name to me again!"

"Is he the reason you betrayed me?" Vincent pressed, convinced he had the full truth of it now.

"I didn't betray you," Lou snarled. His eyes were sharp and clear now, dilated to the point of almost total blackness. "And Phil wasn't my fuckin son."

Vincent was surprised by that. "The fuck you talkin about?"

Lou glared up at him, teeth bared. "His mama was a fuckin whore. Nobody really knows who Phil's father is, but I know it wasn't me! He was born three months too late to be mine. I was doin time up in Carson City, remember?"

Vincent nodded thoughtfully. "I do remember."

"Dumb bitch was sleepin around on me as soon as I went inside. When I got out, I was sure the little bastard wasn't mine, but I took care of him when Trina OD'd, anyways. I always knew he would be more trouble than he was worth. When we found out he was talkin to the Feds, I had no problem puttin him down. *I'm* the one who gave the green light, remember?"

"And what about his son, Patrick?" Vincent said. "Maybe he's trouble, too."

Fear ran across Lou's face like a skittering animal. "No! Patrick had nothin to do with any of this! Please, Nephew, I'm *beggin* ya! Don't hurt the kid. He's nothin like his daddy. He's all I got left."

"Why was he there that night?" Vincent wanted to know.

"I was just giving him some contacts out in New York, in case he wanted to make some moves on his own sometime. I was teachin him the ropes. You know how it goes."

Vincent nodded. "I do."

"Please," Lou begged. It was the closest thing to being human Bolan had ever seen in the man. "Please don't do this. Don't hurt 'im."

Vincent seemed to be thinking it over. At last, he uttered a heavy sigh. "Fine," he said. "But if he ever strays too far from the line, I'll send him to you in hell in little fuckin pieces."

Lou nodded. "I understand. He's a good boy."

Vincent stepped in front of him, cocked the revolver. "Anything else you wanna say? I owe you that much, Uncle."

"I've told you already, boy," Lou grunted. He drew in a deep breath, hardening himself. Bolan had to give it to the old geezer; he was defiant until the very end. "Go fuck yourself—you and your little *turds*." He leaned forward in the chair as much as the zip ties would allow and spat on the concrete in front of Bolan's boots. Then his eyes turned up to meet Bolan's.

"I didn't like you from the start," he said through bared teeth. "My nephew wanted to hire you. I told him no, not a good idea. But, as usual, Vince don't listen to those who know better'n him. But I can see right through you, O'Brien. You're a fuckin snake. I don't know how, but I know it was *you* who did this." Then he looked back up at Vincent, straightening himself in the chair to hold onto whatever bit of dignity he felt he had left. "Do what yer gonna, boy. I'll see you in hell before too long."

Vincent pressed the trigger. The gun went off like a cannon in the silence. The bullet struck Lou on the bridge of the nose, smashing through brain and bone in a red spray that struck the front of Vincent's turtleneck sweater and spattered the wooden support beams holding up the barn's second floor hayloft behind him. Lou's arms and legs trembled and jerked, and then he went limp, his head resting against the back of the chair as what was left of his face stared up in death into the darkness above.

For a moment, Vincent just stood there, gun still pointed forward in his hand, smoke drooling from the barrel as the smell of cordite drifted faintly into Bolan's nostrils. Nobody dared move. Bolan could hear the blood pouring out of the back of Lou's head as it splatted wetly on the floor beneath him. Taking a deep breath, Vincent dropped the .38 into his pocket and turned back to Bolan. His face was stippled with his uncle's blood, making him look utterly mad.

"You got us here, *you* clean it up," he said in a low, hushed voice. And then he brushed passed him, reached out his big hands, and flung the barn doors wide, allowing in a sudden flood of gray, January sunlight. With the other two men joining him inside the Escalade, Vincent drove off into the bright, frigid morning, leaving Bolan and Benny alone with his uncle's steaming corpse.

CHAPTER EIGHTEEN

1.

Vincent had been right about one thing: war with the Murphys had begun.

Jack Murphy was an old man who used to run guns with Vincent's granddad back in the day before a disagreement over money (some said a woman, but no one really knew except Jack himself) caused the two of them to split and go their own ways. The guy was eighty-two years old and, in spite of his vast age, still ran his organization with an iron fist and a mind just as strong. He'd been plagued with seven daughters, so he never had a son to whom he could hand over his crown. Seeing no one in this current crop he thought was capable or competent enough to take over, Jack simply stayed at the head of the table and ran his business as usual, even when everyone around him told him he should retire.

"What am I gonna do, spend the rest of my days golfing?" he'd asked, laughing at the idea as he cut into his huge 32oz steak, which he still had the teeth to chew, to everyone's surprise. Everyone else at that dinner had laughed at his little quip, but none of them thought it was particularly funny. Jack had a lot of nephews and grandsons and great-grandsons, all of which had their greedy little eyes fixed on his throne.

Jack Murphy was also completely old school in the way he ran his business. He believed in being hard but fair, subscribing to one of the oldest laws in the universe, where every action had an equal or greater reaction. So when he'd heard that one of his trucks had been hit on the road and found out the guns had ended up in Lou Manga's possession (it was no secret to anyone on the Murphy side that Jack had a spy in the Manga camp), he demanded a swift and brutal response.

"Blood for blood," he announced from his seat at the head of the table. His office looked like a boardroom meeting, and every one of his officers sitting around the large mahogany table were dressed in fine suits, just like Jack—the old man demanded it. He paid his men very well, and thus expected a certain level of style and sophistication from his subordinates, believing the world had lowered its standards too far over the last sixty-five years or so. It was often said jokingly (but not in Jack's range of hearing) that if the old man had it his way, they'd all be carrying Tommy Guns and calling the Feds *coppers* everywhere they went. "Nobody hits my truck and walks away from it, you hear?"

Every head at the table nodded. No one was going to disagree with the old man. He was tall and hugely-built with a large head, massive hands, and size sixteen feet. He wore a nasty diagonal scar on his face that ran from his right eyebrow to the left corner of his mouth, a memento from a ghastly wound he'd sustained during a knife fight when he was nineteen years old. The other guy had ended up much worse. The police found his body floating face-down in the

Chicago River with his entrails bulging out through a gaping wound in his lower belly. By the time they dragged his body back to shore, the fish had completely eaten his lips and eyes.

Because of his immense size and disfigured features, his men liked to call him Jack Munster behind his back (or just *The Munster* when they were really drunk and certain the old man wasn't within hearing distance), but all of them were scared of him. In their world, Jack Murphy was Caesar incarnate, and his word might've come from the lips of the devil himself.

"What do you want us to do, sir?" someone on Jack's left asked. It was never *boss*. Jack Murphy was to be addressed as *sir* or *Mr. Murphy*. The first (and last) time one of his men called him *boss*, Jack threatened to cut his throat and dump his body off on his mother's doorstep with a note stapled to his forehead addressed to said mother about the poor job she'd done raising her son without manners. The man never uttered the word *boss* to anyone the rest of his life.

Jack peered at the man who'd spoken sitting two yards down the monstrously-long table and said, "I want you to do what you're *paid* to do, and wipe these degenerates off the face of the earth. Hit them where they eat, hit them where they sleep, hit them while they're on the toilet taking a shit; I don't care how you do it, I want it *done*. Any more questions?"

He looked at each man up and down both sides of the table. Everyone nodded and mumbled their agreement. Jack smiled and nodded back. "Good. Now make it happen."

2.

The funeral for Louis Bedford Manga was a surprisingly large event. It occurred to Bolan from the start that Vincent hadn't told anyone the truth about the circumstances surrounding his uncle's death, nor the manner in which it happened. The story he was hearing as everyone began to arrive at Vincent's house where the wake was being held was that Lou had been ambushed by a group of hired guns working for Jack Murphy, was held down as he valiantly struggled to single-handedly fight them off, and was then shot in the face as he was about to overpower them all. Bolan found this fairy tale amusing, though it had an aftereffect he hadn't anticipated: there was now talk of open war against the Murphys. This was likely to complicate things on his end, he knew very well, but overall it really didn't change things all that much. One way or another, Vincent was going to die. It mattered to him not one bit whether the bullet that did it was his, or one from a Murphy man's gun.

Lou's body was displayed in the foyer as you walked in. Of course the casket was closed (Vincent had used a hollow point round that had mushroomed when it made contact with Lou's face, smashing everything above the nose into jelly); standing in front of it was a large, blown-up photo of the old man smiling and holding a beer, encapsulated by a beautiful array of flowers all around it. Men who'd worked for the Manga clan for years lined up all the way outside, heads down and shuffling against the cold, just pay the deceased their respects. The line extended out to the front gate, where young boys in nice suits were making tips for parking cars.

They filed into the house in pairs, stamping their feet and brushing the snow off their shoulders. They were greeted by a dour-faced Vincent in a five thousand dollar black suit and tie, and Lou's grandson, Patrick, whose face was red and puffy, and who looked like he'd been hitting the bottle hard since he received the news of his granddad's murder.

"Such a great man," some were saying as they shook Vincent's hand in passing, "taken too soon."

"Thank you," Vincent would say, nodding and allowing their hands to clap him reassuringly on the back. "He would've loved this, he really would've."

"Great man. Won't be the same without him."

"Thank you, you're too kind."

"We all loved Lou. No one better at poker, that's for sure."

"You mean no one better at cheating at poker, eh?" Laughter at that one, because everyone knew it was true.

"Yeah, he loved playin cards, alright. Thank you for your kind words."

"Fuckin Murphy scum. We'll send 'em all off to hell. You'll see, Vince."

"We can talk about that later, Stan. But thank you for your

support."

It went on like that for almost two hours. When the last of the mourners came through, the doors to the house were locked and everybody started to drink and swap stories about Lou. Bolan walked around the place (he'd bought a black suit just for this occasion, and couldn't wait to strip it off and throw it in the garbage) with a beer in his hand, listening to what they were saying, inwardly shaking his head. The things these people celebrated about a guy like Lou sickened him.

One overfed asshole told a story about how he and Lou paid a visit to a man who'd been abusing some of their working girls by smacking them around after getting his rocks off. When he got to the part about Lou snipping off one of the guy's thumbs with a pair of bolt-cutters to teach him a lesson, he threw his head back and guffawed with laughter. The men standing around listening to this shit soon joined in, toasting Lou as if he was a martyred saint.

He overheard another story where Lou and his son, Phil, kicked in some mook's door and duct-taped him to a chair. After Lou had tenderized him a bit with his fists, he ordered Phil to go out to his car and fetch him a gas can from the trunk, which he then proceeded to pour over the man's head, and then lit him on fire with a cigar. "And what's Lou do the whole time this piece of shit is screamin?" the guy asked his rapt audience. "The mean old bastard sits down in a chair across from 'im and *smokes the rest of his stogie while the guy's skin is cracklin off!*" More gales of laughter and solemn head shakes. Bolan felt his stomach lurch and had to walk away.

They're like hyenas wearing human faces, he thought, and shivered a little.

These types of stories went on and on, getting grander and more violent depending on who was telling them, and by the end, Bolan was convinced there had to be a real and literal hell for guys like Louis Manga. He'd never been much of a religious man, but he had to believe that.

Next came the speech. Vincent called everyone's attention to where he stood in front of the massive stone fireplace dominating the living room, with those mounted elk heads presiding over the assembled audience like the graven images of pagan gods in some forgotten temple. He spoke fondly of his uncle (ironic, considering he was the one who murdered him), of the things he learned from him as a boy, and how Lou and his father had built this organization up from the ashes of a post-Prohibition America, like it was just the two of them rolling up their sleeves and bleeding and sweating down in the trenches. Everyone in attendance knew it was all bullshit, that the *real* men who fought and bled to build the business that gave Vincent this immaculate home were the ones whose bones were buried out in the graveyard. But everyone just smiled and nodded, pleasantly buzzed and thinking only about when the food was going to be served and how they might be able to slip out with one of the pretty girls working the crowd without their wives finding out.

After the speech someone put on some traditional Irish music and the dining hall became a dance floor. Those not participating gathered in groups along the wall, watching as the younger men and women moved the furniture out of the way and worked themselves up into a sweaty, sex-fueled frenzy of traditional Irish dance. Bolan sat in a plush chair back in the corner, watching the dancing with mild distaste, when a pretty girl with fire-red hair and the most gorgeous green eyes approached him and asked him if he wanted to dance with her. He politely turned her down. She smiled and leaned in closer, running her hand up his inner thigh, asked him if he would prefer something else. Face flushed, he gently moved her hand away and told her no thanks. She looked at him with a curious expression and told him she'd be here all day if he changed his mind. He informed her he would not, but thank you, and she sauntered off, a little sulkily, and found another mark who apparently had no problem taking her up on her offer as she led him out of the dining hall by the hand, casting a reproachful look back at Bolan as she went. *Your loss, buster,* that look said.

By the time the sun was bleeding into dusk, the dinner had started. There was one long table for the guests, and four separate tables for their children. Bolan sat at the same table as Vincent, though way down on the end with the rest of the muscle. They were only one tier above eating in the kitchen with the help. Bolan almost preferred that to sitting here listening to these guys noisily chomping their food and talking across the table at each other at the same time.

He ate slowly, not because he wasn't hungry, but because he was trying to pay attention to what was going on at the head of the table. Vincent was addressing his officers, leaving most of his food untouched, but Bolan couldn't make out much of what he was saying with all the yapping and food-smacking going on around him. To Vincent's left, sulking and drunk, was his nephew, Patrick, who kept throwing Bolan dirty looks where he sat down-table.

Does he know what really happened to Lou? It was possible. Even working for a scary guy like Vincent, people liked to talk. And men were just as bad—or worse—as women when it came to shop gossip.

After the dinner, most of the men retired to the cigar lounge, where girls in short skirts served them drinks and cigars on little round black plates. Bolan leaned back on a soft, red plush couch and saw Benny walk into the room. *Even in a room full of assholes, he stands out as King Asshole,* Bolan thought without humor. Benny was wearing a black suit, black shirt, black tie, black wingtips. His hair was slicked back, heavily oiled, and curly at the tips. When he saw Bolan—even his smile somehow managed to look greasy—he swaggered over and joined him on the couch.

"You believe this shit?" he whispered out the side of his mouth. He looked like a gift-wrapped turd. "Vince's got all these dumb asses believin his uncle was one of the 300 Spartans or some shit." He laughed. It was a short, choppy, ugly sound.

"You get me the location of the two shooters who killed my daughter yet?" Bolan looked at him brutally.

Benny held up a cautious hand. "Easy, man. Not here, for fuck's sake."

Bolan leaned forward, resting his elbows atop his knees. "Benny, I'm tired of fucking around here. I want this over with, you hear me?"

Benny licked his lips. His tongue flicked out like a soft, pink snake. "Listen, I know they run out of Duluth."

"You told me that already."

"Word is, Vincent's bringin 'em down for this offensive they're about to launch against the Murphys. Says he needs some heavy hitters."

Bolan was frustrated. He felt like this was taking way longer than it should, and began to wonder if maybe Benny wasn't purposefully stalling him for some reason.

He hates Vincent as much as I do, though.

Does he? Are you sure?

He wasn't sure, though, and he *needed* to be sure. He looked up and saw Patrick Manga leaning against the bar, swirling his drink in his hand as he gazed around the room through eyes glazed in grief and booze. The man looked haunted.

"What's his story?" Bolan asked.

Benny shifted his gaze towards the bar. He was sweating lightly. "Funny you should ask."

"Why's that?"

"Because he's been askin around about *you*."

"Asking about what?"

Benny shrugged. "Who you are, where you came from, what prison you were in."

"You think he knows what happened to Lou?"

"I think he doesn't believe the official story. And Lou never liked you, so there's *that*. He and Patrick were very close, closer than Lou was to his own kids."

Bolan thought of Phil, dead from a bullet to his liver. "No doubt."

"My guess?" Benny went on. "Lou filled the kid's head with all sorts of shit about not trusting you from the get-go."

"That doesn't prove anything," Bolan reasoned, but it didn't help, and he suddenly had a bad feeling about the guy.

Benny shook his head. "No, it doesn't. But if he finds anything on you that might cast you in a bad light in Vincent's eyes—like your murdered daughter, for instance—it might be enough to put you in a dangerous situation. Vincent seems to the rest of the world like he's got his shit together, but like any petty dictator, he's deeply paranoid. You saw how he killed his own cousin, and then his uncle. You were there for both of 'em, so you know what I'm talkin about. If Patrick finds out your daughter was killed on Vincent's orders, Vincent might think maybe you set Lou up to take a bullet to get to *him.* Which you did."

"So we kill Patrick, too," Bolan said simply. He didn't see any other way around it.

Benny uttered a bitter little chuckle. "Why not just kill *everybody* while you're at it?" He shook his head. "You keep piling up the bodies, my big bearded friend, you'll draw their attention for sure."

He was right, and Bolan knew it. "So what do I do about him?"

Benny was watching Patrick, trying to make it look like he wasn't. "Nothing right now. Business as usual. Vincent never wanted a war with Jack Murphy, but now he's got one. His officers won't let him brush off Lou's death. They want blood and Vincent has to give it to them. This whole thing is like a big pressure cooker. You let out some steam once in a while, or the whole thing explodes in your face."

"Shit," Bolan said with a sigh.

One of Vincent's bodyguards suddenly appeared in front of them, stone-faced. He was built like a brick shithouse and Bolan could see the bulge of his hand-cannon under his black suit jacket. "Vincent wants a meeting," he said in a flat, uninterested tone.

Benny looked at Bolan and grinned. "Shit is right, my friend."

3.

It was a quarter to ten when everyone gathered in the meeting room. It was here that all major business decisions were made in the Manga outfit. Tonight, Patrick had been asked to take Lou's seat, the implications of which had everyone's eyebrows raised. Patrick was well-liked among the younger men, respected, but many of the older cats viewed him as too sullen, too moody, with a flare for the psychotic. Even Benny had called him a psychopath in training, Bolan recalled as he took a seat at the far end of the table.

Most of the men sitting in the meeting Bolan had never met but had seen in passing. He didn't know any of their names, nor did he care to. What he'd told Benny earlier was correct in that he was losing his patience with all of this and wanted to finish it. Every passing day he did Vincent's bidding made him angrier and angrier about his daughter's murder going unpunished, and more than once he had to actually talk himself down from blowing the man's head off right then and there.

Now, as everyone at the wake (those who mattered in the organization, anyway) piled into the room and found their usual seat, Vincent stood at the head of the table like the living image of the iceberg that smashed the Titanic and sent it reeling to the icy bottom of the Arctic Ocean.

"My friends, I hate that we had to gather here tonight under these grim circumstances," Vincent said, laying it on nice and thick. Benny shot Bolan a crooked grin from across the table. Bolan ignored him. "But I have an announcement tonight that, frankly, was a long time coming. I know Lou would be happy about it."

"Amen," somebody three chairs to Bolan's left said, nodding his big head. "Lou was a great man, Vince. He'll be sorely missed."

"Here, here!" Others around the table rapped their hairy, meaty knuckles on the tabletop. Bolan just looked around, hands folded in his lap, and said nothing.

Vincent smiled and nodded, holding up a hand for silence. The knuckle-rapping stopped with the suddenness of a slashed throat. *The man definitely commands their respect,* Bolan thought to himself.

"Lou was my executive officer, and now that he's gone, I've decided to give his chair to my dear nephew, Patrick." Uncomfortable shifting in their chairs and quick, darting looks between them, Bolan noticed, though no one dared uttered any challenge. Vincent's rule was absolute. "So without any more bullshit, I give you all your next Executive Officer of Affairs, my nephew and Uncle Lou's grandson, Patrick Aiden Manga!"

More knuckle-rapping as the young man stood from his chair and addressed them each with a nod. He was drunk but he handled his liquor quite well. His red-rimmed eyes met and held Bolan's for the briefest moment and something ugly slithered across them, though his grin never faltered.

"Thank you," Patrick said, holding up a hand for silence. It wasn't as sudden or absolute as when his uncle did it, but everyone quieted down. "I want to start by saying that I know I have some big shoes to fill, but my granddad taught me everything I know. I can't promise to be just like him, but I can give you my word that everything I do will honor his memory and help my uncle here move this organization into the future!"

"Here, here!" Heads bobbing, knuckles knocking on the tabletop like a stampede of tiny horses. Vincent was beaming and put his arm around Patrick, drawing him close with a hefty squeeze.

"I love ya, Nephew," he said, and there were genuine tears in his eyes. *As genuine as a crocodile can be, anyway,* Bolan thought darkly. "And I just know that Uncle Lou is smiling down on you from wherever he is, giving his blessing."

Patrick wiped his eyes with the back of his hand and nodded. "Thank you, Uncle." Vincent gave him a reassuring clap on the back and sat down. Patrick took another few moments to get himself together, and when he looked up and glanced around at the upturned faces around the table, his entire bearing had changed. Twenty years of prison had taught Bolan the importance of reading body language and sensing the shift in the atmosphere of a room. It literally could mean the difference between life and death. And what he saw change in Patrick at that moment gave him chills. It was like a shadow passed over him and sat down behind the controls inside his soul. There was such a sudden darkness come over him that he almost looked like a different person entirely.

"All that being said, my uncle and I have talked it over and we have both come to the conclusion that this long-time rivalry between the Mangas and the Murphys has to come to an end. As most of you now know, they attacked my granddad—ambushed him like the spineless, sackless cowards they are—and murdered him in cold blood. He gave his life for this family and this business, and they took it from him just like *that!*" He emphasized this with a dry, hard snap of his fingers. The sound echoed out across the room like the first shot of a long-awaited conflict.

Like obedient cattle, the men situated around the table nodded and applauded with more of that irritating knuckle-knocking Bolan was seriously starting to dislike. Patrick was basking in the praise, smiling this dark, secretive smile, like he knew something in that moment that no one else in that room knew. Bolan was beginning to despise this man, and he'd never even spoken to him.

"Whaddya want us to do, Patrick?" a middle-aged man sitting next to Benny asked. He was short and stocky, wearing a thousand dollar suit and smoking a shitty-smelling cigar. The guy even wore an obscenely large, gold pinky ring set with an equally large and obscene ruby that glittered merrily in the light like a bright drop of blood when he moved his hand. *Can you even be more of a cliché?* Bolan wondered, rolling his eyes. Benny caught his reaction and giggled quietly to himself.

Patrick's eyes zeroed in on the man with the pinky ring. "I want to hit them where it hurts, Wallace. Hit them fast, hit them hard." He paused, gauging the room for maximum effect, and then said, "We're gonna to hit the Murphy Truck Depot."

It was like someone was slowly letting the air out of a dozen or so balloons; every man in that room uttered a hiss of disbelief at the exact same time. What Bolan didn't know then was that the Murphy Depot was all the way up in Chicago, in the very heart of Jack Murphy's territory.

The mood in the room shifted then, and Bolan watched as many of these guys, all of them lifetime cutthroats and thieves gift-wrapped in expensive suits, exchanged uneasy looks across the board. Patrick wasn't taking the reaction so well. His confidence cracked in that moment, on the verge of dissolving completely when Vincent brought his huge hand down hard on the tabletop. A steel ashtray with the Express Continental logo embossed on it jumped noisily. Everyone's head snapped to the head of the table, mouths closed.

"This ain't the time to be questioning what we're doin here," the big boss said, smacking down their sudden reluctance with all the weight of his indomitable personality. If it was one thing Vincent Manga couldn't stand, it was timidness among his men. "What's the matter with you all?" he demanded. "Are you wolves, or are you sheep?"

A long, clockless moment passed. Everyone at the table (except for Bolan and Benny) shifted uncomfortably in their seats. Finally, Pinky Ring (his name was Wallace, Bolan remembered) cleared his throat and said, "It's ain't that we're scared, Vince. Hittin 'em where it hurts is one thing. But the *Depot?* That's Jack Murphy's base of operations."

"So?" Patrick's voice was insolent. A tremor of rage rippled through him. Standing there at the head of the table with the former generation looking down on him while the younger men (whose loyalty he'd worked very hard to secure) weren't allowed inside the meeting made him feel outnumbered and outmatched. It put him on the defensive.

"So," Wallace explained slowly, "he never has less than two dozen guys hangin around that place on a *slow* day. You just want us to go in there guns blazin and tear the place apart?"

Patrick's face darkened at that. "That's exactly what I want you to do," he said.

Wallace couldn't help it. He let a chuckle slip as he looked around at the faces of his old friends. "Why the fuck would we do that? What does it accomplish to bust in there?"

Patrick's eyes were wild, crazy, just the sort of thing these older cats feared in the upcoming generation. "I want the ground soaked with their blood, Wallace. I want the whole place brought down in fire and ruin. I want the ground scorched and salted like Ghengis-fuckin-Khan rolled into town, so that *nothin* ever grows there again, not even a fuckin golf course. I want the world to know that when you draw a Manga's blood, you and your whole family gets thrown in the meat grinder. *That's* what we'll accomplish."

After a moment of thoughtful silence, Wallace with the pinky ring asked, "Who's gonna lead this search and destroy mission?" It's what everyone was wanting to know, the moment it flew out of Patrick's mouth. "This kinda shit was right up Lou's alley. But he's gone, and so is Lee and his crew, God rest their souls." Wallace made the Sign of the Cross, along with everyone else around the table. Bolan wondered (quite cynically) when the last time any of these degenerates had actually been to church.

Patrick smiled at the question, as if he'd been waiting for it. "I will."

That obviously didn't sit right with everyone there, but the hard stare Vincent gave each and every man from his place at the head of the table prevented any more dissent. This was going to happen, whether anyone in that room wanted it to or not.

Benny was right. Patrick wants blood, and Vincent has to give it to him. Bolan suddenly realized it wasn't the older generation Vincent was trying to appease. It was the younger—the Patricks of his organization—he feared. *Otherwise, it'll be Vincent's wake next time.*

After a really long, awkward moment of silent contemplation, Wallace lifted his head and looked around the table. "For Lou," he said, giving the table a single knock with one hairy knuckle.

"For Lou."

"Definitely, for Lou."

"Get some payback for Lou."

"What they did to Lou wasn't right. Make 'em pay in blood."

Bolan watched as the smile stretched across Patrick's face like a bloodless scar. *He's crazy,* was Bolan's final thought before Vincent stood, embraced his nephew one last time, and then adjourned the meeting.

4.

"Hang back a sec, O'Brien."

Bolan was almost to the door, bringing up the tail-end of the group shuffling out of the meeting, when Vincent motioned him over. Benny gave him a tap on the arm and told him he'd meet him at the bar, then left. Bolan noticed Patrick watching him and Vincent with a peculiar look; that secretive grin never left his face as he departed through another door leading into one of Vincent's trophy rooms and closed it behind him, leaving the two of them alone.

Vincent patiently waited until the room had cleared, then said, "What do you think of my nephew?"

"Seems pretty broken up about his grandpa."

Vincent nodded slowly. "Yeah, he is. He's one of those guys who can't just let things go, no matter what. And that's a problem for me." Here he tapped Bolan's chest with one big, blunt finger. "And you."

Bolan frowned. "What're you talking about?"

"Patrick's been askin all kinds of questions about how Lou was killed," Vincent explained. They could hear people talking and moving in the hall outside the room.

"He doesn't believe it was an ambush," Bolan said.

"No, he doesn't." Vincent paused, his eyes flickering on Bolan's face. "He thinks you had somethin to do with it. Lou never trusted you, and he wasn't quiet about it. And my uncle, rest his black soul, told Patrick everything."

"Well, he's not wrong," Bolan conceded. "So what?"

"It means this is a problem I don't need right now. I'm not keen on starting a war with the Murphys, but that cat's already out of the bag, isn't it? So I need to let Patrick have his revenge, and maybe put the hurts to Jack Murphy's operations in the process—two birds, one stone, so to speak." Here his eyes took on a dangerous look. One hand fell lightly on Bolan's shoulder. "Patrick can't come back from the Depot."

Bolan looked at him. "You want your nephew killed." It wasn't a question.

"I'm still not convinced he had nothin to do with that truck bein hit," Vincent said. "No way Lou did it by himself, and Patrick loved the old man. He'd have done whatever he was told. And as crazy as he is—you saw him, how wild he looks—it's just the sorta thing he'd be into."

Bolan agreed. The guy was batshit. "How the hell am I

supposed to pull that off with all your guys around?"

"There's going to be a lot of shooting, lot of bullets flyin around. If Patrick happens to take one in the midst of all that chaos . . ." He trailed off with a shrug of his meaty shoulders, leaving the unspoken part hanging in the air between them.

Bolan mulled this over for a whole five seconds and realized he had no problem with killing another member of Vincent's family. It was just one more rung up the ladder, as far as he was concerned. "I'll take care of it."

Vincent grinned hugely. "You're gonna go far in this business, O'Brien. I gotta feeling."

You're right, Bolan thought as he left the room, feeling like he needed a shower. *I'm going straight to the top.*

CHAPTER NINETEEN

1.

Jack Murphy wasn't waiting on the Mangas to hit him first.

The Murphy patriarch had been busy on the phone, gathering his forces from the four corners of his vast kingdom to hit back at the Mangas for their attack on his truck. He brought in heavy hitters from New York, Philadelphia, Chicago, and New Orleans. They made a plan to strike back at Vincent and his crew with extreme prejudice, hitting them where they could find them—whether it was in broad daylight or under the cover of darkness, they didn't care. Jack had cops and lawyers and judges on his payroll, and he would call in as many favors as necessary to make the Mangas pay in blood for what they did to his men in that truck on that cold, January night.

What transpired over the next several weeks would go down in the history books as the bloodiest days of the short-lived war between the two factions, and several FBI investigators would go on to jump start their careers on the how and why in the bloody aftermath.

2.

Randall Whitaker was nervous as he drove the unmarked Peterbilt down an isolated highway in the crashing rain. He was going on his third month working as a driver for Express Continental, and this was the second time they had put him in an unmarked truck with specific orders to avoid any and all major highways and interstates, and that these runs must be done in the middle of the night. That, and he was sure the man sitting next to him in the passenger's seat smoking a cigarette was carrying a gun.

He'd taken this job because the pay was exceptional compared to the other offers he'd received over the last seven months, and now he had a growing (and frightening) suspicion that he knew why. When he'd arrived at the loading docks he was never told what it was he would be carrying, and the men locking and sealing his truck had all been armed with military-style rifles. They met his questions with stony stares and dead eyes, until he stopped asking them altogether and climbed up into his truck. It wasn't until he was about to pull out of the loading area that the man now sitting next to him had climbed into the passenger's seat and ordered him to keep his mouth shut and drive. Randy had no idea what was in the back of the truck as he drove north through western Ohio on his way to New York City, but it scared the hell out of him.

This is definitely the last one, he told himself as he struggled to see the road through the lashing rain. He glanced over at his passenger and tried to make small talk. "Helluva night, huh?"

The man, dressed in a dark leather jacket and jeans, simply stared out the passenger side window, watching the rain. He made no response.

"Say, you think we might stop for a bite to eat?" Randy asked nervously. "My blood sugar's a little low."

The man turned his head in the glow of the dash lights with the same slow, methodical movement of a Terminator. "No stops," he said in a low, dead voice. "We drive until we get there."

"All the way to New York?" The man's pale gray eyes regarded him silently. Randy swallowed and nodded. "Alright. Whatever you say."

The silence stretched out between them as the miles fell away behind them. Randy had to take a piss, but he wasn't about to ask the man to stop again. He had an idea (crazy, but it felt true enough) that this man would easily take the wheel and continue on if something unfortunate was to happen to him—like, say, a bullet to the head. The thought made Randy shiver.

"You cold?" the man in the seat next to him asked.

Randy shook his head. "Nah."

"Then why'd you shake like that?" The Terminator's eyes seemed all-knowing in the glow of the dashboard.

"I told you, my sugar's a little low." Randy's eyes jumped back and forth from the road to the man in the passenger's seat, and back to the road. "I'll be fine."

The man sighed through his nose, took out his phone. He pulled up his GPS, scanned it for a minute or two, then clicked the phone off and returned it to his jacket pocket. "There's a truck stop about a mile up," he said at last. "We'll get some food and get back on the road. That alright?"

Randy nodded, though it didn't make him feel any better. "Sure. Thanks."

"No problem."

They turned off the next exit and, sure enough, there was a truck stop glowing in the dark and rain like some polished jewel. Randy breathed a little sigh of relief and began working the brakes on the decline until they were turning left onto a broad, empty highway. A minute and a half later, he was pulling into the lot.

"Want anything?" he asked, cracking the driver's side door a little. The cigarette smoke was burning his eyes and choking him. The guy smoked one after another, often lighting the new one with the butt of the one he was mashing out into the ashtray.

"Double cheeseburger and fries," the Terminator told him as he opened his own door and dropped down into the lot with a squash of gravel. "And get some extra ketchup."

Randy nodded, said, "Okey dokey," and then went inside, leaving the guy leaning against the side of the trailer.

The truck stop had a fuel desk on one side as you walked in. This whole area was basically a convenience store where you could buy snacks, drinks, motor oil, washer fluid, and cheaply-made hats and T-shirts at exorbitant prices. To the left was a restaurant with booths along the outside walls and a dozen rows of tables and chairs in the center of the black and white checkered tile floor.

He wasn't sure if he'd ever been here before; twenty-seven years of driving truck, all these places started to look the same. The restaurant was mostly empty this time of night, with only one other driver sitting in a booth and sipping coffee and wearing a battered cowboy hat. Randy nodded to the man, the man nodded back, and then he took a seat at the counter. A sour-faced waitress saw him, placed a bookmark in the novel she was reading, and ambled her way down to where he was sitting.

"What can I getcha, hon?" she asked in a tired, disinterested voice. She was chomping her gum slowly, like a cow chewing its cud.

"Two double cheeseburgers, two orders of fries, and a couple of Cokes."

"Don't got Coke," she said, her pencil pausing on the notebook on which she was writing down his order. "Pepsi okay?"

Randy nodded. "Pepsi's fine."

"Be a few minutes," she said, and before he could thank her, she flipped the notebook closed and disappeared through a pair of stainless steel bat wing doors into the steaming kitchen beyond.

Still needing to take that piss, Randy got up and glanced out through the big plate glass window at the front of the restaurant to check on his truck (a habit he'd developed after his first truck had been stolen, trailer and all, outside of Detroit back in '99), saw it was still sitting there idling, and then went into the men's room.

Like every restroom in a place like this, it stank of urinal cakes, disinfectant, and a lingering odor of turd and old vomit. Randy picked one of the empty urinals and unzipped. No sooner than he'd made ready to let loose, a hand landed hard on his shoulder and spun him around without a word.

"Zip it up," the stranger standing in front of him said, glancing down at Randy's wide-open fly. Randy wracked his brain in those few seconds, but he couldn't remember hearing the man enter the bathroom behind him.

He was waiting for me in the stall, he thought, zipping his pants. But that was crazy. Who'd be waiting for him in some disgusting bathroom in some unknown truck stop in the middle of nowhere?

"Excuse me?" Randy said, more than a little rattled. He wasn't the sort of man that angered easily, but this sudden and brazen intrusion had got his hair up. "Just what the hell you think you're doin?"

The man in front of him was tall and completely bald. The sterile white light falling from the fixtures in the ceiling painted bright spots all over his freckled scalp. The guy didn't even have eyebrows, now that Randy had a chance to get a good look. His brother-in-law had a condition where he couldn't grow hair—not pubic, not eyebrows, not on his head—anywhere on his body, leaving him as smooth as a baby seal. This jerk in front of him looked like he might have that same disorder.

"You drivin that red Peterbilt outside?" the man asked casually. He had a slight Southern accent and was wearing a green Army jacket with his long arms resting at his sides like a pair of dead snakes. "The one from Express Continental?"

Randy, flustered, nodded dumbly. It never occurred to him to ask how the man knew what company he was driving for when there was no logo of any kind on the side of the trailer. "Yeah, it's mine. What about it?"

The hairless man smiled faintly, shaking his head. "Nothin. That's all I needed." He then reached into his jacket before Randy's brain could register that he was in grave peril, and pulled out a large-caliber chrome revolver and placed the barrel about an inch from Randy's face.

"Nothin personal, friend," he muttered, pulling back the hammer so that the gun's loaded cylinder made a single turn with a hollow, metallic *click*.

"Wait!" But that was all Randy Whitaker managed to get out before the Smith & Wesson went off and the right side of his face disintegrated in a spray of blood and tissue and teeth.

The bald stranger, smoke rolling thinly from the barrel of his revolver, watched Randy's convulsions as he slid down the wall, leaving a thick smear of blood and brains on the way down, with a fascinated, clinical detachment before making the gun disappear back into his jacket and calmly walking out of the bathroom. He hardly noticed when the driver in the cowboy hat jumped up from his table, muttering, *"Sombitch!"* as he lurched towards the bathroom door to see what had happened, and the sour-faced waitress was nowhere to be seen when he walked past Randy's order that was now sitting neatly on the counter, all bagged up and ready to go with a receipt stapled to the bag. He calmly took the burgers and double order of fries as he walked past, and made his way outside.

When the police arrived ten minutes later, Randy's Peterbilt was gone, leaving behind another body lying crumpled in the gravel where it was parked when Randy went inside. The man they found, dressed in a dark leather jacket and jeans, had three gunshot wounds to the chest. He had apparently pulled his own gun before his death, but never had the chance to use it. Randy's truck would only be found three days later on a back road in western Ohio, completely burned down to the frame. The trailer, and whatever was in it, was never found.

3.

Georgie Mendoza had been doing runs like this for Vincent for over fifteen years now, but something about tonight felt wrong.

First off, the son-of-a-bitching rain. It was the end of freaking January and it was *raining*. Georgie had never liked the rain, even when he was a kid. And now, as he drove the van along the two-lane access road in the middle of nowhere, the rain was coming down in sheets and he was forced to slow down and turn on his bright beams, which only seemed to make things worse, and it put him in a vile mood.

The second thing that tipped Georgie off that this night wasn't going to be like the rest was the job itself. Killing someone who needed killing had never been a problem for a man like him. Georgie had killed his first man when he was eighteen years old and had never looked back.

The person he shot had been a homeless man who'd matched the description of a guy a girl Georgie liked claimed had tried to rape her one night when her and a few friends had been out late trying to get someone over twenty-one to buy them alcohol for a party. According to this girl (her name was Becky-something; Georgie couldn't remember her last name), she'd offered the bum an extra fifty bucks if he could get them a bottle of vodka and bring it back to them. He'd agreed, took her money, and when he returned with the bottle, he demanded she give him a blowjob along with the extra fifty. When she refused, he'd grabbed her hair and tried to force her, only Becky wasn't having any of it. She screamed and kicked the guy square in the balls, snatched the vodka from his hand, and she and her friends took off running.

Later that night, after telling the story to Georgie and his younger brother, Harry, Georgie decided to go looking for the dude. They cruised the neighborhood until they found some guy sitting in a doorway putting new laces in a pair of shoes and minding his own business. Georgie didn't think the guy looked like the raping type, but he'd been half-lit and hopped up on adrenaline and so he grabbed the guy, forced him into the alley behind the building in front of where he was sitting, and asked Becky if he was the one. She didn't seem too sure at first, and the guy's face was a doughy white moon of surprise when Georgie placed the barrel of his piece against the side of his neck. "This him?" he asked her at least three times, and finally she nodded, tears in her eyes, and Georgie shot him through the throat.

In the end, Georgie had killed the wrong guy because Becky had been high on who-knew-what at the time, and it was something that had destroyed his brother in the process. Harry had held the man while Georgie shot him, and for years afterwords, Harry went into a downward spiral of guilt and remorse that ended with him hanging himself in his garage with a garden hose.

This job, tonight, had the same feeling as the night Georgie and Harry went looking for that homeless guy who'd grabbed Becky— which was to say, it didn't feel right at all.

"You sure you're gonna be able to keep this thing on the road, Georgie?" Jesse asked from the back. He and Georgie had been on many of these midnight runs together, and some of them had gotten a little bloody over the years. In a firefight, there was no one better to watch your back than Jesse. But Jesse was a worrier—something that always set Georgie's teeth on edge.

"You worry about keeping the safety on that rifle, and I'll worry about getting us there in one piece," Georgie barked back at him. He was not in the mood for any of Jesse's crybaby shit tonight. He threw a glance to his right, watching Val as he seemed to be dozing off in the passenger seat. Georgie liked Val. Val was the quiet, thoughtful type, who never said anything unless he actually had something worth saying. *Why can't they all be like that?* Georgie lamented as he worked the steering wheel to keep the van from hydroplaning through the heavy puddles of rainwater now swallowing the edges of the road.

"So where we goin, anyway?" Burt asked. Like Jesse, Burt was a good soldier to have at your back when the shit hit the fan, but he had an annoying habit of asking too many questions, which made him and Jesse two peas in a freaking pod, as far as Georgie was concerned. On a night like tonight, with it raining like Noah's Ark and the boss telling them they had to take out a couple of Jack Murphy's boys to send a message back to the old devil himself, Georgie wasn't in the mood to deal with any of it.

"Same place I told you about ten minutes ago when you asked," Georgie snapped.

"We're goin to just roll up on these cats and smoke 'em? Just like that?"

Georgie took a calming breath, let it out slowly. His eyes shifted to the rearview mirror where he could see Burt's big stupid face looking back at him lumpishly. *A good soldier, but a fuckin moron,* he thought nastily.

"That's right, Burt," he said. "We're gonna roll up on 'em, light their asses up, and then get the hell outta there. Any more fuckin questions, or can I just drive the van?"

Burt's big dumb face frowned, but that was the end of his questions. "You don't need to be a asshole, Georgie," he said defensively.

"Take it easy, both of you," Jesse said, playing the referee as he often did. "We're all a little wound up tonight. Just chill out."

No sooner had the digital clock on the dashboard turned to 1:15 am, Georgie turned down a narrow gravel road that ran back through a heavily wooded area surrounded on all sides by cornfields and cow pastures. It wasn't the kind of place you'd expect to find a group of men you were hired to kill, but Georgie knew this is where their targets would be from the briefing Vincent's pencil-dick nephew, Patrick, walked him through. He didn't like Patrick at all and, more importantly, he didn't trust him. The guy was only like twenty-two or twenty-three years old and already running things? Georgie was in his fifties now, been taking out the Mangas' trash for more than two decades, and this skinny little red-headed prick gets a promotion because his psycho grandpa got smoked? It was enough to trigger his acid reflux.

They came to a small wooden bridge spanning a deep ravine that was now swollen with rain and runoff. Georgie stopped the van, put it in park.

"This the place?" Jesse asked from the back. Val yawned in the passenger seat until his jaw popped, sat up blinking through the rain-smeared windshield. He had an AK-47 resting on the floorboard in front of him, propped between his legs.

"This is it," Georgie concurred. He sat with his hands on the wheel, squinting through the rain. Up ahead was one of Jack Murphy's off-the-books warehouses, according to Patrick Manga. It was an old farmhouse with a large barn with a sloping roof and several smaller outbuildings huddling in the rain like souls who'd gotten lost on their way to hell. Georgie had no idea what this place was used for, but it was important to Jack Murphy, and so Patrick had decreed that they kill whoever they found on-site and torch the place. Simple.

Only it's never that simple, Georgie thought bitterly. He looked out at the cold, driving rain with a miserable scowl, wishing he was back home in bed and under his heavy blankets.

"What's the plan?" Val asked. It was the first time he'd spoken a word the entire trip.

"We split into two teams," Georgie said, pulling his own piece from a shoulder holster he wore snugly under his heavy winter jacket. It was a Springfield Elite with .45 ACP rounds; it was compact and it packed a hell of a punch. "Jesse and me will take the barn. Burt, Val—check the house and any of those little sheds you come across. You see anyone that isn't in this van, you shoot to kill, no exceptions. Understood?"

Everyone nodded without a word. Georgie killed the van's engine and popped his door. "Let's go."

"What the fuck is that smell?" Burt asked as they mounted the bridge. He looked like a man who'd just taken a bite out of a cupcake full of worms.

"Pig shit," Val told him, grinning. He was sniffing the air like a dog. "This must be an old hog farm or something."

"It doesn't matter!" Georgie hissed irritably through the rain. "You all know what to do! Now, let's go!"

They didn't have to worry about being quiet as they moved across the bridge and spread out in two different directions. The rain was coming down in a constant roar that made Georgie's ears ring. And Val had been right about the pigs. As they moved in closer, there was the stench of manure layered beneath the rain that made Georgie gag. He and Jesse stayed low with their weapons ready. Both men were soaked through their clothes to the skin by the time they reached the barn. There were lights on inside—Georgie could see through the spaces in the boards naked yellow bulbs hanging from the rafter beams—but no sign of life from where he was standing. He threw a quick glance toward the house, which sat up on the crown of a low hill in the dark like something out of a horror movie. No lights on in the windows there; the whole place was dark and dead and menacing in the rain. He saw Val with his AK-47 and Burt carrying a pump-action shotgun moving along the side of the house, peeking in through the blackened windows before they disappeared around the back.

Georgie signaled Jesse to go around the back of the barn, to another set of doors, while he remained here in the front. Jesse nodded grimly, his face running with water and making him look like a melting wax statue in the dark, and then he was around the corner and out of sight. A moment later, Georgie, looking through a crack in the side of the barn, saw him reappear at the doors across from him, waiting.

Georgie still had that bad feeling, but it wasn't sitting as heavily on him now that the whole place looked deserted. Taking a deep breath, he slid the barn door open with one hand, raising his pistol up in front of him with the other. Jesse, at the other set of doors, did the same.

Walking into the barn, Georgie was confused and relieved at the same time. There was no one here, yet all the lights were on, and the floor, a thick slab of cracked concrete, had been tidily swept and cleaned.

"What gives?" Jesse asked, looking around with a confused frown on his face. There were no boxes or crates or anything to suggest this was a warehouse at all.

Georgie shook his head. *Maybe that little red-headed prick was wrong about this place,* he thought, remembering Patrick's big grandiose speech before they'd left. He took a mean little pleasure in the idea of returning home and telling the cocksucker better luck next time.

"Let's go check on Val and Burt," Georgie said. No sooner did the words leave his mouth, however, a gunshot rang out in the dark and Jesse's head exploded like a rotted pumpkin hit with a sledgehammer. The big man didn't make a sound as his blood and brains burst from the crater that opened the entire left side of his skull, and he went down to the barn floor like a sack of stone.

Ambush! Georgie's mind screamed. *It's a fuckin ambush!*

His eyes wide and his face dripping with Jesse's blood, Georgie raised his pistol, only to drop it with a cry of pain as another shot, this one coming from outside the main door through which he'd entered, filled the barn's empty space like a cannon blast. The slug struck his knee, blowing it apart so that most of the lower leg just hung there by a mess of bloody gristle.

"Fuck!" he screamed, falling onto his side. He looked to his right, and with an expression of sickness and horror dawning on his sweaty, gore-splashed face, he saw the toe of his shoe lying only a few inches from his face, sitting at an angle that was impossible for a fully-functioning foot to achieve.

"Oh, God!" he bellowed, feeling a wave of nausea sweeping over him as he reached his hand out towards his severed leg. His .45 lay on the concrete next to him, but he didn't dare go for it as four men suddenly stepped into the dry warmth of the barn from out of the rainy darkness. They were soaked to the bone from the rain and making wet squishing sounds when they moved, like horrors washed up on a blackened shore. All of them were armed with military-style rifles and shotguns, and they looked down on him like hyenas looking down on a wounded zebra.

In the distance, Georgie heard Val and Burt screaming as more gun shots punched through the roar of the rain outside and the drumming of the rain on the barn's metal roof above. The smiles that etched themselves across the faces of Murphy's men when the silence swept back in told Georgie everything he needed to know: his crew was dead. And he was next.

"Pick him up," one of the men standing in front of him said. He was a small guy wearing a black baseball cap and a fleece-lined denim jacket. Georgie had no way of knowing for sure, but he believed this was the asshole who'd blown his leg off.

"Go fuck yourself," Georgie sneered, trying to crawl towards his gun. The pain coming from his disintegrated stump was like someone had dipped his leg in a vat of molten fire. "Come near me, and—"

A shotgun butt crashed against the side of his head, turning out the lights. When they came back on, Georgie was outside and couldn't move. The rain had slowed to a trickle. Georgie's right eye was swollen to the size of a goose egg, and his head throbbed in rhythm with the pain coming from his severed stump.

"What the fuck is goin on?" he asked sluggishly. He shook his head and looked in front of him. He was zip-tied to a chair by his wrists and the one ankle he had left, watching as a group of about a dozen or so hogs inside a wooden pen were playing a nasty game of tug-o'-war with Val's bullet-riddled corpse. Eventually, the bigger hogs won, tearing the dead man in half with a sickening sound like someone ripping off a piece of Velcro. Val's insides spilled out into the cold, wet mud like some nasty soup, and the winners of the game shrieked and squealed in delight, burying their muzzles into the hot, steaming mess. Burt was lying next to him, missing his nose, his lips, and both of his ears, while three more hogs stripped the skin and muscles from his leg bones with their champing teeth. Another hog was on top of Jesse, grunting greedily and pulling his entrails out of his body through a ragged hole in his ribcage, gobbling them down like a chain of big, wet, red sausages.

"Please," Georgie begged, delirious with pain and fear. *"Please, I can't go out like that!"*

The men standing around him didn't say a word. They simply picked Georgie up, chair and all, and slowly lowered him face-first down into the hog pit. The last thing he saw in this life as he wept and gibbered and struggled against his bonds was a giant hog shambling over to him, giving him a quick, inquisitive sniff before it opened its dripping jaws and nearly swallowed his face whole as it tore his head from his shoulders.

4.

Larry Krieger was one of Vincent's top lieutenants. He'd been raised alongside Vincent by Victor Manga, Vincent's father. Larry's father, Daniel Krieger, had worked for the Mangas his entire adult life, until he was killed on the job when Larry was seven years old. So distraught over her husband's sudden and violent death (he was cornered in a grocery store parking lot between two well-placed cars and shot so many times it looked as if someone had ran him through a wood chipper; the FBI's forensic unit would later determine that the weapon used was a fully automatic machine gun, possibly mounted and concealed in the back of a utility van), Melanie Krieger swallowed an entire bottle of tranquilizers and washed them down with a fifth of vodka, leaving her only child, Larry, with nowhere to go. Her family had excommunicated her long before Larry was born, after she began dating Danny (Melanie came from a long line of good Catholics who knew exactly the type of man Danny Krieger was and, more importantly, the kind of men he *worked* for), and everyone on Danny's side of the family was either dead or in prison. So Victor, out of kindness and loyalty to one of his best soldiers, took Larry into his home at the age of eight and raised him alongside Vincent as his own son.

Larry and Vincent grew up as close as peanut butter and jelly, and as Vincent began to take the reins of power in the organization, he tended to rely on Larry more and more, so that everyone knew that a word from Larry was the same as a command from Vincent himself. His importance to Vincent, along with the fact that Larry was also an avid hunter, would eventually spell his doom.

One morning Larry took a group of his most trusted men and decided to head up into Michigan and do some goose hunting. Larry, also a shrewd investor and money-man in his own right, had bought a nice patch of land outside Kalamazoo; every year he liked to go up there between October and February to hunt waterfowl, and so today, he was hunting geese.

They arrived at the spot near a small lake surrounded by forest that was still in the skeletal grip of winter. The air was crisp and cold, the sky a fragile blue that looked as if it, too, was covered in a thin rime of ice. It was the best sort of day, as far as Larry was concerned. He wasn't a summer/tropical type of guy like most. He preferred the cold of winter over the heat and humidity of summer any day of the week.

Larry arrived at his favorite hunting spot around six in the morning, before the sun was even up. He was a tall, painfully thin man with big calloused hands and a deeply-lined face for someone in their mid-forties due to his love of hunting and being outdoors in general. This morning he was wearing his camouflage jacket and fur-lined cap, and the bright, almost neon-orange vest that told other hunters he was off-limits. Not that there were any other hunters here on his property (most locals in the area knew better than to poach anything on Larry Krieger's land); Larry owned everything as far as the horizon, and even a few hundred acres beyond that point.

So that morning, three heavy-duty pickup trucks pulled up to the small lake surrounded by reeds and pine forests and killed their engines. Larry and eight of his men climbed out their trucks with their shotguns and thermoses full of hot coffee, and waited for the sun to come up. While he was waiting, Larry decided he needed to relieve himself after the long ride north. He'd been up since four that morning and had already finished off two pots of coffee by the time they arrived at the lake.

Telling his men he was going to take a piss, he wandered off into the trees to do his business. He was almost down to a dribble when he heard the first gunshot echo out over the lake, sending a squall of birds shrieking and flapping up out of the tall, frozen grass.

"Son of a *bitch!*" he exploded, yanking his zipper up as he turned angrily and made his way out of the trees and back to where his men would be waiting with the trucks and guns. "Who the fuck did that? You sons of bitches will scare off the—"

Larry stopped, the rest of that sentence hanging in the air while his mouth fell open like a broken trap. His bodyguard, Jerry, was lying across the hood of Larry's Silver Dodge Ram, his brains splattered over the spider-webbed windshield, while the rest of his men just stood there, transfixed, and ogled him with eyes bulging from their sockets like golf balls.

"What the hell?" he finally managed to say as a line of men holding rifles suddenly materialized out of the nearby woods like vengeful spirits. They opened fire.

Larry hit the ground as the forest and lake erupted into a war zone. The bark of automatic fire was relentless and brutal; as he crawled on his belly, the snow and frozen mud around him was littered with a ghastly harvest of brains and blood. Men spun on their feet as the bullets tore them to shreds. Some of Larry's guys managed to fire off a few shots, only to be ripped apart in the return fire. Some of them had pieces of their faces literally blown off their skulls; others attempted to flee while holding their bulging intestines in with trembling, bloody hands, only to be gunned down as they ran.

When it was over (and it was over very quickly) they found Larry, the only survivor, cowering underneath his truck, trembling as he groped for a shotgun that had fallen out of Jerry's hand when the first shot of the massacre took off the top of his head. Without a word, they grabbed Larry by the ankles and pulled him out from under the truck. They loomed over him, ghoul-like, in the early morning, gripping their rifles.

"P-please," Larry pleaded, his face running with sweat. "I have money, if that's what you want! Take it!"

"We don't want your money," one of them said in a cool, calm voice of reason. He was a sleight man with a pencil-thin beard running along his square jawline. He was wearing a black driver's cap and a double-breasted Navy Peacoat. "We need you to send a message back to your boss."

For a moment, Larry dared to hope. *They need me alive,* he thought, and almost sobbed with relief. "Anything! Anything you want!"

The other men exchanged looks and laughed coldly. "So much for his big, badass reputation," one of them smirked.

Larry, scared as he was, rankled at that. "Fuck you, buddy! Do you know who I am?"

"Pretty sure we do," the man in the Peacoat said. "Which is why we need you to carry our message back to Vincent for us."

Larry took a deep breath, exhaled. "What is it?"

The man in the Peacoat turned and nodded to someone Larry couldn't see. Larry then watched in dawning horror as the crowd gathered around him parted to make way for a large man holding what looked like a very sharp machete in his fist.

"What the fuck is this?" he demanded, though his voice cracked like a pubescent boy's, revealing his sudden terror.

"*This* is the message," the man in the Peacoat answered, dropping a nod to his associate holding the machete.

What happened next wasn't battle, but butchery—frantic, bloody, impelled by a cold and calculated fury that only men in this sort of world would understand when it was all over. Some of the men, hardened as they were by a life of violence, nevertheless had to shut out the sight of that dripping blade that rose and fell with the sound of a butcher's cleaver, and the strangled, gurgling cries that at last dwindled away and ceased.

What was left when the man with the machete finally stopped was something that no longer resembled a human being. If they hadn't left most of his face intact and floating atop the gory remains they'd placed inside one of Larry's own heavy-duty Igloo coolers they'd found in the bed of his Silver Dodge, no one would've known whose mangled corpse it was inside that cooler at all.

5.

Vincent was in a meeting with his nephew, Patrick, and a few of his top officers when Gina, his maid, came to the door with a hesitant knock.

Every head turned in her direction as she cleared her throat, and for good reason. She was a beautiful young woman with long, lustrous hair piled on top of her head in a pile of black foam, held in place with a bronze clip. Her uniform, a simple, sleek black and white blouse-skirt combination, accentuated her athletic figure, tempting every man she passed to take a second look.

"What is it, Gina?" Vincent barked at her, causing her to jump a little.

Gina swallowed, her hand going instinctively to her throat. She tried to ignore the looks of the five men sitting around Vincent's desk (especially the young red-headed man with the rat-face; she couldn't remember his name, and didn't want to) by focusing on the fierce eyes of her boss, who was crouched behind his wide desk like some great primordial beast about to pounce.

"Sir, a package has arrived for you," she said with a slight tremor in her voice. She knew what it was her boss did to earn his millions, she wasn't stupid, and the last thing she wanted to do, after the news he'd received about one of his shipments being hijacked, was anything that might upset him further.

"Set it on the table in the hall," Vincent ordered. "I'll get to it later." Gina, visibly nervous now, cleared her throat again. Vincent looked back up at her, a fierce light kindling in his eyes. "Something else I can do for you, dear?"

"The man who brought the package said it was urgent, that you needed to open it right away."

Every man in that room exchanged worried looks. Vincent heaved himself up from his chair and followed the maid into the hall. On the table beneath a large, gold-framed mirror, sat a huge blue and white Igloo cooler, the kind campers who plan on doing some heavy drinking in the woods might bring along.

Vincent just stood there in the hall, glowering at it while Gina fidgeted nervously behind him. At last, he approached the cooler and gave it a little shake with his right hand. It didn't feel like there was a bomb hiding inside of it, but you could never really know for sure. He shook it again, a little harder, and heard something soft yet heavy shift inside.

He turned on the maid, a light sweat beading his forehead. "Who dropped it off?"

Gina, eyes wide, shrugged. "Just some kid," she said.

Vincent's gaze swiveled back to the cooler. "He say anything else? Like where it came from?"

Gina shook her head. "No, sir. Just that it was for you, and that you needed to open it as soon as you received it."

Vincent reached out and picked the Igloo up by the handle, gave it another brisk shake. Did something *squish* inside? He could swear it had, though that seemed unlikely. Bombs don't squish, last he checked, and when he shook the cooler for the third time, something inside definitely *did* squish, he was certain of it.

"Thank you, Gina. Why don't you take the rest of the day off, come back tomorrow."

Gina nodded, breathing a little sigh of relief, and then she thanked him and disappeared down the hall, the rubber soles on the bottoms of her tennis shoes squelching on the freshly-buffed floors.

When Vincent came back into the office carrying the cooler, everyone stood from their chairs and watched with bright, curious eyes as he sat it down on top of his desk.

"What the hell is that?" Patrick asked. He didn't like the way his uncle was looking at the thing one bit. Made his skin crawl.

Vincent shook his head. "Dunno. Gina said some punk kid delivered, said I had to open it right away." A small bead of sweat rolled lazily down Vincent's broad, sloping forehead and disappeared into one bushy brow.

"Let's see what it is," Carter Solverson offered. He was a short, thin man in his late forties who ran collection for Victor in Detroit's Eastern District. Vincent's father had sent him down to keep an eye on his son, Vincent was sure, but Carter was a stand-up guy.

"Could be a bomb," Leroy Carradine suggested. He was a huge

man with no neck and no way to see his balls when he took a piss. He was sitting next to Patrick, smoking and adding to the heart disease that would eventually kill him. Vincent always thought of him as Humpty Dumpty in a twelve hundred dollar suit. Normally, the thought would crack him up, but not at this particular moment.

"It's not a fuckin bomb," Vincent grated. He was genuinely sweating now. His armpits were soupy, and it was running down his back and into the crack of his ass.

"How do you know?" Leroy asked, looking slightly aggrieved.

Vincent's eyes slowly rolled up to Leroy, making the fat man wiggle nervously in his chair. "The thing squished when I shook it. The same way you squished when you waddled in here."

Leroy's big, doughy face went pink. His mouth snapped shut with an audible pop.

"Squished?" Patrick asked.

"Yeah. Like something soft and wet inside."

Everyone exchanged an uneasy look. They'd all been in this business long enough, and with the ongoing war with the Murphys in high gear, it didn't take much for their imaginations to fill in the blanks on this one.

"What're you gonna do, Uncle?"

Vincent just stood there, sweating and looming over the problem without saying a word. At last, he said, "Fuck it," and popped the cooler open, rolling back the lid. When he looked inside and saw what remained of Larry Krieger's face looking back up at him, he visibly paled. Again, the five men sitting around the front of Vincent's desk exchanged open looks of concern, until Patrick stood up and joined his uncle and looked down into the cooler for himself.

"No fuckin way. You gotta be shitting me."

"What is it?" Carter wanted to know, leaning forward expectantly in his chair.

Vincent's eyes were haunted when he said, "It's the fuckin end of Jack Murphy, *that's* what it is." He slammed the igloo shut, took out his cell phone, and made some calls.

CHAPTER TWENTY

1.

Bolan was busy sweeping up when he heard someone knock on the barbershop door. It was after five and Rick had gone home to get some rest (at Bolan's insistence) and he thought maybe the old man had forgotten something. He emptied the dustpan into the trash bag, set the broom aside, and went into the front of the shop.

"We're closed," he said with a smile through the open blinds.

"I can see that," Sara said, smiling back at him from the street. The rain from the previous few days had finally stopped, leaving what little snow was left a filthy, slushing mess everywhere you looked. But it was still cold enough that he could see her breath against the glass when she spoke.

"I was just finishing up," he said as he shut and locked the deadbolt behind her.

She wore a heavy wool coat and scarf, with her purse slung over her right shoulder. "I hope I'm not bothering you."

He shook his head. In truth, he was glad for the distraction. He'd been unable to turn his mind off since Vincent told him he wanted him to kill his nephew. "No, you're fine. Want some coffee? Rick has a pot in the back." He grinned. "One of the rules he has is that it never goes empty."

"Sure, sounds great."

He motioned her to sit in one of the waiting chairs and disappeared through the door leading into the back of the shop, emerging a minute or two later with two mugs of steaming coffee.

"We're out of cream and sugar," he told her, handing her a mug. "Sorry."

"That's fine," she said. "Since I quit smoking, black coffee suits me."

He looked at her, surprised. "You quit?"

"Going on two months now."

He smiled. "That's awesome."

She gave him a playful scowl. "Doesn't *feel* awesome. Can't sleep sometimes, and I don't know what to do with my hands. And when I get stressed out, I just want to light one up. They tell you to chew gum, but that shit doesn't help. At least, not for me."

"So, what's up?" he asked.

Sara lowered her mug, cupping it between both hands in her lap. "I haven't seen you in a while. How're you doing?"

"Pretty good," he lied.

"Everything alright?"

He looked at her, not really knowing what to say. It was obvious to him at this point that, in spite of all the years they'd been apart, she could still read him like a book.

"It's fine," he told her, hoping to drop it. "Just a lot of stress right now."

She frowned. "What's wrong?"

"Rick. He found out he has stomach cancer a while back. I've been keeping an eye on him." *Among other things.*

Her hand went to her mouth. "I'm sorry."

"Me too. The guy has gone out of his way to help me these last eight months or so. I don't know where I'd be without him." He flashed her a tired smile. "He even got my parole officer to cut me some slack so that I only have to report every month now instead of every two weeks."

She leaned forward and placed a thin, warm hand on his wrist. "I'm sorry to hear that. Is he taking chemo?"

Bolan uttered a bitter little laugh. "Rick?" He shook his head. "Hell no. Says he won't go out like that. Wants to enjoy the rest of his time without being sick and bedridden every day."

Sara nodded understandably. "I get that. Hell of a thing. You need anything?"

"I'm fine, but thanks. Where's Abby?"

Sara sat her mug down on the little end table beside her chair and unbuttoned her coat. It was warm in here. "She's doing really good. Jim took her with him to see some family in Florida." She smiled. "They're at Disney Land right now. He's been sending me pictures every few hours or so."

"That's really great. I'm glad she's okay." He paused, not really sure if he should ask, but decided to anyway. "She ever talk about Samantha and Roger?"

The smile slowly faded from Sara's face. "All the time. She asks when Mommy and Daddy are coming back." She lowered her head. "I haven't had the heart to tell her anything. I mean, how do I explain to a two-year-old that her mommy and daddy are gone?"

Bolan's heart hurt for her. He wanted to put his mug down and wrap her in his arms and hug her and tell her not to worry, it's all gonna work out, but he couldn't move. He could only look at her and feel that deep, aching rage smoldering in the pit of his gut, like some living thing waiting to be freed from its prison.

"I can't imagine what you're going through, Sara. I'm sorry."

She wiped her eyes on a tissue she took from her purse. "It's okay." She seemed to get herself together in a quiet show of strength that reminded him why he'd fallen in love with her in the first place. She quickly wadded the tissue up and placed it back down inside her purse. "Anyway, Jim wanted to maybe take her mind off things and have some grandpa time." She stopped, her eyes fluttered open as she suddenly realized what she'd said. "I'm sorry. I didn't mean—"

Bolan waved it away. "Don't do that. We're good. Jim's been there since the beginning. I respect that."

"You're right. I'm sorry. It's just all so fucked up lately." She was fidgeting with the sleeve of her coat. Bolan could tell she wanted to say something else.

"What is it?" he asked.

She looked up. "What?"

He nodded towards her sleeve. "You do that when you want to tell me something but you don't know if you should."

She looked down at her hand and immediately stopped picking at the loose thread sticking out of the seam of her sleeve. "I still do that, huh?"

"You do. What is it you want to tell me?"

She took a deep breath, let it out. "You're going to think I'm a horrible person."

I doubt I'm the best judge of something like that. "No, I won't."

"You will."

"Sara, just tell me what it is."

She was quiet for a moment, thinking—maybe even trying to decide if she was going to change her mind. Bolan let her. Finally, she looked up at him and said something he never would've thought possible after all these years. "Would you like to have dinner with me tonight?"

He looked at her in stunned silence. She was watching him, gauging his reaction with a dawning expression of regret.

"Never mind," she said at last, and she gathered her purse and stood up. "I should never have come here. I have to go, I'm sorry."

He jumped up and caught her by the arm as she went for the door, turned her to face him. "I could eat," was all he could think to say in the moment.

She was searching his face now, and he could see something in her eyes he hadn't seen since before the night he was arrested all those years ago. It stirred something in him, too; something that a little voice in the back of his mind told him this was a bad idea.

"My house," she said quietly, "around six."

He nodded. "I'll be there."

She gave him a little secretive smile (though there was always a small shadow of sadness to it, lurking deeper within) and walked out of the barbershop into the freezing, drizzling rain.

What the hell are you doing? that little voice inside his mind demanded. *There are no happy endings. Not for you, anyway.*

Bolan ignored it, turned the deadbolt, and went back to sweeping.

2.

Across the street, Patrick Manga and another man named Lenny Brockhaus watched as Sara came back out of the barbershop, got into her red Buick, and pulled away, her bright red taillights making phosphorescent smears in the sifting rain as she passed through the traffic light and turned onto West Park Drive.

"You think he hit that?" Lenny asked with a big-toothed grin once Sara's car was out of sight. "I mean, she was only in there for like half an hour, but still . . ."

Patrick flashed him a distasteful frown. "Who gives a shit?"

Lenny, a small, greasy man with lanky black hair and a patchy scruff on his jaw that would never be considered a real beard for as long as he lived, laughed. "I was just bein stupid, man. Lighten up. So what's up with this O'Brien guy? You seem to have a real hard-on for him."

Patrick was watching the big plate window in front of the barbershop. He couldn't see Bolan inside from here; the rain made the glass look like molten silver in the glare of the streetlights.

"Granddad didn't trust him," he said after a long moment. "I don't either."

Lenny followed his gaze through the windshield. "What did he do?"

Patrick wasn't sure if he was comfortable going over this with a man like Lenny. He hadn't known him for very long, and there was no telling to whom his eyes and ears really belonged. After what happened to Lou, Patrick didn't feel it wise to readily trust anyone until he was sure about O'Brien.

Choosing his words carefully, Patrick said, "My dad, Phil, was killed not too long ago. You hear about that?"

Lenny nodded. "We all heard about that. Was he really a rat for the Feds?"

Patrick had never harbored much love for his pop, but he had his doubts about him being a rat. He said, "That's the rumor. He was shot to death in Detroit a few months back. Guess who was with him when he died?"

Lenny's brow wrinkled in thought. "Who?"

Patrick nodded through the windshield towards the barbershop. "O'Brien was the last man to see him alive."

Lenny was quiet, soaking it in.

"And when O'Brien and that Benny piece of shit went along to hit that truck after Christmas?" Patrick's grin was hard, devoid of humor. "They were the only two to walk away from it. Then, miraculously, the guns in the back of that truck ended up in my granddad's storage unit. A suspicious man might think something nefarious was goin on, don't you think?"

"Son of a bitch," Lenny said, shaking his head. "So what're you thinkin?"

Patrick took a long time to answer. Finally, he said, "I wanna follow him and see what he gets up to when he's not goin off on some mission for my uncle."

"Well, here's your chance," Lenny said. Patrick looked at him. Lenny pointed towards the barbershop across the street. They both fell quiet, watched as Bolan stepped out into the rain and locked the door, then jumped into the Jeep Cherokee Vincent had given him to replace his shot-to-hell Nova, and drove off in the same direction as Sara Lewis had in her red Buick.

"Dollars to donuts, he's meeting up with her," Patrick said, more to himself than Lenny.

But Lenny, galvanized with the prospect of actually *doing* something other than sitting in this car, sat up and drummed the dashboard with his fingers. "Let's go find out."

Patrick considered him a moment. "You strapped?"

Lenny looked insulted for a second. Then he pulled back his jacket to reveal the butt of a .38 Special jutting from his belt. "Always, brother. Never leave home without it." He uttered a little cackle that set Patrick's teeth on edge. "Don't lose 'im."

Out of the blue, Patrick's phone rang.

"Yeah?"

"What the fuck you doin?" Lenny asked, wide-eyed when he

saw Patrick answering the call. "O'Brien's gettin away!"

Patrick silenced him with a held-up finger. "Who's this?" He listened for a moment, then said, "You fuckin serious right now?" Lenny stared at him, unsure what to make of it all. Patrick nodded as the unknown person filled his ear with words Lenny couldn't make out, and then he said, under his breath, "That motherfucker. And you *know* this?"

The man said something. Sounded like he was asking a question. Lenny couldn't be sure.

"I'd rather not do this over the phone," Patrick said at last. A quick reply, and then Patrick asked, "And what's your name?" More words, and Patrick's eyes lit up. "Well, preacher-man, I wouldn't trust me, either. Especially if you're tryin to bullshit me. You dig?" Another short spiel from the man on the other line, and then Patrick said, "Where?"

To Lenny, who had leaned closer to Patrick's side of the car so he could better hear what was being said, the person sounded like the adults in a Charlie Brown cartoon—it was just a bunch of wonky gibberish. When Patrick finally thanked whoever it was and put his phone down, he just stared out of the windshield into the falling rain.

"Who was that?" Lenny asked after a heartbeat of silence.

Patrick put the car in gear and did a U-turn. "Someone who says they have information on what O'Brien and my uncle are up to."

Lenny gave a cartoon expression of surprise. "Are you fuckin serious?"

"As a heart attack."

Lenny chewed on this a second, said, "Did I hear you right? Did you call him *preacher-man?* That some kind of code name or somethin?"

Patrick shook his head. "No. He said is name was Jacob Murphy. That he's the pastor of some church in Cambridge."

"Murphy?"

Patrick nodded. "That's right. Coincidence? I don't fuckin think so."

"But what the fuck would some preacher know about O'Brien and your uncle? You don't find that a little weird?"

Lenny had never been the smartest guy on the block, but he made a good point as far as Patrick could see. It *did* seem a little strange that the call came at that exact moment, and that the man on the other end was a Murphy.

Claiming to be a preacher, no less.

It definitely didn't add up, and if there was one thing Patrick hated more than anything, it was that feeling of being lost; whether it was literally or figuratively, it didn't matter. He suddenly had this overwhelming feeling like he was being watched, and it gave him the creeps.

"Weird or not," he told Lenny, "I need to check it out. You're free to get out and walk if you're worried."

Lenny scowled. Questioning his manhood always got his hair up. It was a byproduct of him being molested by an older male cousin when he was a boy. The rape had gone on for years until Lenny, at the age of ten, shot his cousin in the groin with the man's own gun. He spent three years in juvenile detention, where he was bullied and beaten and formed into the brutish, low-IQ sack of shit he was today. His cousin, on the other hand, ended up dying with his throat slit in a prison riot in Wabash Valley. No big loss.

"I ain't worried," he insisted. "I'm with ya. So, what're we gonna do?"

"I'm gonna meet this Jacob Murphy, hear what he has to say. If what he tells me is legit, then . . ."

He left the rest to Lenny's imagination.

3.

Sara made spaghetti and garlic bread. They ate it at the kitchen table that night over a few beers while the rain pattered against the windows. It was full dark outside.

"How was it?" she asked after Bolan had finished and pushed his plate away.

"Pretty good. I never took you for a cook, back in the day."

She grinned. "I'm not. Spaghetti's really the only thing I'm good at, besides Mac and Cheese and hot dogs."

"Trust me," he said, taking a swig from his beer, "compared to prison food, that sounds like a gourmet meal."

She wrinkled her nose. "That bad, huh?"

"Worse. I wouldn't feed a starving animal the slop they gave us inside. But a man has to eat."

"I don't know how you made it in there, Bolan," she said, poking at what was left of her spaghetti with her fork. "I don't think I could do it."

He sat the beer down in front of him, wiped at the condensation with the pad of his thumb. "You'd be amazed at what you can do when you don't have a choice."

They both sat for a moment, listening to the sound of the rain running across the rooftop like the tiny hooves of thousands of wild horses. Sara dropped her fork onto her plate and cleared the table, running a sinkful of hot, soapy water. Bolan just sat there, watching her back as she filled the sink, thinking about all the time they could've had together if things had turned out differently.

Stop it, a voice inside of him scolded. *You can't dwell on what might've been. It'll drive you mad.*

But he couldn't help it. All those years, sitting in his cell alone or working out in the rec yard with only his thoughts for company, he had imagined what life might've been like if he had never gone to

Tommy's party that night. Back then he was interested in joining the military, specifically the Army. He'd gone and spoken with a recruiter, taken the necessary tests, and passed them all with high enough scores that his recruiter wanted to fast-track him into Ranger School when he was finished with basic training. Of course, none of that ever happened. As soon as he was arrested and charged with felony assault, his dreams of military life vanished with the suddenness of a popped bubble. No recruiter in the world could've gotten him in after that

"So Jim's in Florida," he said, changing the subject. He watched Sara sort of freeze up for a moment, and then continue wiping off the plate in her hands.

"Something you want to ask me?" she said without turning around.

"Why did you invite me over?"

She put the plate down and turned around. "What?"

Bolan shrugged. "I'm just curious."

She was mopping her hands with a towel she pulled from the handle of the oven. "You've been on my mind lately, I guess." She seemed to lose interest in the towel, dropped it on the counter. "The house has been quiet and I've been doing a lot of thinking about the old days."

"That's never a good idea," he said, smiling.

Her return smile was weak, forced. "I know. But I can't help it. I've been calling that detective working Sam's case every single week, too. Palmer, I think his name is. He tells me the same thing every time, but he never has any answers." She started to tear up, and Bolan's heart went out to her. He wanted to get up and pull her close, but he couldn't move. It was like his feet were planted in cement. "How does someone invade another person's home, kill them, and no one seems to know anything?" Her composure broke then, and her face seemed to melt beneath the weight of her emotions.

Now he did get up. He approached her the way a cowboy might approach a skittish colt—arms out and open, and slowly. But to his surprise, she didn't push him away or wave him off. She walked right into his arms and laid her cheek against his chest.

"I don't know," he said, in answer to her question. "Prison's full of those who get caught, but they never tell you about the ones who don't."

She was crying now. He could feel the heat of her tears through his shirt. Her entire body was quivering, and all he could do was stand there and soak it in.

"I hate those sons of bitches, whoever they are." Her voice was muffled against him. "I want them to suffer for what they've done."

"So do I." He thought about it for a moment, wrestling with himself; and then he said, knowing it was probably a mistake, "What if I told you I could make that happen?"

She slowly pulled away from him, looked up into his face with tear-ringed eyes. "What the hell are you talking about?"

You really want to do this? that little voice inside of him wanted to know. *This bell can't be unrung.*

"Sit down," he told her, gently guiding her towards the table. The look of sudden, curious worry that passed over her face like a cloud almost changed his mind.

"What's wrong, Bolan? You're freaking me out."

"Just sit down. I need to tell you something."

She sat down, her eyes wide and wary. "Okay, I'm sitting. What did you mean by that, when you said you could make it happen?"

He took a chair, planted it in front of her, sat down so he was looking her in the eye. Then he told her everything.

4.

"Son of bitch," she said when he'd finished. "Please tell me you're fucking with me."

Bolan shook his head grimly. "Not fucking with you."

Sara was speechless. Her eyes, red-rimmed and glazed with tears, were searching his face for any sign that this might all be just one big joke. She saw nothing with which to give her hope, however. "How did you figure all of this out when the cops don't even know?"

"You gave me the first clue," Bolan said. He took the business card from his wallet and laid it on the table between them. Sara stared at it like it might jump up and bite her.

"The pastor's card I gave you?"

"Yep."

She slowly picked it up, turned it over in her fingers as if seeing it for the first time. "I still don't understand what some preacher has to do with it."

"Roger was raised in a religious home," Bolan explained. "He looked at his pastor the way most Catholics look at their priest, as a man he could confide in. He told Pastor Jake everything. Pastor Jake then told me."

The grim finality of his words jarred her for a moment. "You didn't . . . *do* anything to the preacher, did you?"

"No. I threatened to, but I think he wanted the truth to come out as much as anyone else. He seemed to genuinely care about Samantha and Roger."

Sara put the card down and fell into deep thought, her hand lightly covering her mouth. At last she looked up at him. "So that night you asked me about the church they went to—you were planning this out, even then."

"Yes."

She just shook her head. "My God."

After a long moment of quiet contemplation she looked at him, and something in her eyes made him want to smile at her, though he kept his face as immovable as stone. She had a dangerous look to her all of a sudden, the way a cat crouches and lays back its ears when it sees a mouse skittering through the grass. She said, "If you're really going to do this, you kill them all."

He grinned. He couldn't help it. "That's exactly what Rick told me."

"He's right. You have to kill them all. These cops don't know their asses from a hole in the ground, and even if they caught the guys responsible, they'd probably walk on a technicality anyway."

Bolan didn't doubt that one bit, and said so. "It wouldn't surprise me."

Sara leaned forward and stabbed the table with the tip of her right forefinger, hard. "Every time I call, they tell me they don't have any hard evidence to even *name* a suspect." She shook her head in disgust and disbelief.

"All that matters is that *we* know who's responsible," he said. "And I'm not waiting for the police to get their shit together."

She got up from the table and went to the refrigerator. Her hand was reaching for the handle when she stopped and turned back to look at him. "Why did you tell me all of this?" she asked. "What if I'd decided to turn you in to your parole officer, or call the cops? Why tell me at all?"

His answer—the most honest thing he'd ever said in his life, he would come to realize later—surprised him at how easily it fell out of his mouth.

"Because I love you."

Those brushstrokes of color swept up her cheeks. Her eyes fluttered a bit as her brain computed this sudden, surprising dump of information. "Bolan, I . . ." She turned back towards the fridge and stared at the smiley-face magnets pinning several pieces of paper that used to seem important to her to its stainless steel skin. After composing herself, she turned around and recoiled a little when she saw him standing in front of her, his fierce blue eyes like two open wounds in his hard, bearded face. She hadn't heard him get up or walk around the table. For a man his size, he could move as silent as a ghost, it seemed.

"I've *always* loved you," he told her, his voice low and tremulous. He reached out, gently ran the back of his hand down the left side of her face; and before he could pull away, she stepped in and planted a long, slow, invasive kiss on his mouth.

When the kiss was over they just stood there, looking at one another—*into* one another—and Bolan broke the spell by saying, "What do we do now?"

She didn't answer. She slipped her hand into his and quietly led him through the kitchen, across the dining room, and then up the stairs.

5.

"Jim didn't just go down to Florida to visit some relatives," she informed him after their lovemaking.

She was sitting up in bed with her back against the headboard, naked as the day she was born, her long, lithely legs crossed on the mattress in front of her. Her blond hair spilled over her shoulders and the swells of her breasts, long enough to pool on the sheet beside her.

Bolan was lying next to her, head on the pillow, covered up to his nipples with a sheet. In spite of the chill outside, it was warm up here in her bedroom.

"You don't have to tell me anything you don't want to," he assured her.

"I *do* want to," she insisted. "Jim and I have been over with for a long time now."

Bolan grinned. "You tell *him* that?"

She gave him a playful elbow to the shoulder. "Ha, ha. Of course I have. It was his idea, actually." She looked down at her hands that were folded on top of her belly, which was still hard and flat despite the fact she was nearing forty. *She's really taken care of herself all these years,* he thought with some admiration.

"What's the matter, then?" he asked, propping himself up on one elbow.

She sighed. "Don't get me wrong. Jim is a great guy. But he hasn't been taking Sam's and Roger's deaths very well at all. He spends a lot of time with Abby, but sometimes I feel like he just wants to get out so that he doesn't have to deal with it anymore." She flashed him an imploring look. "Sam was his whole world, Bolan. I can't have any more kids. Did you know that?" Her smile was weak and bitter. "I had a tubal done when Sam was born, so that I couldn't conceive again. Jim knew this when we met, but I think it still bothers him. I sometimes think he feels like he's wasted his life with me."

Bolan reached up and gave her arm a stroke with the backside of his hand. Her skin, glazed in drying sweat and golden-hued in the light of the bedside lamp, was soft and supple. "I doubt he feels like it was a waste," he said.

She shrugged. "I don't know. He's never said that, but I think it's true."

"So, is he leaving, then?"

She nodded. "Yeah. He's looking at a house down there right now. It's close to his mother. She's like eighty-something."

"What happens to Abby?"

"She'll stay with me, of course."

"I mean, what happens when Jim is no longer around?"

Sara thought it over for a second. "She'll just have to

understand, eventually. I don't know what else to do."

This poor little girl, Bolan thought, but didn't say. *Has to grow up with her mommy and daddy ripped away from her, and now Jim —the only grandpa she's ever known.* Bolan hadn't liked Jim the moment they'd met, but he did seem to love Abby like she was his own flesh and blood. Regardless of what he might think of the man, it wasn't fair that Abby had to lose out on someone else who loved her because of a series of events she had nothing to do with and no control over. The more he thought about it, the angrier it made him. *Just one more thing Vincent will have to answer for.*

"If there's anything I can do, I will," he told her.

She smiled, reached out and tweaked his beard with the tips of her fingers. "I appreciate it. But I don't think there's anything anyone can do in this situation." She got up and went to the bathroom door connected to her bedroom, flipped on the light. Seeing her standing there, naked and limned against that soft golden glow made him want her again. "I'm taking a shower," she said, and then shut the door behind her.

CHAPTER TWENTY-ONE

1.

Pastor Jake was sitting in his office when his secretary knocked lightly on the door. He looked up. "What can I do for you, Joni?"

"Pastor, you have someone wanting to speak with you," Joni said with a nervous little smile. Whoever was with her was out of sight, just to the right of the door.

Jacob didn't need to be told who it was that was waiting in the foyer. He'd called the man himself, after all. "Let him in, Joni. And good work today. Go on home."

Joni smiled, nodded. "Thank you, Pastor. See you in the morning."

"God bless."

Joni left, and then the man in the foyer stepped through the doorway. He was skinny with a shock of bright red hair and cruel green eyes. He was wearing a pair of designer jeans, a white button-down shirt, and a black leather jacket that fell to mid-thigh. When he saw Jacob sitting there behind his desk with his scattered pile of open books, his grin was curious.

"Hope I'm not interrupting anything," Patrick Manga said.

Pastor Jake shook his head. He didn't stand. "Not at all." He gestured to one of the chairs in front of his desk. "Please, have a seat."

Patrick sat down. He rested his right foot on the ball of his left knee and adjusted his jacket to a more comfortable position. Pastor Jake saw the gun hidden in there, hanging in a leather shoulder holster, but it didn't rattle him a bit. Before he went to Bible collage to become a minister of the Lord, he'd been raised around criminals his whole life. He'd even seen his father, Horace Murphy, beat a man to death with a baseball bat when he was in kindergarten. Afterward, Horace and his brother, Robert, silently wrapped the man in plastic and dumped him into the trunk of a car that Jake never saw again. That early exposure to violence, combined with his faith, made it so Pastor Jake was rarely rattled by the men of this world, no matter how big and scary they might be.

Except for Sam's father, Bolan, he thought. *That man scares the hell out of me.*

"You said on the phone you have information about O'Brien and my uncle," Patrick said, as if the pastor's thoughts had been flashing in bright neon across his broad forehead. "Let's hear it."

Pastor Jake cleared his throat, folded his small, thick hands in front of him on the desk. "Since last May, I have been working closely with Mr. O'Brien. He has recently been released from prison after a twenty-year sentence, you know."

Patrick nodded, but said nothing. This wasn't news to him.

"Since that time, I've gotten to know him pretty well," the reverend went on, "and ever since some time after New Years, I started to notice some oddities in his behavior."

"What does that mean?"

"He's been withdrawn, moodier than usual, and sometimes I get the feeling he's expecting someone to come after him, like he's paranoid or something. I asked him several times about it, but each time I did, he just shook his head and said it was nothing."

"I don't give a rat's ass about his psych profile. Get to the point."

Pastor Jake held up his finger in a *hold on* gesture. "One morning he was here, in the sanctuary, sitting in the first row of pews and staring up at the stained glass window above the platform. I happened to be in the office and heard someone, so I came out to see who it was. When I saw him sitting there, hands in his lap, just staring off into space, I again asked him what was bothering him. That's when he told me."

Patrick sat forward in his chair. "Told you what?"

Pastor Jake was accustomed to working crowds of dozens, even hundreds of people any given Sunday. He was working Patrick the very same way now, without the younger man even realizing it. "He was distressed," he went on. "Told me he'd done something that might either get him killed, or sent back to prison. I assured him that whatever it was, God would forgive him if he simply confessed and made an effort to turn things around." The pastor leaned back in his chair, eyeing Patrick with a cold solemnity that made the little hairs on the back of Patrick's neck stiffen. "I wasn't prepared for what he would say next, let me tell you."

"And what was it?"

Like a dog licking his chops for a juicy bone, Jake thought to himself.

"He told me he was the one who attacked your truck and killed your men." The statement hung in the air for a moment, gathering weight before it dropped. When Pastor Jake was sure the hook was thoroughly embedded in Patrick's mouth, he said, "He also confessed to stealing some guns and planting them in your grandpa's storage unit."

Patrick's reaction wasn't exactly what Pastor Jake had expected. He just sat there, looking at him across the desk, as if the statement flew right over his head. Finally, he said, "Why would he do that? Tell *you*, of all people?"

Jake shrugged. "To unburden his soul, I suppose. Many people tell their pastors things they would never tell another living soul. It's about trust."

Patrick's eyes narrowed. "Then why are you telling *me?*"

Pastor Jake let his breath out in a long, dramatic sigh. "After confiding in me, Mr. O'Brien went on to threaten my life, said he would kill me, too, if I ever spoke to anyone about it. He also, in no small terms, made it clear he would harm my parishioners if I didn't keep my silence. The man is unhinged and dangerous. Threatening me is one thing, but when he threatened the well-being of my flock . . ." He shook his head gravely. "I can't abide that, Mr. Manga. I don't want to see anyone else get hurt."

Patrick flashed him a razor grin. "You do realize what I will do to him, right?"

Pastor Jake nodded. "I do, yes."

"So much for no one getting hurt." Patrick chuckled.

Pastor Jake bristled at that. "I do not make this decision lightly, sir. I can't have this man threatening violence against innocent people."

Patrick was quiet. After some thought, he said, "So why not go to the cops?" He was watching the preacher's every move. Something felt off about all of this, he just couldn't figure out what it was.

The pastor shook his head severally. "He made it very clear where he stood on that. I couldn't risk it."

"So you come to me, hoping I'll take your trash out for you. Is that it?"

Pastor Jake leaned forward, his eyes hard and pleading. "We have *children* who come here, Mr. Manga. And besides, he's *your* trash, too."

Patrick thought this over and realized the preacher was right.

O'Brien was definitely dangerous. Anyone who could take down Lou Manga was no one to underestimate. Patrick had never seen a tougher, smarter man than his granddad. Patrick himself had done some time over the years, too—drinking and driving, a few misdemeanor battery charges—and he'd seen what prison could do to some people. In many cases, they came out of the penitentiary more animal than man.

"How do I know you're telling me the truth?" Patrick said. "You're a Murphy. That got anything to do with this?" The Murphys certainly had their own axe to grind with whoever hit that truck. It occurred to Patrick that this could be a clever plan on their part to worm their way inside and play his family against each other. *It's something they would do, too,* he thought.

To his question, Pastor Jake seemed a little taken aback. "I assure you, sir, that my family has nothing to do with what I'm saying today. I have no connection with them or the things they do, and I haven't been in contact with any of them in years. I am a man of faith, and the Gospel is the only business I'm about. I left that life of sin and death behind me the moment I went to college"

Patrick was silent for a long time. Finally, he said, "So O'Brien just up and told you he killed our men and stole our guns. And then planted those guns in my granddad's storage unit." He paused, gauging the pastor's reaction, then added, "Did he tell you why he did it?"

Pastor Jake hesitated. "He did."

"I'm all ears, preacher."

Pastor Jake licked his lips. *Here goes nothing.* "He said he did it on your uncle's orders."

Patrick looked as if someone had just walked up and punched him high in the belly. His face went white as a sheet. *"Vincent?"* he managed, almost choking on the word. "My uncle—*Vince*—gave him the order? He said that?"

The pastor nodded gravely. "He did."

"Did he say why Vince would do this?" Patrick was as helpless as a fly struggling in a spider's web now. The pastor knew he had him at this point.

"He said that Vincent was paying him to eliminate a growing threat inside his organization. According to Mr. O'Brien, Lou was growing too powerful and had too much influence with Vincent's officers. He explained that Vincent needed to find a way to take Lou out so that everyone would see it as a legitimate move."

All the blood seemed to have run out of Patrick's face. He stood up from the chair abruptly, knocking it over with a bang. The look on his face made Pastor Jake rise up and hold out his hand in concern. "Are you alright?" he asked.

Patrick waved him off. "I'm fine. I have to go." He took a moment to get himself together, then looked at Jake across the desk. "You've answered a lot of questions I've been having lately, preacher."

Pastor Jake fidgeted. "I hate that it has come to something like this. I'm a man of God, you understand. But I cannot abide someone threatening my church."

Patrick looked at him with mild contempt. "In the end, we're all sinners, preacher. Even you."

Pastor Jake let that one pass. "What will you do? I can't have Mr. O'Brien coming back here and doing something crazy."

The grin that spread across the lower half of Patrick's face was awful to behold. "Oh, don't worry about *him*, preacher-man. He won't be bothering you, or anyone else, anymore." *And neither will my uncle,* he thought, but kept to himself.

Jake put a hand over his heart, let out a deep sigh of relief. "Oh, thank goodness for that."

"One thing before I go, preacher."

"Yes?"

"You don't say a word to anyone about what you just told me. You hear?"

Pastor Jake nodded. "I understand. I truly do."

Patrick studied him a moment, and when he was satisfied, he turned and left the pastor's office.

2.

Patrick got to his car and took out his phone. His hands were shaking, but not from fear.

"Lenny. It's me. Hey, I need you to get the boys together."

"What's goin on?"

Patrick glanced back towards the church. It was full dark now. He could see the pastor looking at him through the blinds. The light from the desk lamp gave the window a soft golden glow. "You remember that shit about my uncle we've been talkin about?"

"Sure, man."

"Well, I was fuckin right, Lenny. He killed my granddad, set his ass up."

"Shit. What'd the preacher say?"

"Just what I told you. Vince used Bolan and that rat-fuck Benny to hit that truck, then planted the guns on Granddad so he had a legit reason to take him out."

"No fuckin way," Lenny breathed.

"I need you to get the boys together for me," Patrick said. His adrenaline was humming now. He could taste the blood in the water and it was giving him a hard-on. "When I get there, we're havin a meeting."

"What about this depot thing?" Lenny asked. "Everyone's hyped for that shit."

"Trust me, Len. Once we deal with my uncle, we're gonna wipe the fuckin Murphys off the face of the earth."

"Whatever you wanna do, Pat, me an the boys are with ya. You know that."

"I do. And with what I just heard, I'll be knocking my fat-ass uncle off his throne once and for all."

"No shit?" Lenny's voice was full of wonder.

"No shit, man. Hurry the hell up and make those calls. Tell everyone to get *strapped*. I'm on my way."

"You got it, Pat."

Patrick hung up, tossed his phone into the passenger's seat. He took one last look towards the church, and then started his car and pulled out onto the highway.

3.

When Patrick's taillights disappeared over the hill and he was sure the man wasn't coming back, Pastor Jake dialed a number in his phone and waited for someone to pick up on the other end, which they did in only two rings.

"Yeah?"

"It's done," Jake said.

"You sure?"

"I am."

"He buy everything you said?"

A smile slithered across the pastor's round, sweat-slicked face. "He did. I wasn't sure he would, at first, but as soon as I mentioned that it was Vincent who gave O'Brien the order, he was hooked."

A dry cackle on the other end. "Hooked right through the sack! Patrick's always been stupid. This was almost too easy."

"And you're sure none of this will come back on me?" Pastor Jake wanted to know.

"Of course not, Little Brother. I made sure of everything. Don't worry."

Jake breathed a little easier. "Thank goodness for that." He paused. "Are you sure I did the right thing?"

"I wouldn't have you do it if it wasn't the right thing. Don't I always take care of you?"

Jake had to agree. He always had. "Yes. I'm sorry. I'm just nervous."

"Don't be. The blood's not on your hands, Little Brother. It's *O'Brien* who got his hands dirty first. We're just making things right."

"Okay."

"I'll call you later."

"Sure. I'll be here."

The other end hung up. Pastor Jake snapped his phone off and sat it face-down on his desk. He decided to go into the sanctuary and pray.

CHAPTER TWENTY-TWO

1.

A few days later, Bolan got a call from Benny about the depot job. It was on.

"What's the matter with you?" he asked. "You sound nervous."

"Fuckin right, I'm nervous!" Benny was breathing heavily and Bolan could hear him messing around inside his car, like he was looking for something. "There it is! Fuckin *knew* it was in here."

Bolan frowned. "What're you talking about?"

"Huh? Oh, yeah." He chuckled. "I'm outta smokes and usually leave a single in my glove compartment for emergencies." Bolan heard the snap of a lighter. "That's the stuff."

"Would you knock that shit off?" Bolan snarled. "What're we doing?"

"This shit's getting crazy," Benny said, ignoring his question. "You hear what they did to Larry Krieger?"

"I don't know who that is."

"They chopped the man up with a fuckin *machete,*" Benny gasped. "They chopped him up into so many pieces they put what was left of him in a beer cooler!" He uttered a little laugh that sounded absolutely mad. "I didn't even know a human body could *fit* in a freakin cooler."

Bolan closed his eyes, trying to be patient. "Benny?"

A quick intake of breath, then a long exhale of smoke. "Yeah?"

"What are we doing?"

Benny seemed to calm down for a moment. He sniffed loudly. "We're 'sposed to meet with Patrick and some of Vincent's officers this afternoon."

"Where?"

"At the Express Continental offices. They want to do a briefing or some shit, and then hit the depot tonight."

"Why are you coming along?" Bolan asked. "You're just a bookie."

"That's the same thing I asked Patrick when he called me this morning," Benny said. "I have no fuckin clue. This shit's got me worried, man. Like, something about all of this ain't sittin right with me, ya know?"

Bolan could relate. He remembered there were times in prison when he would walk into the chow hall and five hundred inmates, who were normally screaming and hollering and yapping back and forth, were deathly quiet. You could hear a mouse fart. It was *those* times you had to watch out for, because it meant that bad shit was about to happen—the calm before the storm. This felt exactly like that, only worse.

"What have you heard?"

"Patrick's been makin some moves, and he's not been quiet about it. He's got a lot of pull with the younger cats in the organization. They're all wanting to move up and make more money, and they're bloodthirsty sons of bitches. Word is, Patrick's been having meetings with them and everyone thinks he's about to make his move on Vincent. It's no secret it was Vincent who had his daddy killed for bein a rat, and most of those on Patrick's side suspect he had the old man killed, too—*which he fuckin did.* Like it or not, that puts us right in the fuckin middle of all this shit, O'Brien. You dig that? We're stuck between the hammer and the anvil, and I don't fuckin like it one bit."

Bolan didn't either. But he didn't see any other way to go forward, except to let things play themselves out. Patrick's power grab wasn't his concern. All he cared about was seeing Vincent dead, and if Patrick could make that happen, then it made his job that much easier.

"Benny, you need to take a breath," Bolan said. "Take a minute and calm down."

Benny exhaled into the phone. "Fuck that. I'm out."

Bolan paused. "Out?"

"You heard me. This ain't worth it. I'm not a professional gun thug, O'Brien. I'm just a money man."

"Who hides dead whores in freezers and breaks legs when his customers can't pay," Bolan dryly pointed out.

"Whatever, man. I told you, this is done."

Bolan switched his phone from one ear to the other. He could feel his face getting hot. He was getting pissed off. "*I* tell you when it's done, you sack of shit! We made a deal, and you're going to stick to it! You got that?"

"No, *you* made the deal," Benny shot back. "You threatened to kill me, and then forced me into this pile of steaming shit you created for yourself because you needed some payback to make you feel better. I had nothin to do with your daughter getting killed, O'Brien. I've done my part."

Bolan's lips peeled back from his teeth in an animal-like snarl. "And the two shooters? How do I find them?"

"I gave you their names. Jack Langston. Henry Cooper. Duluth. Fuckin Google it. I'm out, O'Brien. And if you're half as smart as I think you are, you'd be out, too. Have a good fuckin life."

The line went dead.

Bolan just stood there at his window, watching the snow drift down over the street out in front of his apartment, holding his cell phone in a white-knuckled grip. He took a deep breath, dialed Benny again, only to find the call going straight to an automated message system. After three attempts, he almost threw his phone against the wall.

I guess I'm on my own.

And then he thought of Rick. He dialed his number, praying he would answer. Rick had been sleeping a lot more since his release from the hospital. He hated calling him up to ask another favor, but he didn't see he had any other choice.

"Yeah?" Rick said after half a dozen rings.

Relief poured over Bolan like a bucket of steaming water. "I have a problem."

"Lay it on me."

Bolan laid it on him.

2.

It was a sunny afternoon, but brutally cold. The recent snowfall made most of the back roads impassable, but the plows had been busy as bees in a hive on the highways, for which Bolan was grateful.

He pulled into the gravel lot of Express Continental Trucking and wasn't at all surprised by the utter lack of activity he saw when he killed the Jeep's engine, considering what Vincent's men were planning to do here. The trucks parked along the sides of the docks were dark and cold, and the designated employee parking area was empty. Along the front of the office, however, he saw Patrick's black

Audi and several other cars caked in snow and ice and road salt, but there was no sign of their drivers.

Everyone's inside, he thought. He remembered the panic he'd heard in Benny's voice and reached over into the glove box and took out the .357 Magnum Phil Manga had given him what seemed like a lifetime ago now. When dealing with snakes, you just never knew.

He tried Benny's number one more time. Nothing. Just an automated voice telling him the number he was trying to call was no longer in service, to please hang up and try his call again. He nearly crushed his phone in his fist. After a moment or two, he texted Rick.

I'm here. I don't call you in twenty minutes, be ready.

He waited for a full two minutes before his phone jingled.

10-4, was the reply.

He put his phone away, holstered the .357 in the small of his back, and then crossed the wind-swept lot, squinting against the glare of the sun reflecting off the freshly fallen snow. He tried the front doors leading into the main offices. They were locked. The woman who usually sat behind the desk answering phones and manning the radio chatter for the truckers was gone. The lights were off and everything was dim and dark. Frowning, he moved along the side of the building, his unease deepening. By now, he'd expected to be greeted by someone, but there wasn't a soul to be seen as he approached the side door leading into the loading area. He tried this door, thinking it would be locked, too, and grunted with surprise when it opened freely. Peering into the dimly-lit hallway that greeted him, he stepped inside and made it about twenty-five paces when something hit him hard in the back of the head, causing his legs to give out from under him. Before he could put his hands out to stop himself, the concrete floor jumped up and clubbed him in the face, addling his brain.

"What the hell," he managed to groan, and then he was aware of people standing over him, grabbing him by the arms and legs, manhandling him through the rest of the hallway and dumping him like a deer carcass onto the floor inside the loading bay. He propped himself up on one arm, shaking his head like some big dog shaking off sleep, and he could see he was surrounded by about a dozen men with guns looking down on him like sharks at feeding time.

"Put him in the chair," Patrick told the two men behind him, whom Bolan couldn't see. "Strap his ass down tight."

At the command, Bolan was hauled to his feet and dragged to a wooden chair set in the center of the floor. Without a word, his captors, both of whom were built like prison guards with blocky faces and huge slabs for arms, adjusted the zip ties so that his wrists were fixed behind his back and his ankles secured to the front legs of the chair, and then they stepped back to await further instruction.

"What the fuck is this?" Bolan demanded as Patrick and his crew quickly encircled him like lions closing in on a wounded gazelle. He'd never seen any of these men before, and by the way they were looking at him and deferring to Patrick, he thought about what Benny had told him and instantly knew these were Patrick's guys, and that they would gladly take him apart piece by piece, if he told them to do it.

"This is what you call a day of reckoning," Patrick said. "It's that moment in life when all your bullshit comes back and splatters you in the face."

Bolan spat onto the concrete floor. His head hurt; he could feel warm tendrils of blood running down the back of his bull neck. *They must've laid my scalp open good,* he thought blearily. He felt slightly dizzy, and wondered if he might not have a concussion.

"Go fuck yourself," he told Patrick.

"No, it's *you* who's fucked himself, O'Brien." That shark-like grin widened.

A few minutes later, the loading dock door opened with a rattle, letting in a blast of cold, January air. Bolan turned, feeling like he wanted to throw up, and saw Vincent stroll into the warehouse flanked by an entourage of men armed with rifles. He was wearing a large, fur-trimmed overcoat that probably cost more than what Rick paid in a year to keep his barbershop open. Bolan counted eight men with him, none of whom he recognized except for the short, round fat guy whose name he couldn't remember. *He wears a pinky ring,* Bolan thought crazily. *That's how I remember him. He was at the meeting following Lou's wake.* Then it came back to him. The man's name was Wallace. He was one of Vincent's officers, a loyal old dog.

"Patrick, what the fuck is this?" Vincent asked as he approached and walked around the front of Bolan's chair to get a good look at his face. Behind him, his men spread out in a line across the loading bay, clutching their guns and looking across the room at Patrick's men with hard, mean eyes. The divide between the two groups could not have been wider.

"This piece of shit is the reason Granddad was killed," Patrick said. His men formed up into a firing squad behind him, waiting for their orders.

Benny was right, Bolan thought foggily. *This is about to blow up big-time.*

Vincent looked at Bolan, who saw the spark of worry deep in his eyes, then back at his nephew. "Yeah? What makes you think that?"

"I found out that it was O'Brien and Benny who hit that truck," Patrick said. He had all the confidence of truth behind him, and yet Bolan had no idea how he could've figured it out.

Unless Benny told him, he thought grimly. This was a possibility, and if he was being honest with himself, he should've been smart enough to have expected this. *Why else did he bail at the last second?* But then again, Benny telling Patrick such a thing would put a target on Benny's back, too. A man like Patrick would hunt him to the ends of the earth. None of this made any sense.

Vincent laughed at the accusation. "You think O'Brien and some lowlife bookie took out eight men—four of which were war veterans —all by themselves? They would have to be Rambo *and* the fuckin Terminator to pull that off!" A ripple of laughter from Vincent's men. Patrick's men didn't laugh at all. Their dead, mackerel eyes were watching Patrick with eager fingers resting on the triggers of their guns, waiting for whatever might come next.

"I *know* he did, Uncle," Patrick said defiantly.

Vincent shot a glance at Bolan. Bolan saw the sudden uncertainty in his eyes, but Vincent wasn't ready to buy into it just yet. "Just sayin it doesn't make it so, Nephew. How do you know this?"

"I talked to his preacher," Patrick said proudly.

"Who?" Vincent asked, dubious.

Patrick regarded Bolan with a contemptuous look. "Seems O'Brien here found religion inside the penitentiary. His pastor told me he got some kind of *crisis of conscience* and admitted to killing our guys and stealing the guns, *and* planting those guns in Granddad's storage unit."

My pastor? What the hell is he talking about? And then it hit Bolan in the face like a baseball bat.

Pastor Jacob Murphy.

Why hadn't he seen it before?

Because you don't normally associate ministers with gangsters.

But why would he do such a thing? And how the hell could he have known about the truck and the stolen guns?

That's the million dollar question, isn't it?

"Who's this preacher you're talkin about?" Vincent demanded.

"Jake Murphy," Bolan answered for him.

Vincent turned and looked at him. "Excuse me?"

"Jacob Murphy," Bolan repeated. "He runs a church outside of Cambridge. Looks like he's been filling your nephew's head full of poison."

Vincent turned on Patrick and laughed. "You tellin me you believe a fuckin *Murphy?* Over your own blood? Nephew, your granddad would be rollin in his grave."

Patrick's expression was ferocious. "Don't you fuckin talk about my granddad."

Vincent spread his arms wide like some great oak tree robed in flesh. "Alright, then. How about your rat-fuckin-pop? Like father, like son."

Patrick's hands curled into fists. "Say what you want about my father. He never cared two shits about me. But I ain't like him."

Vincent's grin was cruel. "How long before you turn Judas, too?" He was playing the crowd on both sides, raising his voice for maximum effect. "Or have you already? How many other Murphys you friends with, Nephew?" Men on both sides of the bay exchanged uneasy looks.

Bolan saw it.

Vincent saw it, too.

More importantly, *Patrick* saw it. "Fuck you!" he screamed. He was shaking now. "O'Brien and Benny hit that truck as sure as I'm standing in front of you, Uncle. I don't see *him* anywhere. Do you?" He held his arms out, slowly spun in place. It seemed both Mangas had a flare for the dramatic.

Vincent's eyes darted around the room. He didn't say a word.

Patrick took out his phone, held it up. "Benny's phone is dead. Nobody knows where the fuck he is. Why do you think that is?"

No answer. Vincent just stood there, legs braced apart like tree trunks as he regarded his nephew with a cool expression. Bolan saw his massive fists dangling at his sides, slowly curling and uncurling.

"Wanna know what else this preacher-man told me, Uncle?" A weasel grin spread across Patrick's face.

"If you got somethin to say, Nephew, spit it the fuck out."

"O'Brien told this preacher that it was *you*, Vince, who ordered him to hit that truck and then plant those guns on Granddad." He laughed nastily. "Ain't that some shit?"

An eager shuffling from Patrick's men behind him. Bolan could hear the dull clicks of itchy trigger fingers in the silence that followed.

Vincent pointed at him with one long, blunted finger. "You're way off base here, Nephew. Best you stop now, before you go so far you can't come back."

"Why did you kill my granddad?"

"I didn't kill Lou," Vincent said.

"Yes you did," Bolan said suddenly. It was as if a cannon had gone off inside the loading dock. Every eye widened and every head snapped in his direction.

Vincent turned upon him with the full weight of his indomitable will. There was a strange look of wonder and disbelief mingled with murder in his eyes. "You shut the fuck up," he breathed slowly.

Everyone's attention was on Bolan now. He had no idea what he was doing, just that he knew he had to do *something*. His head was spinning, and not just from the possible concussion. Something wasn't right with all of this, and there was no time to figure it out now. He knew that if he wanted to live, he would have to mix the lies with enough truth and get these two to focus on one another long enough to buy him some time.

Rick, I hope to God you're on your way.

"It's true," Bolan went on, hoping he wasn't about to bury himself, "Vincent killed Lou. Shot him in the face in that old barn.

He wanted me to kill you, too, Patrick. He said so, at your granddad's wake. He told me to make sure you didn't come back from the depot job."

Patrick looked at Vincent. The tension became a living thing between them.

"I fuckin *knew* it," Patrick muttered.

"You know shit," Vincent said. "I don't know what the fuck is goin on here, but somebody is feeding you some bad information, Nephew."

"So you didn't kill my granddad?"

"Lou was ambushed by those shit-eating Murphys," Vincent said, doubling down on the lie. "And now they got inside yer head, kid. You're not thinkin straight. They got you all twisted up. You can't trust a Murphy, never could. It's why my grandfather stopped dealing with them in the first place. Jack Murphy betrayed my grandfather, and then killed the woman he loved when she refused to leave him. There's been bad blood ever since. You understand?"

Clearly Patrick didn't. He looked at Bolan. "You fuckin tell me the truth. Did my uncle tell you to kill me and my granddad?"

"This is boring the shit outta me." Vincent stepped in between Patrick and Bolan. "Let's just kill this asshole and be done with it." He pointed at Wallace and snapped his fingers. "Gimme your gun."

Wallace, looking confused, nevertheless obliged and handed

Vincent a 9mm. Vincent took it, made sure there was a round in the chamber, and then leveled the gun squarely in the center of Bolan's face.

"Patrick, you don't want him to do this," Bolan said without taking his eyes off Vincent. "There's a hell of a lot more to this story than what you know." He was taking a gamble, he knew that, but he had to do something. His eyes shifted to Patrick. "You're going to want to hear it all."

Vincent shook his head. "Nah. Nobody wants to hear anything else you have to say, you piece of shit."

"I do," Patrick said, stepping around behind Bolan's chair. His eyes were leveled on his uncle now. He pulled the .357 that was taken off Bolan when he was knocked to the floor and cocked it loudly, pressing the barrel hard against the side of Bolan's thick, muscular neck. He then leaned down, breathing hotly into Bolan's right ear. "You fuckin say it, or I take your head off right now."

Vincent looked at his nephew with murderous intent. Bolan knew that if Vincent had his way, Patrick wouldn't be walking out this warehouse alive.

"*I'm* the one who gives the fuckin orders around here," Vincent fumed. "And *I* say he's talked enough. Now get the fuck back and let me do what I should've done a long time ago."

Bolan felt the pressure of the gun barrel leave his neck as Patrick raised the gun and pointed it at Vincent's chest. "I want to hear what the man has to say. After that, you can do to him whatever you want."

Vincent uttered a cynical little laugh. "So now I need your fuckin permission to smoke someone? Go fuck yourself, kid. I've been doin this sorta shit since before your mama was spreading her legs for dope and dollar bills."

Patrick's eyes narrowed dangerously. "Watch your fuckin mouth, Uncle. Don't be bringing my mother into this." He gave the back of Bolan's head a hard shove, sending a spike of hot agony through his brain that momentarily blurred his vision. "Go on, O'Brien. Tell me what's on your mind."

Vincent sighed heavily. He looked at Wallace and the others and gave them a big, animated shrug before turning his attention back to Patrick. "Have it your way, you little fuck." And then, without warning, he raised his gun and put a single bullet through Patrick's forehead.

The shot was stunningly loud in that wide, spacious area, making everyone who heard it jump as if they'd all been bitten. Bolan, taken off-guard, threw himself backwards when he heard the blast, and he could feel the chair crack and splinter beneath his weight as it toppled backward and dumped him onto the floor. As his face smacked the cold concrete (loosening a tooth in his lower jaw), he saw Patrick lying next to him, his eyes bulging in their sockets, a small black hole dribbling blood and brains from his shattered skull just above the point where his eyebrows came together. His mouth was a wide O of surprise, like he was trying to shout something when the switch in his brain was suddenly turned off, and the .357 was lying on the concrete floor, a mere few inches from Bolan's face.

What happened next was not the reaction Vincent had expected, though in hindsight, Bolan couldn't say he thought it would've gone any differently.

When they heard the gun go off and saw Patrick's head snap back as the bullet punched through his frontal lobe, someone armed with a pump-action shotgun on Patrick's side took it upon themselves to fire off the first shot and hit Wallace just below the nose. The 12 gauge slug smashed through cartilage and bone, ripping the fat man's lower jaw (and most of his head) clean off, sending a spectacular spray of teeth and blood into the air like a geyser. The man next to Wallace managed to turn his head aside so that only half his upper body was painted with the fat man's gore, and then he raised his pistol and struck the man who'd killed him with three shots to the chest.

The next thing Bolan knew as he struggled to free himself from the shattered remains of the chair was the warehouse erupting into what could only be described as the Battle of Armageddon, only on a much smaller scale. Men were shouting, guns were roaring, and bodies were dropping like bowling pins.

One man on Vincent's side managed to kill the guy standing directly across from him, only to have his head hollowed out by a bullet to the back of the skull as he tried to dive for cover behind a parked forklift. Another soldier on Patrick's side emptied his shotgun, but before he could find cover to reload, he was struck in the shoulder and sent spinning to the floor. He screamed like Bolan had never heard another man scream before, only to have his mouth filled with buckshot that blew the rest of his face apart like a bloody jigsaw puzzle.

Patrick's men were scrambling to find cover, terrified grins plastered to their sweating faces, their eyes bulging with fear, as they willy-nilly shot at anything they could see through the gun smoke, while Vincent's crew, definitely the more disciplined of the two opposing factions, took up a strong position behind a stack of rusted metal crates used to transport auto parts. Both sides exchanged gunfire and curses, filling the inside of that warehouse with concussion after concussion of deafening thunder.

Bolan, meanwhile, managed to slip his hands through the loosened zip ties (nearly cutting through the flesh of his wrists doing it) and grabbed the .357 lying in a puddle of Patrick's congealing blood and brain matter, and rolled behind a metal support beam to catch his breath. He checked the revolver and saw that Patrick had loaded it with six hollow points, and then he looked out from where he was crouched to see if he could spot Vincent in the bedlam.

He found him not twenty feet away, ducked down behind the window inside the shipping manager's office. There was no way to get to him from here, with all the bullets flying. It was a veritable no-man's land. Damn it.

Bolan leaned out from behind the steel beam and took a shot at Vincent through the window, hoping to take off the top of his head in one go. The glass exploded inward and he could hear Vincent yell something over the pounding thunder of guns; and for one second he dared hope he'd hit his mark, when Vincent rose up and squeezed off a couple of rounds in his direction, both his shots going wild. Bolan was certain the walls of the office in which Vincent was taking shelter were made of nothing more than cheap plywood or chipboard covered in Sheetrock, and that a well-placed hollow point might punch right through it and hit soft, meaty flesh underneath. So instead of aiming for the man's head, he put the sights of the Magnum just to the right of the window and squeezed the trigger.

The .357 roared in his hand, bucking like some wild animal, and he was rewarded with a satisfying scream as the bullet passed through the flimsy wood and found its mark. He briefly saw the hole appear in the wall, and then he saw Vincent tumble backwards inside the office with a painful cry, pulling a computer and a bulky old fax machine down on top of him as he crash-landed on his ass. The hollow point slug hit him in the shoulder. It mushroomed as it struck meat and bone and shredded everything in its path.

"You son of a bitch!" he bellowed in a wounded-animal howl. *"I'LL FUCKIN KILL YOU!"*

Bolan waited, not saying a word. He kept the gun trained on the window, hoping Vincent would make the fatal mistake of exposing himself in an attempt to shoot back. But his enemy wasn't taking the bait.

The shooting finally stopped. On the other end of the warehouse, most of Patrick's men were either dead or hunkered down, while Vincent's crew held their position to wait them out. This was now a battle between youth and wisdom, and it seemed wisdom was winning. Vincent's men had taken only a third of the casualties suffered on Patrick's side, and most of the younger cats were almost out of ammo.

Silence now hung heavy in the air, along with the sharp tang of blood and cordite. Bolan's ears were ringing and his head throbbed dully like a bad tooth. He made himself as small a target as he could manage behind the steel beam he was using for cover (not easy to do for a man standing six feet five inches tall) and waited for the nausea to pass. He heard coughing and cursing, but couldn't tell from which side it was coming; and someone was crying out for someone else named Emma, only to have his buddy tell him to shut the fuck up, he wasn't gonna die in a shithole like this.

In the shipping office, Vincent was wheezing and scrambling around like a rat inside the walls, knocking shit over with no regard to how much noise he was making. Bolan deduced he was badly wounded, maybe even dying.

"Vincent!" he called out, and then winced from the sudden explosion of pain in his head.

"Fuck you, O'Brien!" was Vincent's shrieking reply. He was definitely hurt, Bolan concluded, and it was only a matter of time before he made his final, fatal mistake.

Bolan opened his mouth to shout something back, when one of Patrick's men yelled out to no one in particular, *"What the fuck is that?"*

Bolan heard it almost immediately. It was coming from outside. He turned and looked towards the front of the warehouse just in time to see the overhead doors crash inward with a sound of shrieking metal. The force of it sent broken pieces of steel and springs spinning around him, and then he saw Rick's pickup truck come barreling into the room, headlights on and glaring like two angry eyes from the depths of hell. The tires locked and barked on the concrete, bringing the truck to a skidding halt. Before anyone knew what to make of this new event, the driver's side door kicked open and Rick was out and down on one knee, wearing a tactical military vest and holding an M4 5.56mm rifle.

"Bolan! Bolan, you here, son?"

At risk of giving away his position, Bolan said, "I'm here, Rick!"

"Get your ass in the truck, soldier!" the old man cried, falling back into his Vietnam commander voice. *"Move it!"*

Someone interpreted this exchange as his cue to pop his head up from behind the forklift and take a shot at Rick. The bullet struck the pickup's windshield, putting a hole through the center and spider-webbing the rest. Rick ducked at the sound, and then promptly returned a three round burst, missing the man who'd taken the shot at him, but hitting the forklift's propane tank. There was a loud hissing noise as pressurized gas was released in a thick cloud, and then Rick shot the tank a second time, this time causing the thing to burst like a bomb, filling the man full of red-hot shrapnel. Everybody watched as the poor bastard jumped up screaming and on fire, most of his face cut down to the bone where the pieces of the propane tank had fused with what remained of his skull. He looked like he was playing that old kid's game of *Ring Around the Rosie* as he held out his arms and spun around in circles, and then he collapsed in the middle of the concrete floor, his shredded clothes and skin now blistered and smoldering. Someone to his left, hidden behind a metal crate, saw his legs on fire, and threw up violently on the floor in front of him.

Taking this moment to make his move, the door to the shipping office crashed outward and Vincent, holding his bloody shoulder, ran down through the hallway where earlier Patrick's men had ambushed Bolan and clubbed him over the head. Bolan heard another door—the loading dock side door that opened out into the parking lot—open with a bang as one of Vincent's size fifteens slammed against it.

"He's fucking running!" Bolan shouted, nearly biting his tongue in half in frustration.

"Then move your ass!" Rick admonished him, waving him towards the truck. He squeezed off another round of cover fire, and then jumped back into the cab as Bolan took off at a full-on run.

"Go!" Bolan cried, smacking the driver's side door with the palm of his hand as he dove into the truck bed.

Rick didn't need to be told twice. He threw the pickup in reverse and stomped on the accelerator as a couple of men inside the warehouse jumped up and opened fire. Most of the shots went wild, but a few struck the hood and grille, and one managed to pass through the windshield and graze Rick's upper arm. Bolan was holding onto the back of the cab when he saw Rick's body rock back against the seat. But the old man, gritting his teeth, managed to maneuver the truck around in a reverse 180, and then slammed it down into drive and took off onto the highway after Vincent's fleeing Cadillac at almost eighty miles per hour.

3.

"You alright?" Bolan shouted through the pickup's rear windshield. The wind blew his lips back from his teeth in a huge, cartoon grin.

"Hurts like a son of a bitch, but I'm fine!" Rick shouted back over his shoulder. His M4 rifle was lying on the seat next to him, and there was an ugly blood smear where the bullet tore out a chunk of meat from his upper arm. Ahead of them, Vincent's white Cadillac Escalade was all over the road, chewing up the miles at almost a hundred miles per hour now.

"Don't you lose him!" Bolan shouted above the roar of the wind and the droning of the tires on the asphalt.

"You just worry about what you're gonna do when we catch 'im!" Rick shot back. "I'll worry about the rest!"

Bolan grinned. "Fair enough!"

The chase through the countryside was a short one. Bolan stood in the bed of the truck, clamping himself to the top of the cab on either side in a white-knuckled grip, while his ass was freezing off due to the frigid winds scouring his face and neck raw. It was all he could do to hold on as his hands and fingers were starting to go numb from the cold. Up ahead, Vincent took a curve in the road that almost sent the Cadillac onto its side into an empty crop field, and it wasn't until Rick nearly rolled the truck onto its side taking the turn after him that Bolan realized they were bringing the chase up into someone's private driveway.

"Where the hell is he going?" Bolan shouted. His eyes felt like they were being rubbed across a belt sander.

"Not far!" Rick shouted back, half-turning his head. He pointed ahead through the mangled windshield. "Look!"

The Escalade jumped a small embankment separating the farmer's yard from the driveway and came down nose-first into the stump of an old tree, crushing the entire front end of the Cadillac like an empty Pepsi can. Glass blew out of the windshield and doors as if a bomb had gone off inside the cab. Vincent flopped forward into the dashboard like a drunken man, taking the steering wheel full in the face.

The Cadillac's engine was hissing and sputtering when Rick slammed on the brakes. Smoke was pouring up out of the mangled front end. Bolan could see the right front tire was bent at a weird angle. The front axle had been sheared in half upon impact.

The driver's side opened. Vincent spilled out onto the ground. Bolan had the .357 ready as he dropped down out of the bed of Rick's truck and approached. "You move another inch, and I'll blow your head off right where you sit."

Vincent sat up like a drunk who's found himself in the alley behind the bar the next morning, and leaned back against the bent and twisted frame of his car. There was a long, horizontal gash running across the bridge of his nose, dribbling blood over his lips and chin. He let out a hitching gasp through a ruin of broken teeth, blowing bloody froth from his mangled lips.

"Go fuck yerself," he wheezed. "Eat shit." Bits of what was left of his front teeth sprinkled the front of his shirt, stuck in the flowing blood like pinkish-white crumbs.

"Poor taste in last words," Bolan mocked.

Vincent hocked and spat a gob of blood into the frozen mud where his tires had deeply scarred the lawn. "We can work something out, O'Brien. I'm not unreasonable." His words were slurred, barely audible. His breath exited his lungs with the sound of wind passing through a torn sail.

"I think Phil and Lou would disagree," Bolan said. Then added, "Patrick, too, I suppose."

Vincent shook his head. "That was personal. They were Judases, all of 'em."

"I don't give a shit," Bolan said simply. He leveled the Magnum with Vincent's head. Vincent looked up into the barrel of the gun as if he were bored and had seen this movie a thousand times before.

"Do what yer gonna," he wheezed. Blood bubbled on his lips, dribbled from the bulge of his chin.

Bolan pulled the hammer back on the .357. "This is for my little girl, you piece of shit."

The look on Vincent's face, in the end, wasn't fear but confusion. Like he hadn't understood what had been said to him. And it didn't last long. Bolan pulled the trigger. The Magnum jumped in his hand, tearing the entire top half of Vincent's head off, causing his body to twitch and jerk before he laid over and collapsed onto his side. His arms and legs shook and then his body settled as blood and pulverized brain matter poured out of the ghastly wound above his eyes.

"Put that gun down, son!"

Bolan and Rick wheeled back in the direction of Rick's truck. An old man was now standing in the driveway, holding a shotgun on both of them. He was short and stocky, wearing denim overalls over a heavy, blue and white plaid shirt. A fur-lined cap rested on his head, and the wind and cold had made his bulbous nose and cheeks an angry scarlet.

"Do it now, or I'll blow your ass away like you did him!" He nodded towards Vincent.

Bolan and Rick exchanged looks, and then Rick shrugged.

"Easy there, Bob." He held his M4 out in front of him. "Don't you recognize your barber?"

Bolan recognized him now. The old man he'd met in Rick's barbershop the day he got off the Greyhound. He looked different now, wearing a hat and holding a gun, but it was him, alright.

Recognition dawned in the farmer's eyes as well. His expression softened from angry fear to confused concern. "Rick? That you?"

"In the flesh."

"Thought you were sick. Got the cancer, like Henrietta."

Rick frowned. "You never told me your wife was sick."

Bob was scared. He kept shifting his weight from one foot to the other and his eyes were moist and restless. Bolan remembered Rick mentioning Bob had been one hell of a machine gunner back in Vietnam, but it was clear those days were long past him.

"She's up the house, hooked up to some machines. They wanted her in a home, but I told 'em to eat shit."

Rick grinned. "Same here."

"What the hell is goin on here?" Again, he looked down at Vincent's nearly headless corpse and took a deep, shuddering breath.

"There's some bad people out there, Bob," Rick explained.

"Yeah, no shit."

"And they may be coming this way," Rick went on. "We could use your help."

Bob's tongue flicked out of his mouth, moistening his lips. He nodded. "Yeah, yeah. Sure, Rick. Anything to help. I got to call the sheriff about this, though."

Rick nodded, shouldering his rifle with a painful grunt. He looked pale and there was a rime of sweat greasing his forehead and cheeks.

"You going to be alright?" Bolan asked.

"Ain't like I'm not already dyin," Rick snapped back cheerfully.

He didn't like the look of the wound in Rick's shoulder. He felt a sudden hook of guilt sink into the meat of his heart. This man, who had no obligation to give a shit and still chose to do so, was ready to march straight into hell with him. And he'd been willing to do it from the start. There was no one else in Bolan's life about whom he could say that. His mother (she never wanted him in the first place) died years ago, and he never knew his father. Rick was it.

Rick gave him a hard jab with his elbow, bringing his focus back to the here and now. "Get it together, son. We have company." He nodded over his shoulder.

Bolan turned around. Three cars had pulled up onto the side of the road, about twenty yards from where Vincent's crashed Cadillac was spewing smoke.

We might as well have lit a fucking flare, he thought numbly as the doors to each car opened and men with guns suddenly spilled out like some clown show from hell.

"Rick, we need to—"

The bark of an AK-47 abruptly cut off the rest of Bolan's words. He and Rick turned and followed Bob back towards the house, each man running as fast as he could manage while bent double at the waist as 7.62mm rounds went screaming past their heads.

CHAPTER TWENTY-THREE

1.

Bob led them in through the open garage. There was a late model Dodge pickup truck parked alongside a silver Ford Taurus. The place smelled of oil and grease and boxes of things turned musty in the dark damp.

"Help me with this!" Rick shouted as he gripped the overhead door with his good hand. His left arm, running with blood down to the fingertips, was cradled at his side.

Bolan shoved the .357 down the front of his belt and gently pushed Rick aside. "I got it." Muscles rippling, he gave the door a hard pull and brought it down with a loud crash, plunging the interior of the garage into sudden darkness. No sooner had he engaged the lock on the door, he heard the snarled bark of a machine gun, and then several jagged holes suddenly appeared in a warped halo in the galvanized metal around his head, sending tiny spears of white, January sunlight punching into the darkness around them.

"Get inside!" Bob croaked, pulling Bolan down with him as he dropped into a crouch. The three of them moved between the Dodge and the Taurus to a small set of wooden stairs leading up to a door that opened into a large, spacious kitchen. Everything was done in finished wood and white tile. There was a island for cooking in the

center of the floor, crowned above by a spindle of hanging pans and utensils. A giant red rooster cookie jar stared at Bolan from its perch atop the counter as they entered.

"I got to go upstairs and check on my wife," Bob said shakily from his place on the floor. He was sitting between them and the kitchen door that led off into a spacious dining room.

"You go ahead, Bob," Rick told him with a grunt. He placed his back against the side of the island and planted his rifle between his legs. His breathing was elevated, his eyes bright with pain.

"There's a phone up there, too," Bob announced, tightening his big farmer's hands around the stock and pump of his shotgun. "I'll get ahold of the sheriff."

Bolan looked at Rick. "You need to go with him."

Rick laughed, shaking his head. "No way, son. I'm stayin down here with you."

"Listen to me," Bolan reasoned, "I'll do my best to keep them out, but if they get past me, you need to stop them before they can get to Bob and his wife."

Rick didn't like it, but he nodded. "Okay." He reached over and grabbed the collar of Bolan's shirt, tearing it a little in his eagerness. "You better watch your ass, son! Keep your head on a swivel. Got it?"

"I got it. Go on."

Rick gave him one last doubtful look, and then nodded and disappeared with Bob without another word. Bolan heard their boots clambering up the stairs a few seconds later. After about a minute or so, he went to the kitchen window. The trees next to the sidewalk leading down to the driveway blocked most of his view of the front lawn in both directions. Now there was the sound of an engine, which puzzled him. It was faint, but it was growing steadily, meaning it was getting closer.

There's more of them, he thought grimly. He frowned, feeling his heartbeat in his ears. Pulling the Magnum, he made his way into the living room to a big picture window that looked out over the front yard and the deserted road beyond, and watched as a big black SUV suddenly turned up into the driveway and began its ascent up the hill toward the house.

"Bolan, we got more coming!" Rick suddenly called out to him from the second floor.

"I see 'em!" He wasn't taking his eyes off the window. "I'll be up there in a second!" Rick didn't answer.

He instinctively ducked as the SUV revved its engine and came to a stop in front of the porch with a grind of treaded rubber on frozen dirt. Four men climbed out and began to move up onto the porch. He watched them for a second or two more, just to be certain, and then he turned and bolted up the stairs, taking them two at a time.

"Rick!" he hissed through the open door of the first bedroom he

came across at the top of the stairs. He found Rick and Bob standing next to a queen-size bed and speaking in quiet tones with the woman lying there. She was covered up to her chin with heavy blankets. Bolan stepped through the doorway and was immediately caught off guard by the smell of death hanging in the room like a miasma. The woman was hooked up to numerous machines, and there was an I.V. drip hanging on a steel hook above her right shoulder. The face peering out over the top of the blanket was nothing more than a skull with thin, papery flesh stretched over it. The woman's hair was thin and dry as chalk dust, swept back from her brow in a mass of colorless straw.

"This is Henrietta," Rick told him softly as he approached the bed. "Bob's wife. Pancreatic cancer. He's been taking care of her for months now."

Bob was holding his wife's hand in both of his, the shotgun leaning against the wall beside him. He was speaking something to her in a soft tone, and Henrietta nodded. Bob leaned in, kissed her waxy forehead, and then grabbed the gun.

"I managed to get the sheriff on the line," he told them. "They're on their way. We just have to hold out 'til then."

"Rick," Bolan said. "They're about to break their way inside. I need you downstairs."

Rick lifted his head, and for a moment his eyes were cloudy with a sadness Bolan had never seen before. Then something inside of him *turned*—it was the only way Bolan knew how to describe it—

and he pushed past Bolan and mounted the top of the stairs.

"We can't let them get up here," he said grimly over his wounded shoulder. He was trembling, but Bolan didn't think it was from fear.

"We won't," Bolan assured him. He reached out and gave the old man a reassuring tap on the shoulder. "They'll be inside any minute."

Rick handed Bolan the M4. "Take it. I can't shoot that for shit with my shoulder."

Bolan took it. Looked at him, puzzled. "What're you going to do?"

Rick drew his .45 from a tactical holster strapped to his leg. "I never leave home without a backup."

Bolan turned and looked back at Bob and Henrietta. "We'll do everything we can to keep them from coming up those stairs," he said. "But if they get up here—"

Bob hefted the shotgun defiantly. "I was a machine-gunner in 'Nam. I was with Rick when our squad leader was killed and we were outnumbered. We made it through that, we can do it again." He smiled dangerously, suddenly looking fifty years younger and meaner. Bolan smiled back, and then led Rick downstairs.

2.

Back in the living room Rick flattened himself against the wall on the other side of one of the big picture windows. His face was pale. Bolan joined him on the other side, cradling the M4 against his chest as he peered through the curtains.

"You good?" he asked.

Rick nodded. "Always."

Outside, there was no sign of Vincent's men, and Bolan wondered briefly if they'd suspected the sheriff's department was on the way and given up. His hope was shattered when he peeked out and saw that SUV was still blocking the exit through the front porch.

"What're they doing?" he whispered. "You see them?"

Rick nodded out the window. "They're creating a perimeter. In case we try and sneak out of a window or a back door."

Bolan shifted the M4 to a more comfortable position. "Whatever happens, we need to make every shot count."

Rick nodded gravely, tightening his grip on the .45. "We make these fuckers *regret*," he said. "Back in 'Nam, sometimes all we could do was hold our position and make the Cong bleed until our boys could get to us for an extraction." He looked across the window at Bolan, his eyes hard and mean. This was no longer Rick the Barber. This was Rick the Decorated Green Beret, and it was both chilling and inspiring to see. "The sheriff's twenty-five miles from here. No one's going to extract us, son. We have to make it ourselves."

Bolan looked at him, his blue eyes large and moist in the cold, afternoon light spilling in through the curtains. "I'm following *you*, Rick" he said.

Both stood as still as statues, watching as two men crossed in front of the window and made their way around towards the back of the house. Rick whispered, "I'm going to keep an eye on the back door." Bolan just nodded, and Rick slid away into the kitchen as silent as a ghost.

Presently, two men carrying AK-47s came loping up through the front yard, trampling Henrietta's empty flowerbeds with their boots. Bolan's back was to the wall just below the window as one of the men's shadow moved across the floor in front of him. He could feel the intruder stop and look in through the wispy curtains. He glanced towards the kitchen, but he couldn't see Rick. There was no sight-line to the back door from here.

The man moved on and Bolan let out his breath. His blood was thundering in his ears, and his body was dumping adrenaline into his veins at an alarming rate. He wasn't worried for himself, though. After all those years living among murderers and rapists and the general worst humanity had to offer, he had become comfortable with chaos. No, his worry was for Rick and the old couple upstairs.

Slowly, he rose up just enough to peek over the window sill. Saw one of the men standing not a foot away from the front of the house, his back completely exposed. Bolan watched him as he turned slowly and went around to the side of the house to the attached garage.

Someone was kicking at the back door, making it rattle in its frame. Bolan heard the man outside curse violently as he threw himself against it again and again. He got down on his belly and crawled toward the kitchen, cradling his rifle against his chest. Rick was standing to the right of the back door with his pistol pointed up towards the ceiling. His finger was on the trigger and his face was running with sweat as his teeth gritted back against the pain in his wounded shoulder. To Bolan's surprise and admiration the old man, despite his wound, had somehow managed to push the heavy, stainless steel refrigerator against the door, all by himself. It was quick thinking that might've saved his life.

"Somebody blocked the door!" the man on the back step shouted to someone in the front yard. Bolan heard a voice answer him, but couldn't make out the words. *"Alright, alright!"* the guy on the other side of the door snarled. He must've been told to figure it out, because he went around the back and broke out a window in the laundry room, just off the kitchen. The glass shattered and shards sprayed all the way out onto the kitchen tile, skittering past Rick's feet like tiny glittering teeth. Bolan could hear the guy grunting and puffing now as his feet scrabbled against the siding in his attempt to enter through the broken window. He finally managed to pull himself up and wormed his way inside.

Just as he was falling into a sweating, cursing pile onto the floor, Bolan came through the door with his combat knife in his fist and drove it down hard into the top of the man's skull with both hands. There was a dull *thock*, and the guy began to convulse, his legs kicking and scraping against the white-painted wall like a man who just took hold of a live wire. Then he made an inarticulate grunting sound deep in his throat, stiffened, and fell limp.

Bolan viciously ripped the knife free, shaking the blood from it. He stepped over the corpse on his approach to the broken window to see if anyone else might be lurking around the back of the house, took a quick assessment of the back yard, and then returned to the kitchen.

"They're going to realize something's up when he doesn't report back," he told Rick, jabbing a thumb over his shoulder.

"We're ready for 'em," was Rick's reply.

Bolan looked at him. "I can hear another one in the garage."

"You take him, I'll keep an eye on the stairs," Rick said.

Bolan left him there and made his way back towards the kitchen in a walking crouch. He found the garage door entrance they'd used earlier to get into the house. He could hear someone on the other side of the door, bumbling and stumbling inside the garage. He threw the door open. The intruder wheeled at the sound of the knob striking the wall, but it was too late. Bolan closed the distance in two strides, gutting him with the knife with a single, hard thrust. He gave the blade a wicked twist, driving it upward through his belly and ribcage, the saw-toothed edge turning the man's insides into bloody mush, and then he yanked it out with a viciousness that caused the man's entrails to spill out onto the garage floor in a wet *splat*.

He took a moment to make sure his man was dead, then looked out toward the SUV. They'd seen him now. Men were scrambling and running for cover. He lifted the rifle, squeezed off a few rounds to cause confusion, and then ducked back inside the house where Rick had positioned himself at the bottom of the stairs.

"They're coming!"

The cold, January afternoon erupted in gunfire. Bullets punched through the windows and walls, shredded furniture, smashed knickknacks, and chewed through family pictures as glass and plaster rained down on top of their heads. Bolan rose up and fired off two more quick bursts, hitting nothing. Rick worked the . 45, each blast like a cannon going off inside the house. Bolan heard one guy let out a scream. He peeked out through the window and saw the man crawling through the grass holding his belly with a blood-smeared hand. Another guy popped up to help him and Rick put a bullet through his chest.

The gunfire ceased. Bolan checked his clip and slapped it back into place. Rick, abandoning his post at the base of the stairs, came in from the living room to check on him.

"What the fuck are you doing?" Bolan snarled, startled by his sudden appearance. His ears were ringing and he could barely hear his own voice. "I told you to stay in the living room!"

"Fuck that shit!" Rick shouted back. Plaster dust clung to both men's sweaty skin like war paint. It was a miracle that neither of them had been hit by a single bullet. Bolan risked a peek out the window and couldn't see anyone, but he wouldn't allow himself to believe they'd run away.

"You need to get your ass back in there—"

Someone was pounding at the back door again, this time hard enough that the refrigerator was skidding on the tile. Bolan and Rick rushed into the kitchen to push the refrigerator back and a gunshot rang out from the broken laundry room window to their left. Rick fell back against the wall with a garbled curse. Bolan looked down at him, horrified. Rick waved it away. *"I'm fine!"* Bolan ducked to the side of the doorway that led into the laundry room as the gunman came in through the window and took cover behind the washing machine.

Bolan peered around the corner and a pistol cracked. A chunk of the door frame exploded in front of his face, stinging his eyes with hot splinters. He fell back with a *"Fuck!"*, raking his eyes with his hand. Rick's .45 went off with an almost cartoonish *BAM!*, and he looked up in time to see the man crumpling against the wall behind the washing machine.

"Thanks," he muttered, shaking his head. His left eye felt as if he'd gotten a nail lodged in it.

Rick opened his mouth to say something when they heard Bob yell something upstairs. His shotgun went off and then someone else let out a cry and it sounded like something hard tumbled down the stairs. They exchanged looks, both men's eyes wide, and then at once they both ran from the kitchen and saw two men had managed to get in through one of the smashed living room windows. One of them had a pistol, which he raised when Bolan and Rick entered the room, and the other had already made it up the stairs and back down again. He was standing over the old woman with a machete drawn back above his head, her long, graying hair knotted in his fist. The left side of his face was buckshot burned, like he'd just missed having his head blown off at close range.

Good for you, Bob, Bolan thought.

But it wasn't good for Bob. Behind the man holding the machete, Bob's crumpled form was lying in the corner on the stairs' landing with a deep, bleeding gash where his neck connected to his shoulder. The entire left side of his body was soaked in blood. He wasn't moving.

Henrietta was struggling on her belly, clawing feebly at the carpet littered with chunks of wood and drywall, her deathly-pale face twisted in a mask of fear and confusion as she struggled to breathe. She managed to open her mouth and call out to her husband, but Bob didn't move. Both of the intruders were looking at Rick and Bolan with wide, bloodshot eyes and bared teeth.

"You take another step and she's dead," the man with the pistol warned.

Bolan looked down at the pitiful form of the old woman

sprawled out on the floor and bit back a scream of rage. He held up his hands, letting the M4 hang by its strap from his neck. "Easy, man, she's just a sick old woman," he said. "Let her go and let's see if we can work something out."

"This ain't a negotiation," the guy with the machete growled. Bolan didn't know it then (nor would he have cared if he had), but this was the man who'd chopped Larry Krieger into beef stew, using the very same machete he was now carrying. His face was blocky and cut at rough angles, and what was left of the side where Bob had shot him was nothing more than burnt hamburger. "We're not here to make any deals." His eyes, feverishly bright with pain and murder, rolled down to the old woman cowering beneath him.

"No!"

Rick made to rush the guy, but Bolan grabbed him by his vest and pulled him back. "Stop it!" he said. "Just stop!"

Rick's was trembling, but he obeyed and stepped back. "Just let her go," he told the two men. "We're the ones you want. There's no sense in killing a woman who's already dead. Just look at her."

The one with the pistol considered this for a second, and then nodded to his partner. "Let her go, Mel." Bolan and Rick exchanged a quick glance. The man with the gun must have sensed it, because he quickly turned his attention back to them. "Don't you even *think* about it!"

Bolan lifted his hands in a show of good faith. Rick did the same, though he still gripped his Colt. The old woman gave a little whimper and started to cough. It was loud and croupy, clotted with phlegm, and the one with the machete kicked her in the side of the face. *"Shut that shit up, bitch!"*

It took everything Bolan had not to drop his hands and bring his rifle up slinging lead into both of them. "Don't you fucking touch her," he warned through gritted teeth. "Not one more time."

The man holding the pistol gave his partner a reproachful scowl. "What the fuck did you do that for? Can't you see she's no threat to anyone?"

But Mel had a look in his eye (his good one; Bob had put the other one out; it pooled in the socket like a dollop of bloody jelly) Bolan didn't like. He shook his head, saying, "Fuck this shit," and then he raised the machete and brought it down with all his strength.

"NOOOO!"

The flesh of the old woman's neck parted as if beneath a cleaver, and a jet of blood sprayed up out of her in a bright red arc that nearly hit the ceiling. He struck her again and again as she kicked and thrashed her legs. Bolan would never forget those terrible, smacking, wet-meat sounds, or the way her head suddenly came loose with a gush of blood and rolled onto the floor.

Rick screamed and lifted his weapon. The man with the machete had only enough time to look up before the .45 thundered and blew a hole through the front of his throat. His partner, mortified by the sight of the old woman's head slowly rolling to a stop on the bloody floor, turned and vomited. When he was done, he went shakily to his knees as Rick slowly swiveled his gun and trained it on him. It was at this moment when all three of them—Bolan, Rick, and the man on his knees—heard the sound of sirens warbling in the distance.

At least Bob's call went through, Bolan thought deliriously, *even if it is too late.* Suddenly none of this seemed real to him. It was like he was caught in some strange nightmare and couldn't wake up. *There are no happy endings. Not for any of us.*

The smoke and dust had begun to settle around them in a milky-white haze made fantastic and surreal by the shafts of sunlight slanting in through the broken windows. Off in the distance, the sirens were drawing closer.

"You cut her fucking head off," Rick uttered slowly to the man on his knees. *"What the fuck did she ever do to anybody?"*

The guy still had traces of vomit in his beard. He took a quick backward step when he saw Bolan was now slowly advancing on him, too, gripping that terrible knife.

"Look, man, I wasn't gonna kill her!" he pleaded, his eyes jumping from the serrated blade in Bolan's hand to the barrel of Rick's .45. "I told Mel to drop it! You heard me say it! He was always a sick son of a bitch! Please—*God*—you have to believe me!" He squeezed his eyes shut and began to shake uncontrollably. "Oh God, *please!*"

"God's not here, boy," Bolan told him coldly, and then he rammed the combat knife up through the bottom of the man's jaw, just behind the chin, until the tip of the half-serrated blade popped through the soft jelly of his left eye. The man trembled and stumbled back against the wall, ripping the curtains from their rods with his flailing, groping hands, so that the clips holding them in place snapped and went spinning; and then he came down hard on his ass in the corner, coughing and gurgling on his own blood, still trying to grip the haft of the knife and pull it out, to no avail.

3.

That's how the police would later find him: his head cocked back, resting against the wall with his mouth open and clotted with blood. The knife that killed him was never found at the scene.

Neither were Bolan and Rick.

CHAPTER TWENTY-FOUR

1.

Pastor Jake never heard the man enter. It wasn't until he felt the shadow fall over him that he paused in his task of setting out that Sunday's hymnals and slowly turned around.

The bright, summer sun was shining against the man's back through a window along the wall in the sanctuary, painting the front of him in black shadow. All Jake could make out at first was that he was incredibly tall, with shoulders as broad as a barn beam.

"Afternoon, sir," he said, clearing his throat roughly. The man's sudden appearance had shaken him more than he liked. "Can I help you?"

The man's arm shot out with a speed Pastor Jake had not expected, and a hand with a strength like a steel trap closed around his flabby throat, instantly choking off his air. Jake's eyes bulged comically from their sockets. The remaining hymnals he was cradling in his arms went flying as he instinctively tried to beat the man's grip loose with his hands.

"Stop it," the man spoke for the first time. His voice was low and dangerous. "Stop it, or I'll snap your neck right now."

Pastor Jake had no doubts whatsoever the man was strong

enough to make good on his threat, so he obeyed. "W-what d-do you w-want?" he croaked. The blood had been cut off from his lower body and his head now felt like it was on the verge of popping like a kernel of corn in a hot skillet.

"I want some answers," the man replied simply. He began to lead Pastor Jake toward the front of the sanctuary, where he forced him to sit in one of the front row pews. At last he released his grip on his neck and loomed over him. A large, serrated combat knife appeared in one hand as if from magic. Jake hadn't seen him reach for it at all.

"I don't know who you are, but—"

"Yes you do," the man interrupted. He took a step closer, so that the light from the windows fell fully on his hard, bearded face.

Recognition on the pastor's face now. He took in a deep, labored breath, cringing from a sudden sharp pain in the front of his throat. The man's grip was less than a quarter of a pound from crushing his larynx.

"Mr. O'Brien," he said at last. "I didn't recognize you at first."

"You see me now." It wasn't a question. Bolan was wearing a light, dark jacket and jeans, and a pair of heavy black boots. His only weapon as far as the pastor could tell was that monstrous knife, which caught the light and glittered coldly in his fist.

"I do. What can I do for you?"

"I'm going to make this quick and simple," Bolan explained. "I'm going ask you some questions, you're going to answer. You lie, you die." His grin was horrible. "Easy enough a child could understand."

Pastor Jake's face was pale and doughy. His scalp glimmered with sweat through his thinning hair. "Okay."

"First question: why did you tell Patrick Manga I confessed to hitting that truck and stealing those guns?"

Pastor Jake's tongue flicked through his lips, wetting them. "I don't know what you're talking about."

Bolan sighed and then, without warning, he brought the knife down into the top of the pastor's left thigh, deep enough that he could actually feel the blade glance off the femur bone. Jake's eyes bulged like water balloons and he threw back his head and shrieked to the ceiling.

"GET IT OUT! GET IT OUT OF MY LEG!"

Bolan just stood there, watching him for a moment. Then he bent forward, clamped his left hand around the man's mouth and gripped the haft of the knife with his right. "Shut up, or I twist it."

Pastor Jake's body instantly broke out into a sweat. He was trembling all over, and his skin suddenly smelled like onions. His eyes filled with bloody veins and Bolan was afraid he might pass out.

"I pull it out, you don't scream," Bolan told him. "Agree?"

Pastor Jake grunted, nodded his head.

Bolan hesitated, let the pain go a few extra heartbeats, and then he pulled the knife up with a nasty, wet, sucking sound that brought up more blood and shredded meat with it. Pastor Jake practically bit through his lower lip to keep himself from screaming.

"You gotta get me to the hospital," the pastor murmured breathlessly. He was looking down at the ragged gash in the top of his thigh, sickened and amazed at the amount of blood now pouring out. It was running down his leg and filling his left shoe. *"Please."*

"In a moment," Bolan lied. "Right now, you're going to tell me everything. Now answer my question: *Why?*"

"I had to," was the pastor's reply.

"What do you mean?"

"My brother told me it was the only way."

Bolan frowned. "Your brother? Who is he?"

Pastor Jake was trying to hold the blood in the wound on his leg, but it was welling up through his fingers. His skin had taken on a sickly pallor now, and sweat was dripping from the tip of his nose.

"Benjamin Murphy," he swallowed and said. "You know him as Benny."

Bolan just stared at him for a moment. It made sense, now that he thought about it. No one else was there that night. And Benny had bailed on him just before he drove over to the Express Continental office.

"Why?" Bolan asked.

"Huh?"

"Why would Benny do that?"

Jake looked up at him. For the first time since Bolan had met the man, he saw a flash of anger in his pain-clouded eyes. "You don't know?"

Bolan tightened his grip around the haft of the knife. "No more games. Tell me, or I stick it in your other leg."

Pastor Jake shuddered. "Okay, okay. It's because of our younger brother, Ronnie."

"Who's he?"

The pastor met his eyes with such a look of loathing and contempt it surprised Bolan. "He's the one you killed in prison. Eighteen years ago now."

Bolan was caught off guard by that. He just stood there, and remembered everything.

2.

Ronnie and his thug-buddies made a run at him while he was preparing to undress in the shower room. Ronnie had been the one holding the shiv; it was a brutal but effective weapon he'd made out of a twisted piece of metal he'd sharpened to a deadly point. It almost looked like a corkscrew, its design intended to kill and do as much damage as possible, so that the fool who took it in the kidney or liver could not be sewn back together.

When Bolan saw the shiv in Ronnie's hand as he came around the corner, he went berserk, using his superior size and strength to throw his attacker against the wall hard enough that his teeth rattled and the shiv went flying. Before Ronnie had a chance to recover, Bolan grabbed his face and began to smash the back of his head against the wall, again and again, until his skull cracked open and his eyes filled with blood.

The other two who'd joined Ronnie in his attempted murder plot had thrown themselves at Bolan wildly once they saw their leader was dead. Bolan broke the first man's jaw (along with most of his teeth) and landed a punch on the other that snapped his collar bone like a chicken wing. Both men had slunk away, abandoning their plan. Someone must've snitched, because the guards had shown up in record time (which almost *never* happened, as far as Bolan ever knew) and they proceeded to beat Bolan into submission and drag him away to solitary confinement. A few months later, he was handed a plea agreement in court. His lawyer made it abundantly clear what his options were: He would take another fifteen years for manslaughter, or face a life sentence. He chose the fifteen years.

3.

Bolan took a deep breath. "What're you telling me here? Are you saying that Benny ratted me out to Patrick because I killed your brother?"

Pastor Jake shook his head. He was losing a lot of blood. "No. That was just his way of killing two birds with one stone. The Mangas have been a thorn in my family's side for generations. Ben infiltrated them about two years ago, going under cover as a bookie and a loan shark. He figured he could use you to take out Vincent, and still get his revenge for you killing Ronnie."

"Undercover?" It sounded strange to Bolan, that he put it that way.

Jake laughed, but it was more a defense mechanism against the pain than actual humor. "Ben's a cop."

"A cop?" Bolan didn't believe that. *Couldn't* believe it.

The pastor nodded. "That's right. Ever wondered why the Feds never questioned you about that truck being hit and set on fire? Or why they were crawling over every inch of Vincent's life, and yet you never got scooped up with the rest when they raided his home?"

Bolan didn't answer.

Jacob nodded. "Ben works undercover for Cambridge P.D. Organized Crime Division. Been doing it now for twenty-two years." He uttered a dry little laugh. "It's ironic, you think about it. Ben's been protecting you this entire time, ensuring you don't get sent back to prison."

"Because he wants to kill me himself," Bolan figured. It's what he would do, now that he thought about it.

"I suppose so," the pastor agreed. "Ben kept your name out of everything. To the police, you're just a number in some file in his computer. Convenient for you, eh?"

Bolan didn't find any part of this convenient. He remained silent.

"It was our great-grandfather, Jack, who sent him to college, and then the academy," Pastor Jake explained. "We Murphys have always had police and lawyers in the family. My great-grandfather believes it's better that the ones in our pocket are family, rather than some corrupt person who's only in it for themselves. Those people turn on you when it suits them, but blood is stronger than that."

Bolan's mind was reeling, but he kept it from showing on his face. It all made sense now that he was thinking about it. How else would Benny have been able to fool the Mangas, unless he was well-trained and knew exactly what he was doing?

He must've spent years planning this, Bolan realized. *He's been keeping an eye on me since before I ever got out of prison. That's how he knew to have his brother here tell me about Roger—*

Bolan stopped.

He suddenly went cold all over.

He looked at Jake, and something like a cloud of utter doom passed over his face. The pastor saw it, too. He recoiled back into the pew as Bolan slowly stepped toward him.

"My daughter and her husband," he said thickly, feeling like his mouth was full of blood. "He killed them, didn't he?"

Pastor Jake shivered. The blood loss was bad now. He didn't have long. "I had nothing to do with that," he whispered. "Whatever else you might think of me, I am still a man of God."

"Man of God?" Bolan snarled and was suddenly on top of him, pressing the bloody tip of his knife against the soft lower lid of his left eye. "How can you say that to me—to *anyone? Your* brother murdered my daughter and her husband—good people—and you *dare* speak of God?"

Jake was weeping now. The tears rolled from his moist, fever-red eyes, mingling with the beads of oily sweat now running out of every part of his body. "I never wanted anyone to die! I told Ben to let it go, that revenge was for God alone! But he wouldn't listen! He wanted you to pay for what you did to our brother! I loved Ronnie, too, but not at the expense of innocent life!" His breath hitched in his throat and he let out a long, deep sob. Bolan removed the knife and took a step back, giving him some room.

"So Benny killed Samantha and Roger, and then made sure you would send me in his direction," he said. "He *wanted* me to find him."

Jake nodded weakly. "Yes. I only went along because I thought I might still be able to save my brother's soul. I was a fool. I see that now."

"You sent two of your flock to the wolf to be slaughtered."

"You don't think I know that?" Jake exploded suddenly. He was weeping now in big, hitching sobs. Sweat and tears and snot poured out of his ashen face in thick runnels. "I *loved* Sam and Roger! They were *good* people! They helped me build one of the most impressive youth ministries in this district! I never wanted anything to happen to them, but Ben's appetite for vengeance could not be sated! He did what he did without any regard for my feelings on the matter!" He leaned his head back against the top of the pew, took in a deep breath, let it out in a shudder. When he spoke again, his voice was soft, hardly a whisper. "You don't understand him. Once he puts his mind to something, he cannot be stopped."

"Is that right?" Bolan gave the sanctuary at large a contemptuous look, then he zeroed back in on the pastor. "You'll be dead in another minute or so."

"I know."

"There is one more thing you can do before you die, to make this right."

Jake shook his head. His teeth were chattering now. "There's no making this right."

"Call your brother for me," Bolan pressed. "Tell him to meet you at the North Side Diner in Cambridge."

Pastor Jake looked at him ruefully. "So you can kill him, too?"

"Yes. It's the only way this ends."

"Why would I do that?"

"You said you loved Samantha and Roger."

"I truly did," Jake said with a sad little nod of his head.

"Then do this one last thing for them. Then you can say your prayers and make your peace with the Almighty. I'll give you that much."

Pastor Jake fumbled in the pocket of his blood-smeared sweater for his phone. Before he dialed, he said, "Might I make a suggestion to you? As a pastor?"

Bolan's look was cold. "It's your fuse that's burning."

"Let this go," Jake said. "Just walk away and never look back. Let God deal with my brother."

Bolan shook his head. "I can't do that."

"Then you are damned."

"Make the call."

Pastor Jake dialed the number. It was the last thing in this life he ever did.

4.

Detective Benjamin Murphy stepped through the door of the diner and looked around. The place was well-lit but empty at this time of night. A cook in the back, a tired-looking waitress with big, sagging boobs, gigantic hips, and too much makeup were the only ones on the clock, it seemed.

He looked around the room as he passed the counter, but there was no sign of his brother, Jake. When he finally got a good look at the only other customer in the place sitting at a booth facing the door, he froze in his tracks.

Bolan was waiting for him. He wore a black turtleneck sweater, blue jeans, and big black biker boots. A cup of coffee on a saucer sat untouched in front of him.

Son of bitch.

"Detective Murphy," Bolan said as he approached the table. There was the hint of a smirk on his face. "I was wondering if you would show."

Ben took a quick assessment of the room. He then looked down and noticed a large, olive-green duffle bag sitting on the floor next to Bolan's feet, the kind an Army recruit might've carried out of boot camp forty years ago. It was battered and scarred from years of weather and war.

"Leaving town?" he asked, though he couldn't have cared less about that. The fact that he didn't see his brother put him on edge.

Bolan glanced down at the bag and shook his head. "We'll get to that," he said coldly. "Sit." He motioned towards the empty seat across from him.

"Where's Jake?" It came out more like an accusation than a question.

"Sit down," Bolan repeated.

The detective did as Bolan commanded, making sure his enemy could see the badge clipped to his belt and the holstered SIG P226 just behind it.

For a moment, the two of them just sat across the table, studying each other. Benny—*Ben*—looked a lot different cleaned up. He was wearing a slate-gray suit with a white shirt open at the collar, and black, square-toed shoes. His hair—Bolan remembered it being greasy and curly—was neatly-groomed and combed back from his broad forehead. He was clean-shaven and his teeth were no longer crooked and yellow, either.

Prosthetics, Bolan assumed. *He must've worn them to really sell it.*

"I'm not gonna ask you again," the detective warned. Even his accent was different. "Where the fuck is my brother?"

Bolan took a sip of his coffee, set the cup down slowly. He was drawing this out, enjoying the final moments before he finally ended it. "You killed my daughter."

Ben looked at him, a murderous twinkle floating in his eye like a mote. "Getting right to it, I see. Fine. Enough bullshit. Yeah, I fuckin killed 'em. Both of 'em. I made it look like someone kicked their door in and shot 'em. Wasn't hard to do."

Bolan bristled, but kept himself in check. "Because I killed your scumbag brother in prison." Not a question. Both of them knew it very well at this point.

"That's right."

Bolan nodded. "And the two men from Duluth. Who were they?"

Ben shrugged. "Couple of lowlifes I put away ten years ago. Jack is sitting in Terre Haute, waiting for his turn in the gas chamber, and Henry is doing life in Pendleton." He chuckled dryly. "They're even worse shit birds than you are."

Bolan indicated the duffle bag with a slight nod of his head. "I got something here you'll want to see." The detective watched as he bent over and opened the big, heavy bag at his feet. He righted himself and then, again, nodded downward. "Take a look."

Ben peeked over the side of the table and Bolan took a wicked pleasure as his eyes swelled to the size of saucers.

"You motherfucker!" he hissed, gripping the table like a man in the middle of a crippling heart attack. His legs jerked and stamped at the linoleum floor under the table—a quiet tantrum so that he didn't draw the attention of the waitress behind the counter. *"I'll fuckin kill*

you!"

Bolan looked down into the dead, pale face of Pastor Jake from where he was lying twisted and folded inside the bag. His eyes were glazed and his mouth hung open, his teeth crusted with blood from where he'd bitten through his lower lip to keep himself from screaming.

"I had to break his arms and legs to fit him in there, but it worked out, I think," Bolan said mercilessly. He looked back up. *There* was the Benny he knew, staring back at him with eyes now black with murder. "All he wanted was to make things right with himself and the Lord. Well, I don't know about God, but him and me are square."

Benny was gripping the edges of the table with hands that had gone bone-white. He was seething, his chest heaving in and out, and Bolan could see actual tears of rage and grief at the edges of his eyes.

"I'm gonna fuckin burn you alive, O'Brien! I swear to *everything!* I won't stop with you, either! I'll kill your precious Sara and that little girl she took in, too!" He stopped, grinning evilly as Bolan's expression darkened. "Oh, yeah, I know all about them. Some nights I sit outside her house and watch the two of them through the window. Pretty little girl. I'll bet Sara would do *anything* to keep someone from gutting her like a deer. What do you think?" He sneered, weasel-like, and then laughed.

Bolan didn't move, didn't blink. "You're not going to touch

either one of them."

Benny snickered. "What makes you say that?"

"Because you're not leaving this diner alive." Bolan reached behind him and drew the big combat knife, held it in his fist on the table in front of him. "You know that old saying, about bringing a knife to a gun fight?"

Benny's hand went under the table, flicked the snap on his holster to free his draw. "Yeah, I think I heard that a time or two."

"Well, I don't think it's always the case," Bolan said.

"Then you're a dumb motherfu—"

Benny had no time to clear his holster before Bolan lunged at him across the table, sending the coffee cup and saucer flying. He moved with no more warning than a striking cobra; his knife flashed in the glare of the overhead lights. Benny shrieked and his head suddenly flopped at an unnatural angle onto his right shoulder as Bolan's knife descended terrifically on his neck. Once, twice, three times he struck at the side of the man's throat, cutting through meat and bone until Benny's head literally fell back from his shoulders in a shower of blood, the ruined features of his face frozen in a white mask of horror even as it dropped to the floor with a dull thud, rolled a few feet onto the checkered tile, and then came to a stop.

Panting with adrenaline, Bolan took only a second to steal one last glimpse of Benny's severed head lying on the floor before he crossed the room in three strides and pushed his way out of the diner's front doors and disappeared into the night.

5.

A minute or so later, the waitress came out from the kitchen to check on the two men whom she believed to be having a very heated conversation ("Not that it was any of *my* business," she would later say when asked to tell her story on national television), when she unknowingly stumbled into a scene of absolute horror.

One of the men who'd been in the booth was gone ("He was very nice, very handsome, and I'll be *damned* if he wasn't as big as a gorilla!" she would later tell a stone-faced Detective Palmer, who would spend what little time he had left on the force investigating yet another brutal murder) and the other fellow's headless body lay slumped over, the ragged, severed stump of his neck pumping blood across the table in weak little arcs as his heart finally came to a stop. Following the blood trail to the floor, she saw the man's head lying in a wide pool of blood, his eyes bright bulbs of surprise. But it wasn't until she saw the corpse twisted and broken inside the bag, its dead, pale face staring up at her, that she started to scream.

EPILOGUE

Bolan found them at the park on a warm Sunday afternoon. When he saw Sara sitting there on the red bench beneath an old, bent oak tree, he almost lost his nerve and left. Then he noticed Abby running and playing and screaming with the other kids near the bottom of the big blue twisty slide and decided he needed to do this.

This is the last time you may ever see her, he thought as he crossed the street and began to ascend the narrow concrete walkway leading into the playground. *You might not get another chance.*

"This seat taken?" he asked as his shadow fell over her. She craned her neck and looked upward, squinting into the sun. Her hair, honeyed gold, was braided and long enough to coil on the bench behind her. He'd never wanted her more than he did right at that moment.

She smiled. "Not at all." She moved her purse and placed it under the bench with Abby's diaper bag.

Bolan sat down. He looked around the playground, watching the army of children as they ran and laughed and played, smiling to himself. His first memory of this place was when he was five years old, just starting kindergarten. His mother had brought him here to burn off some energy so she could get some of her reading done. He had always been a high-strung kid.

"Did you come to say goodbye?"

"Yeah," he said.

She waited for a moment, then said, "So where you goin?"

"I don't know. Rick says he wants to go out and see the Grand Canyon before he dies. I think we'll go there."

"How's he doing?"

He shrugged. "Good days and bad. Today's a good one, I think."

"Your parole officer has been calling me every day, wondering where the hell you are," she said. "I don't know what to tell her."

"Tell her the truth. You don't know."

"That's what I've *been* telling her, but she calls anyway. Yesterday she made it clear that she would revoke you if you don't get in contact with her."

"I'll call her."

"Cops have been asking around, too," she said. "They also wanna know where you're at. Said they have to ask you some questions." Her tongue slid through her lips, moistening them. "Does this have anything to do with what we talked about that night?"

He remembered her spaghetti dinner, and then him telling her everything. And the lovemaking that followed.

"What did they tell you?"

"They said some guys got killed a few months back, and that some of them were shot with a rifle registered to Rick. They found his truck, too, shot to shit in some farmer's yard."

"Rick told me his gun and truck had been stolen," he said, grinning.

She didn't find it funny. "The detective told me there was a cop's body found in some restaurant." Her voice dropped to a whisper. "Had his *head* cut off. Sam's pastor was found there, too, stuffed in a bag"

He didn't say anything.

"What the hell is going on, Bolan?" She paused, looked at Abby, then back at him. "Was Pastor Jake part of this?"

He thought about his answer for a long moment, then shook his head. "None of that matters now."

He could tell she wanted to press him further, but she didn't. "They say they have some questions about where you were when it happened. The detective gave me his card, wanted you to call him."

"Palmer?"

She nodded.

"What did you tell him?"

She laughed, but it was a sad sound. "What *could* I tell him?"

He just sat there, watching Abby playing tag with another little boy. After while, he turned and looked at her. "Thanks."

She nodded.

A pause. Two kids were fighting by the jungle gym and had to be separated by their parents. Then Sara asked, "The ones who killed Sam and Roger. They're dead?"

He looked at her, nodded slowly. "Yeah. They're dead." He didn't tell her the rest of it. That it was an undercover cop named Benny who murdered their daughter because of something he did eighteen years ago. Safer to just leave it where it was. The less she knew, the better. "I got them all."

Tears welled in her eyes. She took a deep breath, let it out shakily. "Good. I hope they rot in hell for what they did."

He had a sudden, overwhelming desire to reach across to her and pull her close and kiss her on the mouth. "I'd better get going. I just wanted you to know that it's done. The men responsible will never be able to do that to anyone else."

He stood and turned to go, stopped when he felt her tug on his hand. He looked back and she was crying now. "Thank you," she said, wiping the tears away with the palm of her hand. "You'll never know how much this means to me, Bolan."

He wanted to cry, too, but didn't. Instead, he leaned forward and kissed her on the forehead. "I love you, Sara. I want you to know how sorry I am, for everything. I can never make it up to you, but I will always be here for you. Both of you." His eyes found Abby in the sandbox playing with a group of kids, and he felt an ice pick of pain and regret slide through the muscle of his heart. *I need to get out of here*, he thought, and turned away.

"Will I see you again?" she asked as he started back down the walkway.

He stopped and looked back. "Never say never," he told her with a grin, and then left. When he finally got to his car and drove away, he knew it would be for the last time.

There are no happy endings, remember?

Yeah, I remember.

Made in the USA
Monee, IL
12 April 2024

56833885R00213